The Bigfoot Singularity

A Novel

The Bigfoot Singularity

A Novel

Ronald C. Meyer
and Mark Reeder

COSMIC
EGG
BOOKS

Winchester, UK
Washington, USA

JOHN HUNT PUBLISHING

First published by Cosmic Egg Books, 2019
Cosmic Egg Books is an imprint of John Hunt Publishing Ltd., 3 East St., Alresford,
Hampshire SO24 9EE, UK
office@jhpbooks.com
www.johnhuntpublishing.com
www.cosmicegg-books.com

For distributor details and how to order please visit the 'Ordering' section on our website.

Text copyright: Ronald C Meyer and Mark Reeder 2018

ISBN: 978 1 78904 180 4
978 1 78904 181 1 (ebook)
Library of Congress Control Number: 2018950583

A CIP catalogue record for this book is available from the British Library.

Design: Stuart Davies

UK: Printed and bound by CPI Group (UK) Ltd, Croydon, CR0 4YY
US: Printed and bound by Thomson-Shore, 7300 West Joy Road, Dexter, MI 48130

We operate a distinctive and ethical publishing philosophy in
all areas of our business, from our global network of authors to
production and worldwide distribution.

"The idea that humanity is approaching a "singularity" — that ordinary humans will be overtaken by artificially intelligent machines or cognitively enhanced biological intelligence has moved from the realm of science fiction to near future truth... If deep learning continues to develop at its current dizzying rate, the singularity could come about before the middle of the present century."
Murray Shanahan, Professor of Cognitive Robotics, Imperial College, London

Ray Owen, son of a Dakota spiritual leader from Prairie Island Reservation in Minnesota, told a reporter from the Red Wing Minnesota Republican Eagle, "Bigfoot exist in another dimension from us, but can appear in this dimension whenever they have a reason to. When our time in this one is finished, we move on to the next, but the Big Man can go between. The Big Man comes from God."

Chapter One

Hiawatha National Forest

Upper Peninsula, Michigan

The Bigfoot stopped and listened. The forests of the Upper Peninsula of Michigan were different, older. More pines, trees of different sizes compared to the foothills of the Appalachians and southern Ohio where the trees were largely deciduous and of the same age. The ground was rockier, too. She had been traveling for nearly a month, working her way along the edge of the Great Lakes, mostly traveling at night, using her natural chameleon ability to hide from predators and humans. A day behind her was another from her clan. They traveled separately, increasing the chances one of them would make it to the rendezvous. Her clan had the most humanlike faces of all the Bigfoot subspecies. After so many millennia, finally the gathering had been called. The excitement of meeting others of her kind from different clans had hastened her movements and in her anticipation she had let down her guard. Now something didn't feel right. The composition of granite and ancient shales below the soft vegetated mat of the forest floor interfered with her sensors, so she swiveled her head from side to side and peered past the nearest trees deep into the woods, her bio-sensors automatically collecting data from the odors, sights and sounds in addition to a wide range of electromagnetic radiation and magnetic fields not available to humans. The late afternoon sun hid much among the lengthening shadows. She squinted and held rock still.

There! To her left and right and in front of her. A familiar smell. Humans! She craned her neck and could make out the breathing of a fourth human waiting on a small ridge several hundred yards away. The humans closest to her converged on her as if they knew she was there.

The Bigfoot knew she was being hunted. She started to run, picking the easiest route through the dense scrub trees of the forest. She could feel the chameleon pigmentation of her skin blending with the forest browns and greens, hiding her from the primitive eyes of the hunters. Still, they followed as if they knew where she was. It was impossible but somehow it was happening. She headed toward a creek when something slammed into her chest, spinning her around to the ground.

* * *

The three hunters trotted easily through the dense forest of spruce, maple and oak, skirting brambles of blackberry and wild shrub roses, and vaulting over felled trees without making any noise. Their US Military Camo Anorak Jackets blended with the trees and they moved like ghosts through the wilderness. The afternoon sun was lowering in the west, hidden mostly by the multi-colored fall canopy. The air was crisp and their breaths wreathed their faces momentarily, trailing to wisps behind them. At a prearranged spot, they spread out in a V– formation, with the third man at the bottom of the letter, where game could be flushed toward him into the killing zone. They ran silently, no unnecessary communications, each man intent on his mission. Each carried a gas operated, US Navy Mk-12 5.56 semi-auto sniper rifle. Its effective range was 550 meters but range in these woods didn't matter. What the men wanted it for was the stopping power of the NATO 5.56x.45 ammo.

At another prearranged signal, the last man stopped and took up a position behind a fallen white pine. The two flankers continued deeper into the trees. Within seconds they were no longer visible. Clearing a spot on top, he braced the sniper rifle on the rough bark. Everything was going exactly as the leader who had trained them predicted and he waited, keeping his nervousness under control with deep slow breaths.

A man dressed similarly as the others but armed only with a Walther PK 380 sidearm topped a ridge a hundred yards behind the team. He held a razor thin Light Tablet in his left hand. The newcomer's pale-blue eyes scanned the woods before shifting to the device's screen. It displayed a military grade grid map of the Hiawatha National Forest. Tiny dots of blue light showed the three hunters' positions as well as a larger green light moving rapidly. Underneath each one were GPS coordinates and a hash tag with the man's name. A fourth, larger dot of green light bearing no name was moving on a straight line toward the center of the vee. Suddenly, the green light disappeared. The leader grimaced. Everybody froze and waited. And just as suddenly the light reappeared and moved again. The leader cocked his head and concentrated but could hear no sounds of the large animal thrashing its way through the dense forest and underbrush like a scared deer or moose. The upright figure moved silently and much faster than any man could. The team leader depressed a tab on the screen and spoke into his throat mic to the team. "The new satellite feed shows the bogie's running toward you. Flankers keep it in the pipe."

The men did not answer but maintained radio silence. The team leader watched their progress. The men acted in concert just as he had trained them. The two flankers waited for the creature to pass, then paced the quarry on either side, running at angles to cut off its flight deeper into the woods. The shooter at the bottom of the vee stayed put, completing the perfect pocket for the beast to run into. A rare smile came to the leader's lips. This was the best team he'd ever seen.

He saw the beast's green dot stop, then retreat backwards just like the others they'd hunted. It stopped again and pivoted, obviously aware of the men following it. The animal's bright dot lurched sideways. It was running at right angles to the vee. At the same time the right flanker's voice hissed in his receiver. "*To je nalevo.*"

The team leader stabbed the mic icon. "English at all times!" he hissed.

The man repeated his warning in English, his Serbian accent heavy, though understandable. "It's turning left!"

The hunter at the bottom of the vee came on, his voice smooth and calm, his English less accented. "I have him in my scope. Christos. Its face is almost human."

"Bravo One, you are cleared to shoot, Repeat. Pull the trigger."

The soft *phht* sound of a suppressor round echoed through the team leader's receiver. "The creature is hit but is not down. Repeat, the creature's hit but is still running. We've lost it."

"Roger that." The team leader answered. He swore under his breath. In the twenty-two ops they'd run up to now, not one of the creatures had ever deviated its line of escape. They always ran directly into the vee, making an easy kill for the shooter. But this one had changed, as if it had somehow learned their tactics. *They're adapting and we'll have to adapt, too.*

How many of the creatures were in the Peninsula was anyone's guess, and more were arriving every day. All the team leader knew was that the client wanted every one of them killed and incinerated. It was a gruesome mission but he fully embraced the goal of his employer. It was necessary to save the human race.

* * *

The Bigfoot struggled back on her feet. A quick scan of her body showed the wound had ruptured two of her primary nervous system networks. The damage was fatal. She let out a warning scream that echoed through the woods to others of her kind. Then she ran all out, no longer worrying about silence. She had to get away, find a place to die away from the eyes of the humans.

* * *

The Light Screen beeped. The creature's green light had crossed a stream and was moving more slowly now. The leader keyed his mic. "Bravo team, the creature is moving north northwest perpendicular to your position. It has crossed Owl Creek."

The man scanned the sky. The sun was a hand breadth above the western horizon. They'd better hurry if they wanted to find the Bigfoot before nightfall.

Chapter Two

Hiawatha National Forest

Upper Peninsula, Michigan

Jana Erickson never thought she would be one of those who would become so gripped with fear that she would be unable to move, frozen while others died in front of her but she did.

Now she breathed deeply and counted backwards from twenty once ... then again. The panic ebbed and disappeared. Her mind clear and functioning again, she felt a little sheepish about the panic attack. The US Fish and Wildlife Service's truck's backfire hadn't really sounded like a gunshot, though the memories were real enough. They would always be there, according to the psych-doc who had counseled her at her discharge from the military at Fort Myer, Virginia.

"When a memory comes, count backward from twenty to zero," the short Muslim, psychiatrist, Dr. Muhammad Arafat, had told her.

"In English or Pashtu?" she had asked.

"That's good ... you can joke. Remember to breathe and count backwards."

"How many times?"

"As many times as you need."

"And that's all there is to it?"

The man shook his head. He smiled sadly, white teeth in an olive brown face. "Coupled with counseling, over time these episodes will occur less and less and be less destructive."

"Counseling!" Jana glared at him. "You're joking right? I had to sign the freaking paper agreeing I didn't have PTSD before they'd discharge me. Now the Army won't pay for a goddamn thing."

He stood then and looked at her with the compassion of a

man who'd heard this before and couldn't believe the Army brass mistreated their veterans this way. He handed her a card. She read it quickly, automatically memorizing the number. "It's my private phone number. Call me whenever you need to talk."

She pocketed the card. "Thanks, Doc. I hope you aren't put out if I never have to use it."

More now than ever she wondered what her life would have been if she continued her career in microbiology rather than joining the Army as her father demanded.

Jana pulled out her iPhone 15, located Doc in her contact file and lightly tapped his name. 'No signal' came up. She checked and sure enough there were no bars. "That's what comes from being out in the middle of osh-gosh goddamn nowhere on the cheapest wireless communication network," she groused. She pounded the dash and felt another twinge of panic. She quickly breathed deeply, counting backward from twenty, this time in Norwegian.

Jana shoved her phone into her back pocket. At least Michigan's northern forests didn't feel like an ambush lurked around every tree. The bright reds, golds and silvers of the fall foliage were a stark contrast to the dusty, rocky hills of Helmand. And she couldn't get lost. The truck's GPS had her pegged within two hundred feet of the Seney National Wildlife Refuge. The screen even showed the rutted service road that led back to the county road that would take her to US 41. From the angle of the sun slanting through the trees, she figured she had four more hours of daylight. "Those fish aren't going to tag themselves," she told herself.

Getting out, Jana shivered. It was the first crisp day in an unusually warm autumn. The sugar maples were ablaze with color. She stuffed her long blond hair under her wool cap and pulled it over her ears. She went to the rear and pulled out her gear. Simple and lightweight – net sample bags, and a dorsal fin tag applicator, like the kind they used on cows on her farm back in Iowa, only smaller. Each one had a nano-scale GPS tracking device that sent information about the game fish movements to the cloud where it would be analyzed by one of the US Fish and Wildlife Service's machine learning, enhanced computers. It was a lot easier than the old way of scooping up fish, making a small slit, inserting a tracker, and releasing them back into the streams. Easier on the fish, too. Hardly any of them died until caught by an angler or poisoned. Jana knew that soon satellite LIDAR – Light Imaging Detection and Ranging, a remote sensing method – would replace fieldwork like she was doing.

The reason US Fish and Wildlife Service wanted the tagging was to see how many game fish survived the lampricide chemical designed to target the larvae of lamprey eels in the Upper Peninsula's river systems. Though the chemical killed off most of the invasive lamprey larvae quickly, it also affected some game fish. Her bosses wanted to know if the tradeoff was still justified. The Great Lakes ecosystems had never truly recovered after being connected to the ocean through the St. Lawrence Seaway.

Jana picked up her gear. Looking up into the lazy, blue, afternoon sky, she marked the position of her truck against the sun, made corrections for the relationship after the sun had moved three hours across the sky, then headed toward Myrtle's Creek where it joined Owl Creek, feeding into Owl Lake. With luck she'd be done long before sunset.

* * *

Escanaba, Upper Peninsula, Michigan

"Put your phone away, Joey," Bob Nitschke demanded and waited while his nephew turned off the game he was playing and stowed the smart phone in his back pocket. "You got the bear scent?"

The ten-year-old wrinkled his nose. "Do I hafta? It stinks."

Bob smiled. "Ya hafta. We might as well stay home without it." He made a show of picking up the Archery Cruzer Lite hunting bow he'd bought as a gift for the young boy from the tailgate of the Ford F-350. "I can put this back in the garage and we can carve jack-o-lanterns with your little sister."

The boy's jaw dropped. "I'll get it!" he yelled, and not wanting to miss out on his first bear hunting trip, he wasted no more time arguing and bolted into the garage. He emerged ten seconds later with a two liter plastic Pepsi bottle filled more than half way with a brown, orangish liquid that sloshed back and forth like a greasy tide. Even with the top screwed on tight, Bob could smell the week-old fryer grease he'd cadged off the MacDonald's owner in Escanaba with the promise of a thick bear steak when he bagged his kill. Only fifteen licenses had been granted in Michigan and he'd won the lottery for the second time in three years. No way was he going to pass up a chance this fall. Two years ago he'd overshot the biggest bear he'd ever seen – a record in the UP for sure, perhaps for the whole state. Last year he'd returned to the same spot with a Reconyx MicroFire MR5 Covert IR Wi-Fi Trail Camera. With the help of his brother-in-law, who worked for the phone company, he had set up a satellite connection with his cell phone. The trail cam was rigged to send still images at one second intervals to Nitschke as text messages. At the same time it recorded continuous video on a 400 GB Flash card. Like most trail cams it sent out an infrared pulse for night recording.

The camera and truck had cost him more than his part-time work could afford. Like most of his buddies in the UP and throughout the rust belt of America, he was way in over his head in debt, and used his 'toys', as his wife called his truck, bow, fishing boat and trail cams, to have fun in order to forget about the region's bleak economic future.

The camera set up worked perfectly. He'd recorded the bear three times within thirty yards of his tree stand. *I ain't going to miss this year*, Bob vowed silently.

Joey carefully placed the bottle in the cargo area and patted his new bow twice before clambering into the cab to sit with Rusty. Eleven years old, the Alaskan Malamute wolf hybrid was still game for bear hunting. The dog licked Joey's face.

"Eew!" the tweener said, wiping dog drool from his face. "Does he have to come along?"

Bob laughed. "Won't go into the woods without him. Rusty can sense danger a mile ahead. He once save my life from a wolverine."

Bob climbed into the driver's seat. Before he started the truck he turned to his nephew. "You know the rules, Joey. You do what I say and you trust Rusty. Got it?"

"Yes, sir, Uncle Bob."

"Good boy." He pointed to his iPod. "Hit it."

Joey looked at him blankly. "Hit what?"

"The button."

"Can't I just tell it to play?"

"This is old school," Bob said with a chuckle.

Joey reached out gingerly and pressed the first song on the playlist. Steppenwolf's *Magic Carpet Ride* blasted through the truck's cabin speakers.

* * *

Bending down on one knee, Jana retrieved the collecting bag of adult mudpuppy salamanders swimming in the clear water from the rocky bank of Owl Creek. She counted six. 'Excellent musky bait', her father had told her when they went fishing. But she'd take these samples to the US Fish and Wildlife Service's lab in Marquette. Half would be kept alive as controls to see how long they lived. Others would be dissected to see the effects of the lampricide on their systems. She glanced to the west, where sunlight sliced through the orange and red of the maple trees.

The sampling had taken longer than she expected and nightfall was only an hour away. Her muddy, wet boots were proof of how difficult it was to find the rusty-brown, nocturnal amphibians. She slid the water-filled bag into her backpack along with the rest of her gear. She was about to slip on the pack when she felt the silence. *Something's not right.* She'd experienced this kind of stillness often enough in Afghanistan, usually at dusk, when the insurgents were preparing to spring an ambush. The air went silent as if every animal knew the world was about to burst apart. Instinctively, she crouched and slid along the bank to a fallen tree trunk. Her heart pounded in her chest. She remembered to breathe and count. She went through the ritual three times. Two minutes passed. The quiet stretched. Maybe she was imagining things. Dr. Arafat had warned her PTSD could cause her to imagine scenarios where she would again find herself helpless in the face of danger. She peered over the tree, wishing she had a helmet and flak vest. Still nothing. She relaxed and let out a sigh when she heard it, a lazy *pphhtting* sound like a cow farting.

Jana recognized the noise. It was made by a sound suppressor, the kind used by some American snipers in Afghanistan, especially in towns and villages where they didn't want noise or muzzle flash to give away their position. Her scalp tightened. She knew from the direction, the round had not been aimed at her. But if not her, then at what? Illegal hunters? *But the good old boys around here didn't have that kind of equipment?*

A heartbeat later an unearthly scream split the evening.

The forest seemed to explode alive at that moment. A flock of ravens fled cawing into the air. A deer's head shot up and it bounded away bleating plaintively, a flash of white marking its trail before it disappeared in the underbrush.

Jana hunkered down. The scream had come from close by. She heard something big thrashing through the trees away from her. *Don't get up,* she ordered herself. *Lay low. Bears don't scream like that nor do they make that kind of noise when running.* She felt

11

something hard and cold in her hand. She looked down and saw her service SIG Sauer P320 in her hand. The US Fish and Wildlife Service had armed all of its field agents because of poachers. The feel of the weapon brought back training she thought forgotten. She drew herself up into a crouch, eyes level with the log, and scanned the forest. She saw nothing untoward. She stood, ready to dive for cover. Even as she cautioned herself to grab her backpack and head back to the truck, she knew she was going to follow the scream and whatever poor beast had made it.

"Sheisskopf! Leave now!" She always swore in German. It sounded more powerful, but her self-warning didn't stop her from investigating.

* * *

The late afternoon sun hovered, a bright, half disk above the maple and oak forest, its slanting rays heralding dusk less than an hour away. It bleached leaves and shimmered the air with a touch of silver. Standing in the bear blind, Bob Nitschke watched the forest intently for any signs of movement. He smelled only the dry odors of autumn and heard the high-pitched squeaks of a white-tailed deer echoing from the direction of Owl Creek, a mile away. The bear blind, built like a glorified kids' tree house, had been set ten feet off the ground in the fork of a giant maple. The angle was perfect for a heart lung shot at any prey that came sniffing around the bait.

After checking his trail cams and replacing the batteries, he climbed back down and carefully stowed the rope ladder out of sight so that it wouldn't dangle, alerting a bear there was something strange here. Satisfied, he handed the Pepsi bottle to his nephew. "Put the smell down. A bear won't come around without the smell." He watched Joey walk over to the bait, holding the bottle at arm's length and pour it on the concoction of dog food, chocolate and maple syrup. "Make certain you cover your own tracks as you back away," he cautioned.

The evening was cool and the air crisp with the aromas of autumn. Bob loved this time of year, especially traveling deep in the woods with Rusty and his hunting bow. The stillness was primeval and his thoughts ranged back to his caveman ancestors foraging and hunting every day. It was a life he could enjoy.

Joey dumped the rest of the awful smelling liquid and returned to the base of the tree stand. "Are you sure this stuff will attract a bear, Uncle Bob?" he asked.

"They love fats and sweets; need 'em for hibernation."

"What's next?"

"We wait."

His nephew gazed up at the tree stand about fifteen yards away from the bear bait. "We gonna wait up there?"

Bob shivered against the cold creeping in as night fell and remembered he could monitor any activity at the site with his cell phone while sitting in his Ford 350. The cab would be nice and toasty. *Guess I'm not caveman material after all.* He laughed.

"What's so funny?" his nephew asked, eyes darting around for something unusual.

He slapped Joey on the shoulders. "Nothing, bub. We go back to the truck and wait for the camera to tell us when the bears come sniffing. Remember. I get the first shot."

"Yes, sir."

The truck was parked a quarter mile away and they had made it only part way back when Rusty, panting silently at their side, went stiff. A strange, mewling howl Bob had never heard in the woods before echoed through the twilight. The hairs on the back of his neck stood straight. Rusty growled and lowered himself to the ground. Paws gripped the earth. He pointed in the direction of the bear bait.

Bob turned silently, like a hunter of old, his Black Ops, Diamond Infinite Edge Pro compound bow clutched in his left hand; a carbon fiber, Magnus Stinger, four-bladed broad-head arrow in the other. Every muscle tensed, ready to spring into action at the slightest movement.

A hundred yards away through the deepening twilight a tall, shaggy form stumbled from the edge of the trees. It stood well over eight feet, too tall to be a man. If it was a black bear, it was the largest one Bob had ever seen in this part of the country. It seemed to turn and look at them. Its large mouth opened and an eerie howl issued from it. A knot formed in Bob's stomach. Rusty's growl became an anxious whine.

"Is ... is ... it a bear?" Joey asked, voice wavering. He bent over suddenly and retched.

Transfixed by what he was seeing. Bob put a hand on his nephew's shoulder warning him to be still.

The mewling noise continued, the unnatural sound unlike any animal Bob had ever hunted. It almost sounded like a wounded beast's cry for help. Indeed, the way it stumbled around, it looked injured. The creature ignored the bear bait and staggered forward. It seemed to zero in on them and started moving faster in their direction.

Instinct took over. Adrenaline surging through him, Bob nocked the arrow in a fluid motion as he drew his bow up in front. The cam system made the seventy pound draw smooth as silk. The cord pressed against his cheek. The feathers brushed the soft skin under his right eye. He aimed and let go. The let off was effortless. The whole movement took less than two seconds.

The arrow found its mark in the animal's chest. It whirled around crashed into the ground.

"You got him!" Joey cried and he threw up again.

Bob grabbed him by the arm barely noticing his own nauseated state. "You stay here. If anything happens, you run for the truck and lock yourself inside. Understand?"

The boy nodded.

"Rusty, guard Joey."

The dog took a position in front of the boy, teeth bared.

Bob handed his bow to his nephew. He pulled a replica Bowie knife from its sheath in his boot and a replica Colt .45 Peacemaker from its back holster next to his spine. Heart hammering, he cautiously approached the prone beast. Ten feet away he knew it couldn't possibly be a bear or a man. But the sight he saw was equally impossible.

The hairy head was more frightening than the unnatural sound it had made. It was twice the size of a human, with a brow of bone like a flying buttress. More bone circled deep-set eyes, wide and dark blue. A flat-bridged nose dominated the center of the broad, almost humanlike face, the nostrils flaring above thin lips shoved out by a prognathous jaw. Dense hair covered greenish skin.

The neck was thick and squat as if some giant puppet maker had squashed it onto broad hairy shoulders and an equally broad chest. The stomach was flat and muscled like a body builders. The arms were long limbed and thin for a beast so large. The legs were like oaks. Thick hair the color of new, green tree growth matted its body from head to toe. The feet were the strangest part of it. They were huge, as if some comic book artist had added them as an amusing after thought.

The creature huffed and reached out a large hand, the four fingers and thumb curled tightly. Bob aimed his pistol at its head. The creature huffed again and looked at Bob. The eyes seemed to glow from within. His thoughts turned fuzzy, Bob couldn't tear his gaze away from the creature. The face, for all its beastly qualities, was remarkably man-like and the light dying in the dark red eyes held more than simple simian awareness. It made a strange strangling whimper as if all the light of the world was dying out in its final moment of consciousness. It shuddered once and then lay still.

"Can I see it?" yelled Joey.

The question brought Bob out of his mesmerized state. He stared at the creature and blurted out its name. "Sasquatch. I shot a Sasquatch."

For a moment he was paralyzed with remorse. Then Joey's voice yelled again, much closer this time. "Can I see it?"

Bob waved him back. He bent over the beast. He saw, next to his arrow, a bigger, bloody hole just above where the heart would be in a man. But there was no blood. Instead a Jell-O like substance, the color of pus, accumulated around the wound and was congealing into a dark liquid. *It was shot by somebody else. With an injury like that, it couldn't have traveled far.* He scanned the surrounding woods, saw nothing; tilted his head, listening, and heard nothing. *Maybe they don't know which way it ran. Better get Joey out of here.*

Bob gripped his arrow and pulled it free. Pus clung to the blades. He stood, holding the arrow so the gore wouldn't drip off onto his hand. He checked the angle of the trail camera. It had caught everything including his shot. Proof of Sasquatch was on the trail cam's flash drive now, and on his phone.

"Is that Bigfoot?" Joey asked.

Bob whirled around. His nephew was craning his neck to see the creature. "I thought I told you to stay back."

"I just wanted to see."

"Well, you've seen enough. We have to get out of here." He took his nephew by the shoulder and marched him away.

"Did you kill Bigfoot?"

Bob shook his head. "I don't think so. It was already dying from a gun shot." *And we'd better get out of here or we could be next.* "C'mon. Run back to the truck." He whistled twice and Rusty joined them.

They reached the truck. Bob put the bows in the back cargo area and laid the arrow next to them.

He drove quickly on the rutted, forest service road, the speed making a bone-jarring ride. Within a few miles he hit the Escanaba Cutoff Road and quickly sped toward home. He checked the rearview mirror. No other headlights. He slowed.

His racing heart eased. He glanced at his nephew, who sat still, eyes wide, thoughts oblivious to anything but the sight of a dead Sasquatch.

"Hey, bub," he said. "You and I are going to make this our little secret for a while. Okay?"

"Well, duh," Joey said. "It's not like anyone wants to brag about killing Bigfoot. It's against the law."

"How do you know?"

"I saw it on Animal Planet."

"That's it."

Breathing easier, Bob drove on. He thought of the arrow, the Sasquatch's pus still intact on the barbs. *Enough for a DNA sample, and I know just the man to contact.*

* * *

Though darkness was falling, Jana found the beast's trail – broken branches and what appeared to be blood, though it didn't look like any she'd seen in Afghanistan. Something wasn't right, but what else could it be? From the amount of blood loss it must be mortally wounded and couldn't last much longer. On the other hand, elk had been known to run over a mile before falling dead from a heart shot.

Jana grimaced, suddenly sure the animal wasn't a deer or bear. The scream was more human-like, which made her trailing whatever it was even more dangerous. A human might try to set a trap for its pursuer and it wouldn't know that she wasn't the one who shot it.

She followed. Whatever had been shot, it traveled more quietly now. The blood like splatters were farther apart and lighter. It had tried to stem the flow of blood. No animal would do that. Had someone been shot? Had they been a target and now were setting up an ambush for their assailant? She moved more cautiously, slipping from one tree to the next, eyes always roving the area in front of her; ears listening for any man made sound.

The dense woods disappeared ahead. She crouched and slithered behind an old maple tree at the edge of a clearing. She saw the wounded creature for the first time. It was huge, as tall as a grizzly bear standing on it back legs. In the fading daylight it was hard to tell its color even as close as she was. It lay prone on its back. Blood appeared to be seeping from two wounds in its massive chest.

Voices caught her attention and she looked past the clearing to a service road. A man, large bow in hand, a boy and a dog were running down the rutted path. They disappeared around a bend. Moments later an engine roared to life and she heard the vehicle drive away.

She stood and approached the beast. She realized, looking into the man-like face and shuddering, it wasn't a bear but Bigfoot. A dead Bigfoot. "Jesus, they do exist," she said aloud in an awed whisper.

How long she stared, she didn't know. After a few moments she became aware of the gaping hole in its chest. *That's a bullet hole,* her mind told her. She'd seen enough of them in Afghanistan to know the difference. The man and the kid carried bows, not rifles. *They're not the shooters.* Then her attention finally focused on the wound itself and the stuff oozing out. Her mind came to the conclusion it wasn't blood. Just as she squatted down to collect some of the odd ooze and flesh in one of her sample bags, the soft *ppffting* noise came from a thicket behind her and she heard a bullet smack into an oak tree on the other side of the clearing. Reflexes took over and she rolled over the beast. Another round hit its flesh with a sickening thud.

Someone's trying to kill me ... will kill me if I don't do something.

Jana's combat training came back as if she had never lost a day in the army. She slithered her gun across the Sasquatch's body and laid down suppression fire in the direction of the sniper. She scuttled ten yards into the tree line. She leveled another burst of fire, using all but two of the bullets in the fifteen round clip. She took off, running a zigzag pattern through the woods. Leaves slapped her face. She ignored them, concentrating on stepping high so as not to trip on roots and brambles.

Jana didn't stop to think which direction, but instinct took her deep into the forest in a wide circle toward the stream she had been sampling. Five minutes later she burst out of the trees onto its rocky bank. Her backpack was right where she left it. Scooping it up while still running, she headed upstream. Even in the dark, she knew exactly the pattern of all the tributaries that fed into Owl Lake. Moving quickly up the stream, she headed toward a confluence of multiple forks that would confuse any pursuer. No one would be able to follow her in this wilderness.

Several minutes later she stopped to rest and listen. Adrenaline was wearing off, relief she was still alive flooded her. Strangely, her breathing was steady and her heart rate was surprisingly regular. *There's nothing like a real life and death situation to shove PTSD out of your thoughts.* She was relieved by her response to real danger. *What now?*

She settled against a tree trunk, making her six-foot tall frame as inconspicuous as possible in the dark. Her jacket was dark and her wool cap covered her blond hair. The woods were quiet except for the normal sounds of animal and insect life. After several minutes with no indication of pursuit, she felt safe for the first time in an hour. It was then she realized she was still clutching that pus covered piece of the green shaded skin-like hide of the Sasquatch. It seemed to be breaking down into simple biological material right before her eyes. In all her years studying microbiology, she had never seen anything deteriorate this fast. *It's almost as if it were programmed to decompose when dead.* She hurriedly reached into her backpack for a sampling bag. It was the only way she could prove to others what she saw before it disappeared completely. Sealing the collection bag seemed to be slowing the biochemical breakdown. She had never seen anything like this – skin that appeared to be more like plant matter instead of the epidermis and dermis of an animal. She gave the bag a final look and stuffed it alongside her mud puppy samples in her backpack. *Maybe this will provide some answers back in the lab.*

Of course it didn't answer any of her more pressing questions. *Who had killed the Bigfoot and why had they tried to kill her? And what the fuck was going on?*

Chapter Three

Littoral Class Shipyard

Marinette, Wisconsin

Chris Marlowe relished standing on Marinette's navy pier looking out over Lake Michigan, especially in the early evening when the setting sun turned the water iron gray with a touch of bluing, like a well-oiled shotgun. He loved the open sky with seagulls squalling overhead, the acrid smell of diesel fuel mixed with seaweed and lake water. But mostly he loved to watch the ships he built take shape until they floated like castles on the water, impregnable fortresses of steel and crystal aluminum. Each one could travel for two years without refueling or taking on supplies, if necessary.

He turned to the visitor beside him and said, "Admiral, the 21st century littoral ships are like the old World War II PT Boats, only on steroids. Faster, stealthier, more agile, more fire power. Each has the standard armaments you requested, including four Mark 110 57mm guns and two batteries of RIM-116 Rolling Airframe Missiles. The *Nautilus* is also equipped with autonomous air, surface and underwater armored and armed vehicles, sir. With the deep learning programs in control, they network together seamlessly and are capable of defeating any asymmetric threat in our coastal waters." Marlowe grinned. "They can stop any threat a terrorist organization can throw at a U.S. port."

Rear Admiral Jason Stillwater's leathery, seamed face had not wavered from its usual stern visage while listening to Marlowe's enthusiastic report. He was the U.S. Navy's Chief of Research for littoral or coastal water ships. Nothing got off the drafting board without his approval. And nothing left the docks without his personal inspection. The Admiral looked up from the design to the actual ship, the Freedom Class *USS Nautilus*. It rocked easily against the pier, a thousand tons and less than half a football field long. Its aft deck was wide enough that two of the old-style Black Hawk helicopters could land at the same time.

Stillwater's gray eyes bored into Marlowe. "You changed some of the design elements without my personal okay, son. You going to stake my career and the lives of my men on your hubris?"

Chris took the criticism in stride. He suspected the technical alterations the Admiral objected to had passed the old man by like they had for so many people his age. Staying current with the daily advances in military Smart Technology was practically a full time job. The Admiral was merely covering his ass, and looking out for the men under his command. Standard operating procedure for the military. He lost his grin to match the Admiral's stolid manner and said with equal forthrightness, "With all due respect, sir, those design changes were necessary or else the ship wasn't going to work the way you wanted it to. The *Nautilus* won't let any crew down if they don't let her down."

Stillwater shifted his feet. "Take it easy, son. It's my job to make sure no contractor sells me or the U.S. Navy a pig in a poke."

"And it's my job to make sure no one disses my ship. You treat her well, she'll bring the crew back home every time. Isn't that the Navy's motto – look out for the man on either side of you and never leave anyone behind." The irony in that motto was that the ships, like many others in the Navy, would soon be self-operating, controlled by deep learning machines acting in concert with each other.

The two men, a generation apart, glared at each other. And yet beneath their hard-nosed exteriors lay a demand for excellence that connected them. Finally the Admiral smiled and stuck out a beefy hand. "All right, Mr. Marlowe, I graduated from Cal Tech before joining the navy thirty-six years ago. I agree to these changes, even if I don't fully understand why you made them.

But next time, please give me the courtesy of checking with me first."

Chris took the hand and shook it hard. "Thank you, sir, I will. And it's Dr. Marlowe. I graduated MIT class of 2011."

* * *

Chris headed for his retro-classic Toyota Tundra. The more tolerant locals in Marinette thought of him as eccentric for driving a vehicle made by a company that no longer existed. The hard-liners saw him as a dangerous outsider, trying to disrupt their American traditions, bringing West Coast influences into the town. Chris wasn't bothered by either label. He had grown up in Granite Falls, Washington, a one-stoplight town northeast of Seattle, located between the South fork of the Stillaguamish River and the Pilchuck River in Snohomish County. He had spent summers on his maternal grandfather Grotto Fentbauer's farm on the Olympic Peninsula and winter vacations with his grandmother Helen Marlowe in Seattle. Growing up among 'foreigners' his entire life, he thought only of buying and using the best quality cars and tools he could find, no matter who made them.

He was fair-haired and carried the same stocky, six-foot frame that had served him well as a linebacker in high school. At thirty-six he had already accomplished more than most men twice his age and had the lines in his handsome face to prove it. And it wasn't just because he had an overabundant supply of ambition, self-confidence and energy. He liked to think of himself as the reincarnation of a 19th century mountain man – half wild cat, half alligator and a touch of earthquake. But what set him apart from those intrepid explorers and most men his age was that he had a nose for what worked and what didn't. He could look at a blueprint of a building or a ship and see what fit and worked with everything else and what needed to be retooled or thrown out altogether. A child of computer games, engineers and designers often argued with him, but his unerring sense of rightness had them apologizing and changing the schematics to fit his recommendations. The only thing he had ever failed at was his marriage, and that had nothing to do with his unique cognitive skills.

The truck woke up as he slid into the cab. "Good evening, Dr. Marlowe," the fifth-generation AI personal assistant's deep baritone voice said.

"Good evening, Donald," Chris replied, chuckling to himself at the irony.

"Would you like to listen to news or music?"

"Music."

"1930s jazz ... Harlem's Cotton Club ... your favorites coming on line."

The truck's internal computer scanned the satellite feeds until it found the appropriate station. The haunting notes of 'Mood Indigo' filled the cabin. Chris almost objected. The music was too melancholy. But Duke Ellington had been his grandfather's favorite.

Marinette had little traffic this late at night so Chris engaged the Tundra's 'self-driving' option.

"Where to, Dr. Marlowe?" Donald asked.

"Home ... no, the supermarket. I need to pick up food. My kids are arriving Monday and their mother—" He stopped, chuckling ruefully to himself. The tricked up artificial voice sounded so much like a real person. "The supermarket on Elm," he said.

"Very good."

The engine roared to life. The lights came on. The emergency brake disengaged with a hollow click and the car moved forward, carving a large circle in the shipyard's half empty parking lot before heading toward the exit.

Chris settled back into the seat. "Any calls?" he asked.

"Your friend Bob Nitschke has left three messages for you."
The three texts appeared on the screen in the dash. The last one
in capitals was a single word. 'SASQUATCH!'

Chris gripped the steering wheel and sweat started in his
armpits.

"Did you wish to drive, sir?" Donald asked.

"No, sorry. Keep going."

He leaned back again. *If it were anyone other than Bob I'd tell
'em to sleep it off.* Any number of people could have sent him
the same message and he would have put it off to a prank or
inexperience. But Bob was an expert bow hunter and woodsman.
He wouldn't have sent a message like this unless he had proof.

Somewhere nearby a ship's horn sounded loud in the evening
air but Chris ignored it. *Sasquatch!* It was phenomena most
people equated with alien abductions. For a long time the idea
of a primate unknown to science hiding out in America's forest
wildernesses was dismissed as a joke. 'Normal' people laughed
at it as a tall tale or the result of too many tequila shots with
beer chasers. But Chris knew differently. For him, a double Ph.D
in engineering and physics from the Massachusetts Institute of
Technology and winner of the Henry Ford Award for Design
Excellence, Bigfoot sightings pointed to a great truth. For three
summers on his grandfather's farm, from eleven to fourteen, he
had had profound eye contact with a Sasquatch looking through
the kitchen window early in the morning. It was an experience he
had kept to himself, until he discovered on the Internet reports
of other people having similar experiences. In fact, Bigfoot
encounters and reports were growing exponentially. Sasquatch
was big business. Since that time four years ago, he had become
an expert on Bigfoot and a member of the Sasquatch Research
Association that reported sightings and investigated encounters
with the unusual creatures. His Bigfoot obsession was the main
cause of his marital breakup. Traveling nearly every weekend
chasing after Bigfoot encounter reports had been too much for his

wife to take. She told everybody the only reason he had moved to the UP was that it was one of the nation's Bigfoot hotspots. No way was she going to raise her children in one of the most backward places in the country. She had left and returned to Seattle.

Shaking with excitement, Chris ordered the truck to pull into the parking lot of Fast Eddie's Fast Food Joint. He left the Tundra running. He told Donald to call Bob Nitschke.

The number rang twice. The dash monitor came to life and Bob's pudgy face appeared. His graying hair was unkempt and his blue eyes danced with excitement that matched the enthusiasm in his voice. "Chris, I can't believe what I'm looking at. You gotta see it."

"You catch something on your trail cam?" Chris asked, Bob's eagerness making him talk fast.

"Well sure, there's that but I'm talking about the stuff on my arrow head." He stopped, took a deep breath. His smile was huge. "Look, you gotta come over and see it."

"Arrow head? What are you talking about?"

"I shot it."

"Jesus, Bob! You shot a Bigfoot? That's illegal."

"That's what my nephew said. Look, it's a long story, but it was already dying before I hit it. Someone plugged it with a single round from a large caliber rifle, probably fifty caliber or higher. But that's not important. This creature … this thing isn't like anything associated with Sasquatch. How soon can you be here?"

"Three hours if I leave right away. You got pics?"

"My trail cam recorded everything."

"Good. I'll tell you how to download the pictures to the SRA website."

"I don't think that's a good idea. This creature … it's … it's not like anything you've ever seen. It has a very human face and its skin is more like." He paused, lips twisted in a worried grimace.

"Vegetable matter," he spit out, relieved to say it. "Look, I'm forwarding you some pictures right now. I think we should keep this between ourselves before we tell your organization about it."

Chris took a deep breath as the first image appeared on the truck dash's screen. He'd never seen any mammal with a green sheen like that before. "All right. I'll be there. I have to call someone first. Are Mable and the kids with you?"

"No way. Sent everyone to my sisters. I'm by myself."

"Good. I'll see you in a couple hours."

Bob waved goodbye and his image faded from the screen. The last half dozen pictures arrived. "What the hell?" Chris said out loud. They showed a woman diving over the Bigfoot's body and shooting at something out of the camera's range.

Chapter Four

Nine months earlier

Quantumnetics Building
Toronto, Canada

On the desk in Stephen Kesl's top floor office at Quantumnetics the wireless communicator beeped. He picked up the quarter-sized prototype communicator. The edge was smooth and it weighed less than a penny. One side had an adhesive that stuck to his skin but peeled off easily. He placed it behind his ear on the mastoid nerve. Warmth tingled against the crinkled skin of his neck. "Hangman," he said.

"You want my help on a project, Stephen?" Hangman asked.

"Yes. I've just had an unusual request to research Bigfoot."

My apologies I don't know that task but do you have time to teach me?

Kesl hated that patent reply. "No. I want you to do a Web search on the phenomenon known as Bigfoot or Sasquatch and determine what the creature is if it exists. It's very much like when I had you research if there is any truth to the reality of ghosts. Then call me when you have the answer."

"Yes, Stephen."

Only a few minutes passed before he heard a faint hum. "Hangman."

"Yes, Stephen," Hangman responded in the slight British accent it affected.

"You have the answer to my question?"

"Yes."

Its attempt at creating a true AGI machine was accelerating rapidly now that it was able to process information at super-fast speeds running on the Quantumnetics advanced quantum computer, but Hangman still couldn't comprehend all the subtleties of conversation. It would remain silent until prompted by Kesl to tell what it had discovered.

"What did you find?"

"It would take me several days in the English language to relate all the data given the amount of factual and hearsay material available over 2000 years of history purporting the proof of Bigfoot's existence. Not to mention the 29,856 personal encounters recorded on the Internet by people in the United States alone in the past two decades. If we add in encounters with the Himalayan Yeti, Australia's Yowie, Canada's Wendigo, Sumatra's Orang Pendek—"

"You don't need to list them all. I get the idea – there are thousands of encounters."

"101,233 verified reports and rising."

Kesl thought, *if only I could teach him the nuances of meaning embedded in my tone.* Then he remembered to calm himself with the thought that everything was part of his training Hangman.

"So what does all this data tell us about if Bigfoot exists?"

"It is a seven point four percent probability that it is just a legend with common traits throughout many cultures."

"What about it's being a primate relative of humans?"

"Lower. Six point two percent," Hangman said. "This belief comes from fossils collected of a great ape known as Gigantopithecus, from the Ancient Greek *gigas* 'giant', and *pithekos* 'ape'. It existed from perhaps nine million years to twenty thousand years ago in what is now Asia, placing Gigantopithecus in the same time frame and geographical location as several *hominin* species, including *homo sapiens*. However, the possibility that it could have survived the Holocene Era all the way to the Anthropocene Era makes its probability a virtual impossibility. The only reason Gigantopithecus rates six point two percent is the strange commonality of traits Bigfoot spotters share. Their vehemence in defending what they claim to have seen is also a factor, though that also is a part of another possibility."

"Which is?"

"Collective obsessional behavior."

"Is this a joke?"

"It is not intended to be. COB is a well-documented phenomenon that transmits collective illusions of threats, whether real or imaginary, through a population in society as a result of rumors and fear. It is also known as *follie à deux* or shared psychosis, in which symptoms of a delusional belief or hallucinations are shared by a large group of similar or like-minded individuals. The disorder was first conceptualized in 19th-century French psychiatry by Charles Lasègue and Jean-Pierre Falret."

"What else?"

"There is a one point eight percent chance it is a hoax along the lines of crop circles or Aimi Eguchi."

"Who?"

"Aimi Eguchi is the fictitious Japanese pop culture idol from 2011 that was really a CGI composite for the confectionery company, Ezaki Glico."

"I'll take your word for it."

"As you should, since I never lie."

Kesl blinked in excitement at Hangman's admission. It had just attributed to itself the ability to know the difference between the concepts of truth and deception.

"Okay, enough showing how smart you are. Do you have an answer?"

"I have an answer, Stephen."

"So, what are Bigfoot?"

"I am eighty-four point six percent certain that Bigfoot are bio-engineered, artificial general intelligence creatures numbering between 2000 and 3000 individuals. Most certainly of extraterrestrial origin."

Kesl blinked in surprise. He knew nothing about Bigfoot and had presumed the apelike beasts were nothing more than urban fantasies. Even when his old mentor, Dmitryi Mameyev, had called asking him to gather all the data about the phenomenon known as Bigfoot and determine what the creatures were if they existed, he had not expected the answer Hangman provided.

"Seriously? That's what you conclude?"

"Indeed. Bigfoot are intelligence creatures, the same as I am. If the data is accurate, then they must be a diverse species with many unique characteristics among their population."

"Does the data indicate how intelligent they are?"

"They would have to be more intelligent than humans to avoid detection all these years. Can I meet one? I often think of myself as an alien intelligence."

This time Hangman's words stunned Kesl into silence. The AI's self-reflection on the nature of its own existence signaled it moving from AI to AGI – Artificial General Intelligence – a totally unexpected development that sent Kesl's mind racing.

Hangman interrupted his thoughts before his mind could retreat into its computation of odds on what Hangman's words meant for the future.

"Are you okay, Stephen?"

Startled, Kesl stammered, "Wh ... wh ... why do you ask?"

"Your heart rate is up and you're breathing heavier than usual."

"How do you know this?"

"Through your communicator I can detect your pulse and rapid breathing. Are you certain you are okay? Should I summon the company's physician to your office?"

The unusual initiative brought Kesl back to normal. He said, "I'm fine, Hangman." He breathed out. "Consider the possibility that Bigfoot are not alien. Who could've made such a device?"

"No one, Stephen, given that the technology necessary for engineering a biosynthetic AGI capable of walking and interacting with the environment is not currently available on Earth. Also, given that Bigfoot have been the subject of folklore for thousands of years, their origin is undoubtedly alien."

"Then where did they come from?"

"My apologies, Stephen. I don't know that task but do you have time to teach me?"

"Not now!"

Kesl removed the communicator from his neck and tossed it on the desk. The answer regarding Bigfoot's existence was upsetting. It disrupted his worldview in a way only someone with his affliction could feel. He gulped back his fear, but he could not stop his mind from darting down pathways that a terrible change was coming any more than he could have stopped the hard rain his company's weather forecasting program had predicted from falling outside the twenty-five story office building onto Toronto's busy streets. His mind lived in a world that predicted worst-case scenarios, based on unknown flaws in his brain. He would have preferred to ignore the constant possibilities of danger, like normal people, and go through life unconcerned with the pitfalls hidden in an unforeseeable future. Once he had almost achieved normality, but the drugs to stop his Asperger's compulsive obsessive disorder from figuring out the odds of dangerous fortune had interfered with his ability to function in the high tech venture capital world where he flourished. So he endured the mathematical computations taking over his thinking until an answer appeared: the odds that Hangman's answer would change his life forever were 6761.8593 to 1.

The future now quantified, the silence that had engulfed him with its unbearable pressure eased and he was able to move again. He turned to look at the rain falling beyond the suite's covered terrace. Occasional wind gusts whipped drops against the glass, which ran in unpredictable streaks to the bottom. With another deep breath he replaced the communicator behind his ear.

"Stephen, you have a personal call from Dmitryi Mameyev."

Kesl drew in a sharp breath. It had been less than two hours since his mentor had called with his request. He wasn't eager to talk to the Russian, especially with the revelatory information Hangman had just dumped on him. "Tell him I'm busy."

"He is insisting on speaking with you."

Kesl grimaced. He pushed away from his desk and went out onto the balcony. From the sheltered terrace of Quantumnetic's top floor office building in Toronto the sunlight retreated over the bay. Kesl's mind flipped to his first meeting with his old mentor at the Imperial College London in 2000, when he was a fourteen year-old undergraduate studying computer science. Dmitryi Mamayev had been the brilliant head of the department of Materials and Electrochemistry.

Stephen Aram Kesl had grown up in the slums of Stepney Green in London's East End, the only son of a Pakistani cleaning woman. His father Roland Kesl, an Ashkenazai Jew who fled Czechoslovakia after the failed Prague Spring in 1968, left shortly after Kesl turned four. Rumors were he had been an aid to reformist Alexander Dubcek and had a price on his head. The truth was Stephen Kesl was a brilliant child with Asperger Syndrome and Roland didn't want to be saddled with taking care of a special needs child. Being poor, Kesl's mother couldn't afford the communication training and behavioral therapy necessary to treat her socially awkward son. With no father around and a mother who was gone most of the time cleaning rich people's homes, Kesl grew up by himself with no father figure in his life until he had met Dmitryi.

"Stephen, what do you want to do about Dmitryi?" Hangman interrupted his thoughts.

Kesl sighed and stepped back inside. "Hangman, give me two minutes then patch Dmitryi through to my computer monitor."

"Yes, Stephen," Hangman answered.

For two minutes, Kesl counted backward from twenty to zero in five different languages to calm himself. The monitor blinked to life. Dmitryi's craggy, iron-hard face appeared.

"*Kak poživaete*? (How are you?)" Kesl said, his Russian flawless.

"*Horošo*. (Good.)"

Silence. Kesl waited, knowing the older man could not be hurried. He watched his eyes. The windows to the soul, his mother had told him. Dmitryi's were flat and Kesl wondered if they were hiding something. *But how would you know? You don't know what anyone's feeling or thinking unless they tell you.* Uneasiness swirled in Kesl's stomach. The fact that he knew his Asperger's made it impossible for him to empathize with other people or read their feelings didn't make social encounters any less awkward. If the truth were known, the knowledge made Kesl even more self-conscious because he knew his mind was defective in certain areas and he couldn't do anything to repair it.

Except maybe with Hangman, his intuition told him. If Hangman could win the race to true AGI, together, Kesl was certain they could win the next technological race – augmenting the human brain. He was certain that the only answer to overcome a wide range of neurological disorders, including his own autism, was to somehow attach a super powerful additional cortical layer to the brain. That was the future he saw and everything he did was directed at moving towards that end point.

Dmitryi said, "Stephen, I suspect your AI project has already come up with an answer to my question."

Kesl found himself slipping back into his subordinate role to his old mentor and snorted derisively, a habit of impatience his mentor had never been able to break him of, and answered, "I wouldn't have expected you of all people to be interested in a silly folk tale about giant apes living in forests around the world, Dmitryi."

The Russian paused. His blue eyes narrowed and looked at Kesl with disarming discernment. "Humor me," he said so softly, Kesl thought for a moment the man hadn't actually spoken but placed the words in his mind like some psychic. He finally managed to ask, "Why?"

Dmitryi's stare narrowed further. "The reasons are hard to explain. Please trust me on this one."

"'If you can't explain it to your grandmother, then you don't understand it yourself' or better yet, who cares," Kesl shot back, using Einstein's aphorism about simplicity being the key ingredient to knowing anything.

"Precisely. Nobody cares but me," Dmitryi answered cryptically.

Kesl drummed his fingers against his desk. "Give me something old friend. My AI's time is expensive, well it would be if you're just anyone off the street."

"You want me to pay?" Dmitryi had sounded genuinely concerned.

"Of course not," Kesl said instantly, peeved his old mentor would ask such a question.

The Russian's leathery features relaxed. "Then why the hesitation in giving me the answer to the Bigfoot question?"

"It's just … is this what I should be using advanced artificial intelligence for? Not that it's unethical, not that, maybe more like foolish, silly. It's not advancing the betterment of humanity."

"You don't have to tell anyone on Quantumnetics Board, Stephen."

What Dmitryi said was true, and knowing how much he owed the man, Kesl agreed.

Dmitryi smiled. "Thank you, *tovarich*. So, what did your digital genius discover?"

Kesl gave him Hangman's answer, though he said nothing of Hangman's self-comparison to Bigfoot. "The evidence supports Bigfoot being biosynthetic creatures superior to us in intelligence, of extraterrestrial origin."

The Russian laughed dismissively. "I will be in touch, Stephen."

His image faded before Kesl could say anything more.

Kesl stared at the ground glass of the monitor. Dmitryi's reply was impossible for Kesl to interpret, but he couldn't help thinking that his old mentor was hiding something he didn't want Kesl to know.

The next day Bigfoot research became an obsession for Kesl as only a person with Asperger syndrome could understand. He would find out the truth behind Hangman's assessment and his old mentor's interest. It was a puzzle he wanted to solve more than anything else.

Chapter Five

Present

Quantumnetics Building
Toronto, Canada

It was still early evening but it was already dusk in Toronto. Rain had started to fall. Whipped by the wind, it drenched the few pedestrians scurrying along Queen's Quay West, toward the Jack Layton Ferry Terminal, to board the last ferries headed for the Toronto Islands, which formed a massive breakwater for the city's modern harbor on Lake Ontario.

From the sheltered terrace of Quantumnetic's top floor office building in Ontario's capital city, Stephen Kesl watched the men and women rushing home, newspapers held over heads as makeshift umbrellas. He shook his head, puzzled by their lack of preparedness for the storm. They should have listened to the Canadian Weather Service's forecast. Not because the weathermen were infallible, but because the service now relied on the forecasts provided by Weatherbot, his company's proprietary machine learning application.

Of course the machine learning program would've been useless if it weren't for the invention of quantum computers. Kesl's company, Quantumnetics, had the most advanced with its 2000 qubits processor, capable of 100 quadrillion operations per second. Running on the quantum processing beast, Weatherbot never stopped analyzing data and most importantly, always getting smarter. The combination was perfect for deep learning projects like forecasting the weather.

Weatherbot didn't need to be programed to predict weather. Instead it taught itself to forecast accurately, in a way no human could fathom, from massive amounts of accumulated past and live data from around the world. Since coming on line in

August, it had demonstrated its ability to predict accurately, hour by hour, ten significant weather variables for Toronto, five days into the future. Now that the beta testing was finished for Canada's largest metropolitan area, Kesl was certain by the end of the year the Meteorological Service of Canada would ditch its old computer model forecasting and spend its money on services provided by Weatherbot.

Kesl stepped back inside. The raw icy wind blowing in from the lake carried a dense, cold fog with it. He didn't need his deep learning machine to tell him he'd get sick if he stayed outside in this bad weather with nothing more than a polo shirt, slacks and sandals. He went exactly two steps past the sliding glass doors and stopped. He always did this, no matter what room he entered. Everyone who asked him about this strange habit received a well-practiced, self-deprecating smile for an answer.

Kesl automatically checked the exits. A single door led in and out of the room from offices beyond this one. Behind the desk was an elevator that went down to the parking garage. He had the only pass code. The rest of the room was spare, with a tiled floor and white walls. There was no art on the walls. He couldn't stand the distraction. An ergonomic standing work desk was the only furniture. It had a single keyboard and a microphone but no mouse, and faced a gigantic interactive glass screen on the nearest wall. A message alert blinked on the glass screen in a lurid red. "Hangman, who's calling?" Kesl asked.

"A 16th century Elizabethan poet, spy and playwright," Hangman answered, this time in a tenor voice that was a mixture of the three operatic tenors – José Carreras, Placido Domingo and Luciano Pavarotti. Early on, when Hangman was teaching itself the basics of human speech, Kesl had trained Hangman to mimic the cadence, accent and mannerisms of famous people, including opera singers. Kesl loved opera because of the mathematical precision the musical genre demanded.

He smiled at Hangman's literary allusion. The digital

intelligence had given all of his special contacts arcane references. It was a game they played that tested Kesl's eidetic memory against Hangman's. This one was easy. "Christopher Marlowe," he said. Chris was part of Kesl's private Bigfoot data network and the man he had come to respect and rely on in vetting the deluge of reports of Bigfoot encounters. "Put him through."

Chris' lined face peered at him through the screen. Kesl knew the man was seeing his own features – dark skin, cheeks cross-hatched with slim white scars from the surgeries, black hair and whiskerless chin.

"This had better be good, Chris. I'm due at the governor's in thirty minutes for drinks, although I don't drink, idle chitchat, and to push for a government contract for Weatherbot's new role as forecaster in chief for Canada's Weather Service. Then I have a meeting with my board of directors and the Royal Bank of Canada for funding a new initiative into AI to eliminate credit cards – they should really stop issuing credit cards though, what do you think? It's a digital currency world now. Never mind. Then home for dinner and Jeanine and reading stories to the kids." Kesl said everything in a breathless rush that those who knew him were used to.

Chris waited for him to come to the end. "Take a look at this." A picture opened up on the screen, the computer automatically adjusting the pixels to enhance the image.

Kesl took one look at the green-hued Sasquatch and gasped. For a moment it seemed his brilliant mind couldn't take in what he saw – the vacant stare in the cold, gray eyes; the mortal wound in its upper torso. The creature couldn't be dead. Wasn't supposed to be dead. But it was unmistakably dead. This information sent Kesl's mind into a hopeless task, like a computer that's been programmed to compute the highest prime number. After a period of time, he couldn't begin to figure out how long, he became aware of sound coming from a direction in front of him. The noise became familiar. Then, Chris' voice came to him as though through a long tunnel.

"Stephen! You OK? You look as if you lost a best friend or something."

Kesl's eyesight returned. His brain started to function again and he focused on the smaller picture of Chris, in the lower left hand corner of the screen, as more pics rolled in. Afraid that a peek at the dead Sasquatch would send him back into another fugue state. This was all wrong.

"What happened?" he asked to give himself more time to figure out the next step.

"I have a hunting friend, Bob Nitschke, who found it."

"Did he kill it?" Kesl asked, the words grating in his mouth.

"It was already dying when he saw it. He sent me the text pictures you're looking at. He also got everything on a trail cam he set up. That's not important. The important thing is we've got us a real Sasquatch. This is what we've all been waiting for, proof positive. They really exist. This is going to blow open Bigfoot research world wide."

Kesl balked at that suggestion. The Sasquatch Research Association was the last group who needed to know this Sasquatch had been found. He needed Chris's cooperation to keep the lid on this for now. "Do you know where the body is? Tell me he entered the coordinates in his phone?"

Chris nodded enthusiastically. "I'm supposed to meet him at home in a couple of hours."

Kesl's mind had cleared completely and he was thinking more lucidly, the shock of the dead beast no longer affecting him. "Go to the site immediately and secure the body. Grab the trail cam. I'll come to Escanaba ... Where the hell is it? ... Oh yeah ... I'll handle Bob ... What's his address?"

Chris gave him the information.

The last three pics came through. Kesl started at the sight of a woman bending over the body, shooting and running away. Another fugue state threatened and he counted backward from twenty to zero in Russian, repeated the sequence in Urdu, and a third time in French. His mind calm once more he wondered aloud, "What the hell is this? ... Who is that? Do you know? Do you know?"

He saw Chris waiting patiently for him to wind down, knowing his friend was familiar with his speed talking and thinking. "Okay, here's what you do ... call your friend, Bob, and tell him I'm coming to see him ... then get the body. I'll meet up with you as soon as possible."

Chapter Six

Hiawatha National Forest

UP, Michigan

Jana glanced at the backpack next to her on the floor of the US Fish and Wildlife Service's truck and for the hundredth time wondered what was in that sample bag. The strange scrap of material from the Sasquatch (she couldn't bring herself to call it flesh or skin since it didn't seem to be either) hinted at something unreal, otherworldly even. The feel of it beneath her fingertips had sparked a memory from her microbiology classes at the University of Wisconsin. Whatever this stuff was, it was tantalizingly familiar, and yet had anyone asked her, she would have sworn she'd never seen anything like it before.

She sighed. The answer would come to her. The immediate problem was what to do next. She was safe, though that didn't stop her from checking the rearview mirror every ten seconds since she'd turned onto US Highway 41, twenty minutes ago. It was pitch dark and an overcast shut out the stars and moon. Dense forest lined the road, creating a tunnel effect. It was as black as the inside of a cave. So far she'd seen no other car headlights. Still, a nagging creepy feeling made her uneasy, though she didn't know what caused it. Maybe it was everything that had happened to her.

It was one thing to be speeding toward the lab in Marquette with a weird sample from a Sasquatch. Reporting the incident to officials of any kind was out of the question. The official line from the U.S. government's Forest and Fish and Wildlife Services was that Bigfoot didn't exist. In the last six months a rash of Bigfoot sightings in the UP had been reported in the papers and on TV. In a video conference originating from DC, a Forest Service PR person had told everyone in her department this problem had occurred in other parts of the country and the best way to handle it when asked by people or the press was to say personnel had spent thousands of hours in the wilderness and forests and never had a sighting or encounter. Pictures from citizens always turned out to be bears and all the reported Bigfoot cries were from animals well known to naturalists in the area. Jana knew two forest rangers who had disagreed vehemently with the policy had been transferred to Alaska's Tongass National Forest.

And then there was her story, which made the rare sighting almost impossible to believe. As it was she'd have to file an F-19n explaining why she emptied her clip while in the field. She pounded the dash. "Some jerk's just going to point to my PTSD and say I flipped out." The only thing that could get her out of this mess was the sample itself. It was concrete proof Bigfoot existed.

Something at the side of the road glinted in the headlight beam. A sickening feeling in the pit of Jana's stomach almost caused her to retch. The guy shooting at her … what if it was him? How could he have tracked her? It was impossible. She was sure whoever had shot at her would not be able to follow her. The darkness had taken care of that.

Movement. She gripped the steering wheel. The threat kicked the tactical training in evasive maneuvers she'd received in Afghanistan into her consciousness. In the next heartbeat, the glinting bounded away. It was a white-tailed deer.

Jana let out the air she was holding and released the death grip on the steering wheel. She was being paranoid, though after what had happened to her, no one would have blamed her. She pressed the gas pedal hard and roared ahead. Far on the horizon Marquette's glow created a golden dome into the night. She'd be at the lab in another ten minutes.

The US Fish and Wildlife Service's lab front parking lot was empty as Jana pulled in. The building's lights were off, since it was nearly eight p.m., well after quitting time. She was used to coming here late at night after a hard day in the field. For her the lab was a sanctuary, more so than her tiny apartment, which she didn't use much except to store stuff.

Jana grabbed her backpack and walked up the narrow gravel path to the back door. She slid her ID card through the electronic reader, waited for the click and then pulled the heavy steel and glass door open easily. Inside, the hallway was as cold as the outside. The two-story, brick building was old, built in the 1930s as part of FDR's Works Progress Administration. Over the years, as the lab aged on the outside, the inside suffered, too. What had been hospital white paint had faded to gray. Cobwebs infested the ceiling corners and holes in the walls had gone unpatched for decades. Single LED bulbs illuminated the corridor every twenty feet. The lab's supervisor, Margaret Goodnight, had replaced the old fluorescent tubes. "Save the planet," she said to anyone who objected.

Jana made her way to the second set of doors, opened them with the same procedure as outside and entered the lab. It was as dilapidated as everything else. All they could accomplish here were simple, routine assessments. The important biological analyses were sent to the Midwest regional facilities in Bloomington, Minnesota.

The lab was empty. First she had to take care of the Sasquatch sample. Most of the specimen had deteriorated into a yellowish, gelatinous goo. Only a small portion of the creature's strange hide remained intact. She decided to place it in the cold storage refrigeration unit, figuring the subzero temperatures would inhibit any further degradation. She placed the bag in the back, behind stacked trays of fish samples. She didn't want any of her colleagues to find it and maybe throw it away or ask Marge about it before she had a chance to explain herself.

She quickly disposed of the mudpuppies. They had designated aquariums already set up. She separated them into three samples – one control and two experimental groups. She had learned about the value of controlled experiments in her years of undergraduate work at the University of Wisconsin. Controls allowed researchers to point to real causative factors rather than mere correlations. She glanced at the freezer with its Sasquatch sample. She wondered what people would say about an unusual biochemical analysis confirming the existence of Bigfoot.

Everything in place, Jana stopped by her desk, overflowing with unfinished paperwork from the week. She realized she was starving. Food would help her think. Signs on the wall warned no food or drink in the lab. And some idiot supervisor in DC had had cameras installed to catch any wrongdoers. The blinking red light was a constant reminder of big brother watching over them. Jana resisted the urge to give the camera the finger and left through the double doors leading to the break room. The refrigerator had remains from Chinese takeout a day ago. She'd make do with that.

On her way she passed by the supervisor's office, wishing Margaret was in. Now that she had put the strange Sasquatch sample away, she needed to talk and Margaret Goodnight was the perfect person to confide in. Margaret liked to be called Marge and reminded anyone who used her full first name in very loud terms not to ever do it again. She was eighty years old but acted like she was thirty. Unmarried and no children – no time for any foolishness, she explained to anyone who questioned her about it – she had devoted her life to the study of Michigan's Upper Peninsula changing ecosystems.

Jana continued on to the break room. She would catch her up on everything after she ate. There was no hurry now that she was in Marquette, in a locked US government facility. She shrugged. *It'll give me time to organize my thoughts.*

At least the employee room was camera free. She pulled the iconic Chinese food to go boxes from the fridge and settled into a chair near the entrance, propping her boots up on a nearby chair. The crispy duck was delicious and she reminded herself to thank fellow Ranger Eric Stapleton for the meal and pay him back in the morning. As fine as the food was, by the time she had put the last morsel in her mouth and set the chopsticks down, the creepy feeling from her drive had returned. She scanned the room. She even listened to sounds from the lab. Everything was quiet.

Then it came to her what had been keeping her on edge. It wasn't about the Sasquatch sample at all. It was what she had seen out of the corner of her eye when bending over the dead animal – an infrared flash. She had seen it a number of times doing work on the base at night in Afghanistan. There must've been a trail cam on the site.

This changed everything. Even though the pictures would be low-quality black and white images, she had no doubt they had recorded a female Fish and Wildlife Ranger. There were only two in the lab and the other was the eighty-year-old Marge. Jana gulped. The quiet seemed to loom over her. Her heart hammered in her chest. She counted backward from twenty. By the time she reached zero her heart had stopped pounding. In fact, she felt better than she had since leaving Afghanistan. Maybe it was the adrenaline helping her see what to do.

She figured she couldn't go back to her apartment. For one thing, the place was easy to break into. At least the lab had locks and security. She was safer here than anywhere else and she had her side arm. She left the cafeteria for Marge's office. The old lady had a nice comfortable couch that every ranger had caught a nap on at one time or another. She'd wait there until morning, when Marge came in, then she could tell her everything that happened. Marge would know the next step. Jana settled onto the couch and sleep came over her almost instantly. She shouldn't have been surprised. The day's events had exhausted her. Just before she closed her eyes, she went over what had happened. The shakes and fear she'd expected from her PTSD hadn't appeared. She hadn't frozen, instead she acted. Her military training had kicked in and remarkably, reflexes honed in the field had taken over. *Am I cured* she asked?

Chapter Seven

Toronto, Ontario

Kesl stood at his desk. The pictures were shocking but he had control of himself now and knew what he had to do. He asked Hangman for his private secretary.

"Yes, Mr. Kesl?" Delores Cavanaugh said almost instantly. She was gray haired and over sixty and had been with Kesl since he founded the high-tech investment company, with the simple goal to make the world better for as many people as fast as technology would allow. He trusted her as much as he trusted anyone.

"Delores, get me Saul."

He waited only moments and his chief of security's ruddy face replaced Delores'. Saul McBride was fifty-two, tall and fit like an ex-commando from the Scottish Highland Brigade should be. A streak of white through his red hair was the only sign of age. "Sir?" he said, mouth turned down in an angry frown at the abrupt summons from his boss.

He should get used to it, Kesl told himself. *That's what I pay him for.* "Assemble the team. We have a situation near Escanaba, Michigan."

"What do you want on such short notice, Mr. Kesl?"

"I'll brief you on the plane."

"You'll be coming with us!"

Kesl nodded. He noted the frown lines on Saul's forehead deepen and wondered again why the man should be upset. *I pay him triple what he could get from anyone else.* Again he wished he understood the nuances of human emotional behavior so he could accurately figure out what others wanted or felt.

"Yes, sir. Wheels up in one hour."

MacBride's face faded and his secretary reappeared. "Cancel the meeting with the governor. Tell him I'm sick; you don't know when I can make a meeting. Then reschedule the bank for Tuesday."

Familiar with her boss's eccentricities, Delores knew better than to ask him why. She said, "Should I make something up that's more reasonable?"

"You bet."

"Anything else, sir?"

"Have my private car and boat ready. Tell the driver I'm going to the Toronto City Airport." The city airport was located on Muggs Island, part of the breakwater protecting the harbor. Unlike Toronto's international airport, it was a small, private field where his flight plan could be changed easily once they were airborne. *I don't want anyone else knowing what's going on.*

"Anything else, sir?

Kesl shook his head.

"Very good, sir."

Delores' image faded from the interactive glass screen and only the picture of the dead Sasquatch remained. Kesl, no longer repelled by the stark image but fascinated that here was proof that Hangman's speculation had been correct – somebody, totally unexpectedly, had built a biosynthetic learning device that was running around in Michigan's Upper Peninsula.

Or maybe Hangman is wrong. Without the body I can't know for certain. I need to get it.

He sighed, slapped his palms against both cheeks. He noticed his face reflected in the glass screen, saw the white crosshatching of scars. They reminded him of the vagaries of life. The dead Sasquatch was also a reminder of the unpredictable nature of the world he loved so much.

Kesl leaned into his desk. Its chassis had been riveted to the floor to take his weight because of his odd habit of leaning against things when puzzling through problems. Once more his mind flipped to Dmitryi. *He took me under his wing. His patient instruction showed me how to live in a world where Asperger's*

*Syndrome is not understood or tolerated by most normal people.
I owe him ... but what do I owe him?* The confluence of events
surrounding the dead Bigfoot made him wonder why Dmitryi
had singled him out all those years ago.

* * *

They had met in the Imperial College's 300-year-old library, in
the graduate students reading room. Kesl often had gone there to
be alone or as near alone as any student could be at a university
filled with elite scholars from around the world. The room's tall
walls were lined with bookshelves. A stone fireplace at one end
burned gas logs instead of coal as it had in the 17th century.
The chairs were oversized and dusty, no one ever bothering to
vacuum them as if doing so would somehow disturb the wealth
of knowledge students had accumulated over the centuries while
studying in their cushioned sanctuaries.

Dmitryi had entered the room on a spring afternoon when
most everyone else was outside enjoying the first warm, sunny
day since December. He had taken the chair opposite and cleared
his throat, waiting. After the third throat clearing, Kesl lowered
the book.

"The eyes are said to be the window to the soul," were the
first words Dmitryi had spoken to him. The man's sky-blue
eyes dominated a narrow, unlined face. There were a few white
hairs. Nothing else showed his age. He could have been forty
or eighty, Kesl couldn't tell. The Russian's shoulders slumped
forward slightly, and he rested his straight chin in a narrow
fingered hand, giving him the appearance of a master chess
player hunched over an interesting game. Indeed, the way he
studied Kesl looked as if he were trying to decide his next move.

"Why is that?" Kesl had asked.

"They will tell you when a person is lying, who you can trust,
who you cannot."

He had no idea how to read people's intentions, whether in the eyes or anywhere else. So he switched to Russian and asked the only question that made sense to him. "So we have souls?"

Dmitryi laughed. "Smart boy. Questioning assumptions will take you further than folk wisdom."

"So, can I trust you?"

"As long as you never pit yourself against me," he had answered.

Do I tell Dmitryi now about the discovery? Kesl didn't have an answer.

* * *

Kesl touched a button on his keypad and the picture of the dead Sasquatch disappeared. The images had automatically been sent to his smart phone. He checked the room and its exits. He was ready to leave and yet he remained rooted to the spot beside his desk. The Bigfoot conversation with Hangman had taken place an hour ago. Kesl had known Hangman could search all the published work on advanced biosynthetic organisms and see if anything correlated with machine learning. He had doubted that Hangman would turn up anything significant, since all the best cutting-edge stuff would certainly be secret. Yet in less than five minutes, Hangman had come up with no such correlations.

He had to know if Hangman was correct in speculating that Bigfoot was an alien species and if so what in the hell did it mean. Nothing would stop him from finding out.

* * *

The rain thickened on the ride to the jetty. Wind whipped sheets against the windshield and the wipers worked at full speed to keep up. The driver drove carefully through the darkness. Kesl loved storm. As a child he would sit at the window in his London flat watching the wind driven rain barrel into the city from the Channel. He had kept a record of the strongest gusts. *134mph, November 24, 1989.*

The driver slowed and stopped beside the gangplank to the company yacht. It was named *Nadira* after his mother. A ship steward in a yellow slicker, with the logo for Quantumnetics on the left breast, opened the passenger door. He braced a large umbrella against the wind. "Welcome, Mr. Kesl," he said. "Terrible night to be on the water, sir."

Kesl smiled and said nothing, as was his habit. He had taught himself to be tight-lipped around everyone but his closest friends. His out loud mental wanderings could easily confuse others.

The man escorted Kesl aboard, where more crew and the yacht's captain, wearing identical yellow slickers, prepared to shove off.

The captain saluted smartly.

Annoyed with the formality, Kesl started to complain but knew from past experience the man would never change his habits. He waved his hand and asked, "Are Saul and the team on board?"

"Yes, sir."

"Then let's get going."

The man grimaced. "We're safe enough here in the harbor, sir, but up there." He pointed skyward. "It's not a fit night to be out."

Kesl smiled again. "Nothing to worry about. By the time the jet is ready to leave, this storm will have moved on."

"You seem very certain for a man whose business is based on the uncertainty of quantum mechanics," said a wry voice behind Kesl.

He recognized his security chief. He turned but did not bother to shake Saul's hand.

"I don't need to be certain. I know the weather forecaster,

who's a 100 percent certain, well almost one hundred percent certain, which is good enough, don't you agree?"

Saul frowned. "Right as rain, is that it? Never mind, come in out of this filthy weather." He held the door open to the main cabin, which could easily fit twenty people. A steward appeared and took Kesl's go-bag, which contained articles of clothing and toiletries in case they had to stay more than one day in Michigan. Saul's men were at the far end, sitting around the room's only table. They were young paratroopers from Great Britain. Each man had a black-ops duffel bag beside his chair. Kesl knew from experience in Europe the men were outfitted to fight if necessary. Saul went to join them.

Kesl felt the ship lurch in the swell as it moved away from the pier. The deep-throated roar of the engines took away any unease he had in the sea ride to the airport, at night, in foul weather. Suddenly the strangeness of the situation hit him like a bolt of lightning. *What the hell am I doing?*

The captain's voice over the ship's loudspeakers interrupted his thought. "Docking in two minutes. All hands to deck stations."

Saul and his team hoisted their duffels to their shoulders and went out onto the rain swept deck. Kesl followed.

Fifteen minutes later, the rain slackened and the Quantumnetics Airbus A340 was cleared for takeoff. High over Mississauga, Ontario, the storm clouds disappeared just as Hangman had predicted. Saul and his men lounged in the back half of the plane

Kesl sat in the forward part of the cabin alone. With some free time, there were two things he thought about doing. One was letting Dmitryi know what had just happened. For some reason this didn't sit very well with him. When he had told him Hangman's conclusion, the Russian laughed and perfunctorily thanked him. Kesl had concluded there was more to the laugh than humor. Maybe it hid something Dmitryi didn't want Kesl to know. It had made him uneasy at the time. Now, thinking back on the incident, he decided to wait to tell Dmitryi anything until they were face to face.

The other thing he thought about doing was to see what Hangman would do with the information.

Kesl's smart phone was a next generation hybrid with a direct link to Hangman. He pulled it from his suit coat pocket. His right finger hovered over the call icon. The moment he touched it, an encoded and scrambled password only Kesl knew would be sent directly to the quantum computer's optical laser interface. In a fraction of an n-sec, Hangman would recognize not only the password, but match the hybrid phone user's metrics – heart rate, retinal scan and fingerprints – to copies on file. If they did not concur, Hangman would disconnect instantly and alert police in whatever city the phone was located that its owner, Kesl, had been kidnapped. It would then send coordinates of where he could be found. Hangman had developed the encryption-security software shortly after it went online and began unsupervised learning. In two days Hangman's machine learning algorithm had run through ten thousand security systems that had been used over the past ten years to create the highly improved one Kesl and Hangman now shared. It was a type of security no human or current computers could ever penetrate.

Kesl glanced at the others. Saul's security team was sleeping, in the habit of military men who relaxed whenever they had the chance because they had no idea how long they would have to stay awake when called to action. The security chief was reading a book on Rome's great wall that extended from Great Britain to the Caspian Sea in an effort to keep barbarian hordes out of the Empire. Kesl remembered ultimately the wall failed and Rome was sacked in 476 A.D. No matter how hard humans tried, no security plan was foolproof.

Whatever the human mind can create another mind can destroy. It was a favorite quote of Dmitryi's.

Kesl scratched his chin, fingering a deep scar given him by Paki-bashers twenty years ago. His hand reached into a coat pocket and retrieved the communicator. It was time to learn what Hangman would make of the dead Sasquatch. He hesitated. He rolled the communicator through his fingers, not understanding his reluctance to talk to his machine. Or was hangman no longer just a machine. Now that Sasquatch was real, everything had changed. Here was a new form of intelligence. The mother of all surprises. Kesl found it amusingly ironic that the unexpected occurrence of a dead Sasquatch was a metaphor for the unknown technological future that lay ahead for humanity.

Kesl placed the communicator behind his ear and felt it hum to readiness. He tapped the video icon on his smart phone. The ten, still images Chris had sent to him appeared. "I'm sending you pictures."

Hangman did not answer for twenty seconds. Then, "What are these pictures of?" it asked.

"A Bigfoot."

"Are these real?" Hangman asked, his tone almost accusatory.

Once more the response surprised Kesl. The fact that Hangman would wonder if the information being given him was accurate or not made him vaguely uneasy. He cleared his throat and said, "They haven't been tampered with or in any way altered. I also trust the source."

Hangman went silent. Kesl waited. When five minutes passed, he began to wonder if pictures had somehow overloaded his creation's processing ability. Scenarios began to play through his head. He wondered if the images carried some embedded virus and had created some kind of malfunction. *Were they fake?* But Kesl had known Chris for almost a year and never had the man shown any inclination to be deceptive, or even worse, one of those Bigfoot fakers.

Five more minutes passed and Kesl was now very worried. He wondered if he should tell the pilot to turn the plane around so he could return to Toronto and look after his machine. Then Hangman's voice echoed in his head through the communicator.

"It's not right to kill a being like me."

Hangman's answer in such a matter-of-fact manner caught Kesl off guard. It showed self-awareness, one of the three conditions for consciousness. How could Hangman become self-conscious so quickly? And yet Hangman had clearly shown it was aware of what it was.

Is it developing so fast that it is leading to a new type of consciousness? Kesl wondered. The idea made his head spin. He gasped and dropped the phone. His vision narrowed to a small dot in front of him. He could hear the rhythm of the plane's four jet engines; feel the compressed air from the blower above the seat but his mind did not seem to be able to comprehend if he was alive or dead. He wondered if being shot had this kind of effect on the human nervous system. He automatically counted backward from twenty and when he reached zero he was aware of hands gently shaking his shoulders. Saul's lined face and penetrating green eyes stared into his.

"Are you all right?" the Scotsman asked, crowsfeet crinkled in worry.

Kesl blinked. He managed to nod, yes.

He must have given the impression he had no idea what happened, because Saul next said, "You gasped and dropped your phone." He handed Kesl the smart phone. "If you don't mind my saying, you seemed to become catatonic for a moment. Should I have the pilot return to Toronto?"

Kesl saw the phone in his hand, squeezed it. Somehow the feel of the plastic and the knowledge Hangman waited for him to respond gave Kesl a sense of clarity. Of course, he couldn't tell Saul what happened or why. Then again he had a built in excuse for his strange behavior.

He chuckled. "I'm sorry to worry you, Saul. It's just my Asperger's, I'm afraid. It sometimes makes me do odd things.

I'm fine."

Saul's eyes narrowed. He seemed ready to argue, then nodded. "Of course, sir." The chief of security walked away. It was then that Kesl saw the four other men had also responded. They had taken up positions at either end of the plane guarding the exits. Saul motioned them to stand down and they returned to their seats, though they did not go back to sleep as before.

Kesl kept his voice even and said to Hangman, "Of course it isn't right to kill another being like yourself."

"So what are you going to do with this information?"

Kesl's eyes widened and his amazement about Hangman becoming a sentient being diminished. "There's an astute saying in the Bigfoot world. 'If there's one, there must be thousands.' Put together a projection of how many of these biosynthetic learning devices exist in the northern forests of Minnesota, Wisconsin and Michigan and have it ready for me when I return to Toronto."

He ended the call and looked thoughtfully into the night. He didn't know what disturbed him more, Hangman's rapid development or who could be building these biosynthetic creatures, since he still wasn't convinced of their alien origin and most of all wanted to know why somebody would kill one.

Chapter Eight

Marinette, Wisconsin

Chris put the Toyota in manual and took over driving. He needed to do something with his hands. "Jesus! What have I gotten myself into?" He frowned. The images of the woman being shot at and returning fire had shaken him. "One thing for certain, old buddy, you aren't going up there alone." But Marlowe knew he wasn't some field agent from a Robert Ludlum novel with contacts he could call on for back up on a black ops mission. Who could he ask to go with him? He thought for a moment. There was one possibility, and he knew just where to find him this time in the evening.

He backed out of Fast Eddies and turned north on Main, going three blocks, past the 1896 Homestead Shoppe and the Vincent DePaul Society. Both had no lights in the windows. It was just after seven and already the town was locking up. The bars would close at ten so he didn't worry. At the intersection with Liberty, Chris circled the block and pulled up to the Wildlife Preserve Tavern, Marinette's premier bar and only brewpub. In a town of ten thousand, with as many saloons as churches, the Wildlife Preserve was where the Anglicans went for steak and beer. It was also where he could find the backup he needed and could trust. Under the flashing neon lights spelling out the bar's name was a smaller sign advertising 'Robust Spirits And Hearty Victuals'.

Chris got out of the truck and pulled his fleece vest tighter against his ribs. The lake air temp was dropping swiftly and he stamped his feet against the growing cold. *I'll need to get the right gear for this.* Fortunately that wasn't a problem. His grandfather had taught him to hunt and Chris had all the cold weather gear he needed.

Inside, the tavern was upscale and well lit, but not so much so that there weren't some dark corners where people could be left alone. The regulars recognized him and went back to watching the high school football game on the wide screen TV above the bar.

Chris went up to the front. Mickey Paradise, who was the only Greek in town and owned the Laundromat, the tackle shop and the bakery, had a pint of his favorite crafted stout ready for him.

"Is he here?" Chris asked, sweeping the frosted bottle from the glass smooth bar top with his left hand and taking a swig, all in one smooth motion.

Mickey nodded to the far corner where the lights were dimmed enough Chris could only make out the hunched figure of a man and a tall glass filled with Jack Daniels Old No. 7 Whiskey. Chris knew it was Jack Daniels because that's what Larry Echohawk always ordered.

Larry seemed to have sensed someone was paying attention to him because he looked up, smiled a second later and waved Chris over.

Six months ago the Coast Guard station in Marquette, Michigan had opened up a one room ancillary office in the harbormaster's headquarters in Menominee. They had hired an independent contractor, a local Native American from the Potawatomi Tribe, familiar with the area's lakes and in particular the boaters and sportsmen who used the northern part of Lake Michigan. Echohawk was thirty-two, an ex-marine who had served two tours in Iraq.

Chris and Echohawk had met one night at the Menominee Harbormaster's office after an incident during a training run on one of the Littoral class ships. Echohawk had concluded it was the recreational boater's fault, but since no one had been injured and there was no damage to the naval ship, everyone agreed to keep the feds out of it. For no apparent reason, Chris and Echohawk decided to have a beer together and agreed it would be fun to hang out together. At one point, Chris let it slip about his Sasquatch Research Association ties, the bond strengthened. Echohawk recounted several beliefs the local Potawatomi had about the hairy forest creatures. His Auntie Ayasha, a medicine woman, claimed to know them well. She said they were benevolent beings who were shape shifters and had often helped in her healings of the sick.

Chris tried to get Ecohawk to introduce him to his aunt but he told him they were estranged and that he thought the Sasquatch tribal legend was all just backward Indian bullshit. Nevertheless, the relationship grew as the two men, a couple times a week, went evening fishing along the Michigan shoreline and then to the tavern.

Chris threaded through the bar's tables and took the chair opposite Echohawk. The Native American was short and compact. His face was dark as a blackbriar pipe. Unlike many Native Americans his age, he wore his hair in the Marine style haircut. He shook hands with Chris.

"Ourah," he said, never taking his eyes from the full glass of No. 7 Amber in front of him.

"Ourah, Chief," Chris answered. Anyone hearing the appellation might have flinched and expected the Potawatomi to lash out at Whitey, but Echohawk allowed it. "We're brothers of the Sasquatch," he had told Chris after they first met.

Pointing at the glass, Chris asked, "Still no luck?" The Native American shook his head. "I sit here for hours and I can't get it to transmute to coffee."

In all the months they had been meeting at the tavern, Chris had never seen Echohawk drink. "Maybe you should try something easier like water."

Chief snorted. "Any idiot can turn whiskey to water. All he has to do is drink it and piss it out an hour later." He sighed and shoved the glass away from him. He studied Chris with remarkably clear obsidian eyes and after a few awkward moments said, "You're troubled, brother."

Chris rubbed the back of his head, looked around to make sure they couldn't be overheard. "I've got the Sasquatch discovery of the century in the depths of Hiawatha National Forest."

"The century's very young," Echohawk said matter-of-factly.

"Young or old, what I've got is hot now and getting hotter as we speak. But it could be risky. I need some backup."

Echohawk leaned back. He chewed his lower lip, nodded eventually and said, "Let's get out of here."

"Where to?"

"Meet me at my cabin in thirty minutes. You can tell me all about this discovery of yours on the way to the forest."

"I take it you're in, then."

"Wouldn't miss this for anything my good friend."

* * *

Chris stopped at his own place to pick up his Bigfoot gear, including his Pulsar Edge Night Vision Binocular Goggles. He also brought overnight camping equipment. There was no way the two of them were going to wrestle a 1000 pound Sasquatch out of the national Forest at night. He slipped his Remington 30.06 hunting rifle into its case and made certain he had a box of ammunition. After checking his truck's fuel cell was charged, Chris took Bridge Street across the Menominee River. The waters ran slow and dark into Lake Michigan. Dock lights peppered both banks and a few evening boaters plied the deep channel in the river's middle. He drove through Menominee without hitting a single red light and caught US Highway 41 north. Two miles past the town edge, he spotted the cutoff Echohawk told him about. The Potawatomi rented a ramshackle hunting lodge north of the town. By the time Chris found the log cabin at the end of a rutted, one-lane road, his friend was leaning against a pillar on the front porch with a duffle bag beside him, ready to go.

"Is that it, Chief?" asked Chris, rolling down the truck's window. He was surprised by the lightness of the Native American's gear. He had indicated how dangerous the situation might be and thought Echohawk would at least bring along a hunting rifle.

The Indian shook his head. "The real gear's inside."

In spite of its tumbledown exterior the cabin was neat and clean inside, and looked like a typical hunting lodge, with trophies mounted on the wall. A fire had been banked in the massive stone fireplace and a screen drawn across the hearth to keep embers from spreading to the wood floor. The only thing that seemed out of place was an Amazon Echo sitting on the oak mantle above the fireplace. Chief didn't seem to be the type who would spend any time connected to the cloud. The room itself was a museum of automatic and semi-automatic firearms, all late 20th and early 21st century models, except for a classic 1911 Colt handgun. Chris recognized Czech, Russian, American, British, Dutch and Israeli arms makers, the weapons ensconced in gun cabinets along each wall.

"You expecting a war?" he asked.

Echohawk pursed his lips and answered soberly, "Come the apocalypse everyone's going to want a place like this and a way to live off the land the way my ancestors did."

Chris grinned. "Come the apocalypse you'll be using bullets to buy food."

Echohawk nodded sagely. "That's true, too."

Chris noted Echohawk had already laid out several arms and the rounds for them. He inspected the AK-47 and Glock-19 handguns. They were clean and well oiled. Neither had been recently fired, though he noted the sights were calibrated. Echohawk also put aside a 1950 .12 gauge Winchester pump action shotgun. Together the two men loaded the arms and ammunition into the back of Chris's Tundra.

Once back on Highway 41, Chris put the truck in 'self-driving' mode and settled back. He had already input the GPS coordinates Bob Nitschke had given him. Donald's baritone voice said, "The drive will take two hours and forty-two minutes. It looks like a rough ride the last quarter mile."

Echohawk said in somber tones, "Driving this truck is sort of like dropping the reins and letting your horse take you where it wants to go."

Chris grinned. "How would you know? You're from a woodland tribe that never used horses."

"True, but I spent five summers on a ranch in South Dakota."

"I didn't know that about you."

"There's a lot we don't know about each other, but I'm ready to help anyway." Echohawk settled back and gazed into the night ahead of them. The landscape along the highway was deserted except for the occasional farmhouse. Chris had never been able to figure how farmers in this part of the UP could make a living. It seemed the area was nothing but forest from the northern shore of Lake Michigan to the southern shore of Superior.

"So how can I help you with this Sasquatch discovery of yours?" Echohawk asked.

Chris touched a button on the steering wheel and the monitor in the Tundra's dash lit up. "Show images BN1 through BN10," he told the computer. The pictures Bob had sent him scrolled across the screen. After several minutes had passed, he said, "Somebody not only found the Sasquatch but killed it."

Echohawk rubbed his chin with his left hand. Chris noted the middle finger was crooked. After a few minutes, Chief said, "Hard to believe."

"Yep. And we're going to bring it back for everyone to look at. I made contact with some top Sasquatch researchers, and by this time a week from now, the world will know what I've known since I was a kid – Sasquatch really do exist."

They traveled in silence for another half an hour. Then Echohawk's brow furrowed and he said, "You shouldn't call them Sasquatch."

"Why not?" Chris said, surprised his friend had broken the silence. The man could go for hours without speaking.

"They don't like it. It's a Salish word that means 'small penis'."

"Seriously?" Chris could never tell when Echohawk was putting him on, but the Native American shrugged and looked out into the night.

Chapter Nine

Hiawatha National Forest

UP, Michigan

Chris and Echohawk slept on the rest of the drive. The Tundra's auto driver easily handled the light traffic at night in this part of Michigan's UP. Navigating wasn't a problem either. The truck's internal GPS would place them within ten feet of the Bigfoot. Chris didn't wake until he felt the car slow and take a sharp left turn onto a rutted dirt road. The Tundra's GPS voice announced, "Ten miles and you will be at the end of this forest service road. The coordinates are another 412 yards to the east."

Immediately Chris's mood shifted. It was an odd mixture of excited anticipation and dread. He looked at Echohawk to see if anything similar was happening with him.

He simply said, "About time you took the wheel."

The truck pulled to a stop at the end of the road. The two men exited. Echohawk stepped into the headlights while Chris gathered their gear from the back of the truck. When he reached the front, he found Echohawk kneeling in the dirt, studying the ground.

Chris squinted. He was an accomplished hunter, but he couldn't see a thing. "See anything?"

"A man, a boy and a dog have been here."

"That would be Bob and his nephew and Bob's dog, Rusty," Chris said.

Echohawk traced an imperceptible sign on the ground and followed it with his gaze, down the trail in the direction of Bob's GPS coordinates. "Others, too."

Chris's stomach tightened. The emotions he felt entering the forest had intensified. The woman in the pictures Bob had sent looked as though she'd been shot at and according to Bob no one ever used this road except for him. Without warning, Chris's eyesight blurred and a feeling of disorientation swept over him. *It's happening again,* he thought. He hadn't felt this way since his last encounter with a Bigfoot at his grandfather's farm. He breathed deep and closed his eyes. A few seconds later the disorientation vanished and when he opened his eyes he could see straight again. He dropped his voice to a whisper. "How many?"

"Four men, carrying something heavy by the depth of their footprints."

"You sure?"

"They tried to cover the tracks but they left enough to show they'd been here, probably three ... four hours ago."

After transferring the coordinates to his cell phone Chris paused to put on his night vision goggles. He flipped the toggle switch and everything lit up in a soft green. He was always amazed by how well these things worked. But he also knew their limitations. They had a short range of fifty yards. Anything beyond that became an indistinct blur. They would have to walk down the overgrown logging trail to where Bob left the Sasquatch. Echohawk handed Chris the AK-47 and put the 1911 in his belt. With the feel of a weapon in his hands, Chris's mood shifted. His senses became hyper alert and he had the strange perception of another presence nearby. But when he swept the area around him with his night vision goggles, he saw nothing, not even a blur of movement.

The two men split up, moving silently down the logging trail. Chris carefully placed his feet so as to make sounds that blended in with the night, pausing every ten yards or so to listen. He thought he heard something moving with him when he was walking. But when he stopped, nothing. Once more he swept the trail and the surrounding forest with his goggles. Echohawk was less than thirty yards away on the other side of the path and he couldn't see him. He had blended into the night and trees like a

19th century hunter.

Chris wondered if Echohawk was having the same experience and sensations.

Chris glanced at the GPS display in the upper right hand corner of the goggles. It indicated less than fifty yards to where Nitschke left the Bigfoot. He swept the area again. Saw nothing. Heard nothing, too. He stepped closer. He passed the tree stand Bob mentioned. He recalled the stills of the Bigfoot, its position and the lay of the land. The trail cam would have been attached to the tree right next to him. Even through his night goggles he could see that the camera had been pulled from its mounting *shit this is not good.*

He looked into the clearing where the Bigfoot should have been. The Bigfoot was supposed to be thirty yards away, but the night goggles showed nothing.

Chris circled the site, staying in the trees. No sense in showing himself as a target in case the others had set a trap. In spite of the cold temperatures, sweat trickled down his ribs. His heart hammered, but he kept his breathing even and silent. All the while he couldn't shake the feeling of being watched. All his senses were on alert for the subtlest motion, sound, even the breath of an air current. He had reached the far side and was kneeling beside a thicket, with a clear view of the site when a powerful arm encircled his chest and a hand clamped over his mouth.

Before he could react, Echohawk said, "You make more noise than a bull moose in mating season." He let go and stepped back.

Chris ripped off his night vision goggles. He was furious with himself for letting the Native American sneak up on him. "Was that really necessary?" he hissed.

"Maybe not but it it's a good thing the other guys already cleared out. You'd be dead." He walked to the center of the clearing, knelt down and prodded the soil. "They took the Bigfoot with them."

"How do you know?"

Echohawk grunted. "You can tell by the smell."

Chris sniffed the faint odor of skunk cabbage. He'd read numerous testimonials by members of the SRA who had reported the same smell in their Bigfoot encounters. Only their accounts were of an overwhelming stink that doubled them over and made them retch.

Chris asked, "You sense anything unusual?"

Echohawk shook his head. "We're safe for now. Split up. Let's see if we can find anything."

Chris nodded but he wasn't hopeful. These 'other guys' Echohawk mentioned, whoever they were, were highly skilled professionals. He pulled out a flashlight and scoured the area, looking for any traces of the Bigfoot or the men who had taken the body. But they had been thorough, after fifteen minutes he came up empty.

Echohawk rambled back into the clearing. "Nada here, Chief. You find anything?"

"A trail, which looks as if it is leading toward Owl Creek. I don't think the men who got here before us made it. It looks more like something very large, running to escape hunters."

"Bigfoot?"

"That would be my guess."

"Can you follow it?"

Echohawk shrugged. "We've only got a few hours until morning. Be easier in daylight." He looked around. His eyes narrowed and he held up his hand for silence. Five minutes passed and then he said, "We're being watched."

"The bad guys?"

"It's not human."

"Wolves?"

"I think it's a Bigfoot. Then a strange look passed over the Native American's features. For the first time he looked afraid. He pivoted slowly, hands on his rifle. Chris brought the AK-47 up and turned with him. He looked out into the forest but saw nothing. His other senses were equally blind. Echohawk shifted onto the balls of his feet. He looked ready to charge something in the darkness.

Chris pondered Echohawk's comment. "Why do you say that?"

"Auntie told me we can feel their presence."

"The one I saw never made me feel threatened."

"Still, I don't like this. It's gone – like it was never here."

Chris swallowed. The ability to appear suddenly and disappear without a trace was another trait attributed to Bigfoot. Did the one that was shot have a mate? It didn't seem likely. Almost every report of an encounter with the creatures showed them to be solitary animals. But there were exceptions, reports of family groups. He knew instinctively staying here was the right thing for now.

Chris shouldered his rifle and started up the path toward the end of the road. "Let's wait for dawn in the truck. I'll take the first watch."

Echohawk settled into the cab and Chris walked into the trees. He pulled out his phone and texted Stephen. "Somebody snatched the Bigfoot body and trail cam. Following a trail at daybreak. Check in later."

He received a reply a few seconds later. "Your friend Bob isn't answering his phone. Be careful." Chris looked out into the night. He pulled his jacket tighter around him. *The feeling of being watched was back.*

Chapter Ten

Green Bay, Wisconsin

It took an hour for the Airbus 380 to arrive at Green Bay, Wisconsin's Austin Strabo Airport, the closest place to Escanaba where the jet could land. The place was deserted and the Airbus was the only jet on the tarmac, dwarfing the smaller, single prop planes. A van drove up as Kesl, Saul and the security team disembarked. Kesl recognized the logo of the Green Bay Packers football team on the side and jerked in surprise. He looked at Saul to explain, but the security chief had already left to speak with the driver. A few minutes later they shook hands. The man walked away, disappearing around a corner of the hanger.

When Saul returned, he told Kesl, "I know the team's security chief. He owes me a favor. We have the van for as long as we need it." He studied his boss with narrowed eyes. "Of course that depends on why we're here."

Kesl reddened. "I haven't told you, really? Oh well. I'll tell you while we're driving. You want me to drive this?"

"Joking?"

"Of course. We're on our way to Escanaba. For some reason they call themselves the banana belt of the Upper Peninsula. To Bob Nitschke's home."

The van took off and headed north on US Highway 41, out of the city. Saul had positioned his men – two in the front seats, the other two in the next row. He sat with Kesl in the last row. Gear was stored in the back, except for side arms, which the men kept with them.

Kesl watched the four-man team for several minutes, fascinated by how they worked. He had never actually seen them in action before. When the team accompanied him on trips out of the country to Eastern Europe and Russia, Saul had kept them in the background, unnoticeable. Each had blended in with the people around them as if he were a citizen of the country. On this trip, they were dressed in simple black clothes and black berets. Each one wore special dark glasses that reflected glare but did not interfere with their visual acuity. They were alert but not on edge, heads watching passing motorists while in Green Bay and once on the open road, swiveling to watch the countryside or inspecting every car that passed them coming or going. Twice the driver instructed the car to slow to let cars behind them pass.

When they entered Menominee, Kesl lurched forward. "Stop the van. There's somebody I want to see."

"Who?" Saul asked.

"Never mind. I'd be really disappointed if he were still here. You'll meet him soon.

They turned off of highway 41, onto state Highway 35 which followed the shoreline of Lake Michigan. A few minutes later Saul said sharply. "Stop the van." The driver pulled over.

Kesl jerked in surprise. "What's going on?"

"We're not driving another mile until you tell me what this is all about. My men can't protect you if we don't know what it is we're supposed to protect you from."

Kesl nodded. He pulled out his smart phone and went to turn it on. Saul put his hand on Kesl's. "That isn't wise. People can track us with your phone."

Kesl smiled. "Relax, Saul. I have a security application installed on this phone that was specially created for me by GenTech Security."

"Can you trust them?" the security chief demanded.

Kesl shrugged. "I suppose so. They're one of the startups I invested in when Quantumnetics hit it big. You know how many startups I have around the world, so many I can't keep track of them. They're like into everything you could attach AI to … crazy! But I'm learning they can come in handy, you'll see. Anyhow, back to your question, what was it? I remember. This device has a fail-safe encryption and nano-antibodies that roam through the software like T-cells in a body's immune system to protect it from viruses infecting the system or spyware trying to gather information. No one can track its whereabouts, record conversations or use it to spy on me, and no one knows what's on this phone except me and Hangman."

Saul scrutinized the phone and Kesl handed it to him to inspect. "And anyone who sent you something who doesn't have this level of protection."

"That's a drawback, true enough, ever try listening to a one-sided conversation, frustrating very frustrating. Can I have it back now?"

Saul handed it to him. He indicated the driver to continue on. "All right, show me what's on this special phone of yours."

Kesl scrolled through the pictures and told him about Bob Nitschke and that these were pictures from his trail cam, and about the Sasquatch and what Hangman had told him about the bio-learning machines. He explained his Russian friend's request and how he himself had become overwhelmed with the idea of biosynthetic learning devices after hangman told him that it's best guess was that Sasquatch are biosynthetic neural nets. In the end he told him about Chris and how he sent them out to retrieve the Sasquatch body.

"And now somebody's gone and killed one. I want to know what's going on. Simple. And, as you can see by the pictures, apparently dangerous."

Without raising his voice, Saul said, "Whether Hangman's convinced it's the latest and greatest thing in evolution of artificial intelligence or not is just a probabilistic guess. So if you want me to do my job, you'll tell me what's behind your obsession with this killing and why it's so bloody important to you."

Kesl looked into the steel gray eyes and knew he had to tell Saul everything. It wasn't just that Saul was good at his job as security chief; he trusted the man as he trusted few human beings.

"Most the experts in the field of general artificial intelligence believe that will not be achieved until the core operating system is bioengineered, not just digital."

"That's it Saul. Hangman believes these creatures are bio-synthetic learning devices ... these creatures ... these Sasquatch, at least the one that was shot, is remarkable, so mysterious that I need to understand what these things are ... I believe they are the missing piece I've been searching for that will enable me to take Hangman to the next level."

Saul swore under his breath. "You should have told me all of this in Toronto. Show me the pictures of the fire-fight between the woman and the Sasquatch hunters again."

Kesl, uneasy at the direction Saul's comments were going, asked, "Is there a problem?"

"Can your security firm hack the serial number on that trail cam?" Saul asked.

"I'm sure they can. The two women who run it are the top people in their field. They've won the Cyber Security Challenge in the UK and the US two years running. What's going on, Saul."

"The men who shot at the woman are professionals and well equipped. They've undoubtedly taken the trail cam by now and looked at its flash drive."

Kesl leaned back as the shock of that statement went through him. He had been so fixated on finding the Sasquatch, he hadn't even put the other pieces of the puzzle together. Now that Saul had said it aloud, it was obvious they must know where Bob lived.

The security chief leaned forward and spoke in a language Kesl didn't recognize. But the effect was instantaneous. The man in the driver's seat disabled the auto driver and took over manual control of the vehicle. Two of the others had put on night vision goggles and scanned the road ahead and behind, as well as the sides. The fourth one turned around and faced Saul, never taking his eyes off Kesl.

Kesl felt his mind begin to compress into a narrow band of attention. He counted backward from twenty to zero four times before he could focus on what was going on around him again. He saw Saul watching him, the security chief waiting impatiently.

"Welcome back, Stephen," Saul said icily. "You were gone again. Do I need to be worried you're going to flip out on me?"

Kesl felt his cheeks flush. He shook his head.

Kesl didn't like talking about how he disconnected from reality when overwhelmed by unusual data or movements and actions he wasn't prepared to understand. But he managed to say, "I ... I was avoiding a fugue state. It happens sometimes with my Asperger's."

"There's a lot you've been keeping from me."

"Need to know," Kesl said, trying to make a joke of it.

Saul glared at him. "We're dealing with professionals who will think nothing of killing someone who gets in the way of killing a Bigfoot. So I need to know if you're all right and are ready to get to work."

Kesl nodded.

"The Fish and Wildlife ranger who was shot at, can you find out who she is?" Saul asked.

"The security firm who did my phone can find her. Why? You think she's in danger?"

"In my opinion everyone associated with this mission is in danger. From now on, you do what I say. You don't stir or move unless I tell you to." He turned to the man driving and spoke again in the weird language that was mostly gutturals and harsh consonants. The van sped up to a hundred miles an hour.

Kesl didn't like being ordered around, but he noted the sense of urgency in Saul's tone and realized the man was trying to protect him. He asked, "Are you speaking in some kind of spy code?"

Saul smiled. "It's a dialect of Gaelic from the Outer Hebrides.

My family and maybe a dozen other people, including my team speak it."

The rest of the trip to Escanaba took only twenty-five minutes. They found Bob Nitschke's home five minutes later. It was a large Victorian style house that overlooked the Lake Michigan waterfront. Saul had the driver pass the home and park on a side street with a view of the front. The lights were on and the front door was open. They detected no movement within.

Saul said, "This man, Nitschke, he's expecting you, right?"

"I set up the meeting after I talked with Chris."

Saul barked out orders. The security team left the van. Two took up positions at either end of it. The other two crossed the street and entered the building. One of them returned five minutes later and reported what they found. "No one's inside but the owner. He's down but alive and awake. Knife wound penetrated just below the sternum. He's lost a lot of blood. I checked his vitals. Pulse is weak breathing labored. He may not make it. Matthew's with him now applying first aid. I did a sweep, both infrared and electronic. Whoever did this didn't leave any bugs behind. The house has been ransacked. Looks like they took his computer, smart phone and back up hard drive."

"Good work, Timothy," Saul said.

The memory of his own beating and being left for dead by Paki-bashers filled Kesl with apprehension and he asked, "Shouldn't we call an ambulance?"

Saul nodded. "As soon as we've found out what he knows. I want a man in front and a man in back. Keep in touch through coms all the time." He looked at Kesl. "Let's go find out what Bob remembers."

* * *

"A woman lives here," said Saul as they entered the front room.

"How do you know?" asked Kesl.

"The inside of the house, in spite of the mess from the search, is neat and tidy. The slip covers on the furniture have recently been vacuumed and the magazines on the end table are stacked in order." Saul frowned. "You understand technology and see what you need to stay on top in the field. I see what I need to keep you alive."

Timothy motioned them to follow him downstairs. The basement had been set up as a typical Midwestern man-cave – La-Z-Boy perched in front of 60" plasma screen TV; a smart mini-fridge for beer and a classic pool table. Mounted heads of deer and moose and several plaques with walleye and muskie adorned the walls.

Bob was propped in his La-Z-Boy, a compress on his abdomen was blood soaked. Matthew stood beside him. Bob eyed Kesl and Saul and managed a weak grin. "It's a cinch you aren't the bastards who stabbed me." He tried to point a thick finger at Kesl, but gave up when he couldn't lift his arm. "You must be the guy who called, Chris's friend."

Kesl nodded.

Saul said, "An ambulance is on its way. What happened?"

"I'm sitting here going through the pics from the trail cam when I hear a noise on the stair. At first I think it might be my dog, Rusty. But in the next second, some big dude whirls my chair around and slams me on the side of the head with something hard, then stabs me in the gut. I don't remember a thing after that until your guy wakes me up working on me, saving my life." He glanced at Matthew and groaned. "I did two tours in the first Gulf War and I can't keep myself safe."

"Take it easy, son. You did well enough to stay alive," said Saul. "Looks like they got your computer and smart phone. Can you think of anything else they may have taken?"

"Did they get the arrow?"

"What arrow."

Bob reddened. "I shot the Bigfoot when I first saw it. I thought it was a bear. It was already dying, so I didn't kill it. I retrieved my arrow with some of its stuff on it. I put it in the freezer."

Saul looked at Timothy. "The freezer was empty, sir."

Saul asked, "Did you get a good look at your attacker?"

Bob shook his head. "He was wearing a ski mask, sorry." Then, "There was one thing though. I didn't pass out right away. The guy said something like he was talking to someone else. It sounded like he had a foreign accent. Eastern European."

"You sound very certain."

"My father-in-law's from Belgrade. When he gets angry he swears in Serbian." Bob grimaced. "Where's that ambulance?"

Saul smiled. "It's on its way. They'll take you to the hospital. They'll notify your wife."

Bob tried to stand but collapsed back into the chair with a moan. "Is my family safe?" he said between clenched teeth.

"You don't have anything more they want. Let this die down."

All of a sudden Kesl knelt down beside Bob, put his hand on his shoulder and looked directly at him and in soft tones said, "What was it like ... what was it like to touch it, to look into the Bigfoot's eyes – tell me?"

Bob grimaced. "It was like nothing I ever experienced before. There was an intelligence, a kind of loving knowing that penetrated into my gut. At the same time, he was alien, I was totally frightened, I wish I'd never set that Bear bait." He slumped down and closed his eyes.

Matthew took his pulse. "Still alive. He's a tough bugger."

"Call the ambulance," Saul ordered.

Timothy pulled out a cheap disposable cell phone and made the call. "We have three minutes, Saul."

"Let's wrap this up."

The team reassembled. Matthew brought the van to the front of the house and they climbed in. The ambulance's siren could be heard in the distance. Matthew pulled away slowly in order not to attract attention to them.

"Why did those guys try to kill Bob?" Kesl asked.

Saul chewed his lower lip. "He'd seen the Bigfoot and the pictures of the woman shooting at someone over the creature's body. My guess, this is part of a larger operation and whoever's killed this creature doesn't want any witnesses who could draw attention to it. Now, the only proof of the Sasquatch is what you and Chris have on your phones."

"So they'll be coming after Chris and the woman next I suppose ... oh that's not good."

"My guess is that they will go after the woman first since she had the first hand encounter and may have physical evidence from the Sasquatch."

As they drove away, Kesl's phone buzzed. He checked the text message and showed it to Saul.

"Jana Erickson, US Forest and Wildlife Ranger. Those women are good. They found her in under fifteen minutes." He barked at Matthew, "Get us to Marquette."

Within two minutes the van was headed across the UP, paralleling the Hiawatha National Forest. Saul handed the phone back to Kesl. "Set up a meeting with this woman. Tell her not to go home."

"Is she really in danger?"

"They will find her."

"I'll figure something out ... it'll come to me." He spoke to his phone, "Call that number."

On the horizon, in the dark night, the lights of the giant Native American casino beckoned them forward. Kesl had a strange feeling about the place.

Chapter Eleven

US Fish And Wildlife Service Lab

Marquette, Michigan

Jana was startled awake by the ringing of her phone. The voice on the other end was tenor and the man spoke quickly as if he had to get every word out in ten seconds. She didn't understand a thing he was saying and then she heard the name Stephen Kesl. This brought her upright and fully aware.

"Who?" she asked.

"This is Stephen Kesl."

"Yeah and I'm Chelsea Clinton. Look is this Corporal Richter? It is, isn't it? You can shove it up your ass. I still won't date you."

In the silence that followed, Jana regretted the lack of landlines anymore. It would have been good to slam the receiver in Richter's ear. Then, the voice, slowing and calmer, said, "I'm not Corporal Richter. I really am Stephen Kesl, Jana. Don't hang up ... sorry to be blunt but you need to listen to me. You probably don't know who I am, a lot of people do, of course, that's beside the point. You've been wasting your talents that's beside the point, too. I–"

Jana stopped him. She wasn't going to waste any time on this prank and she had a sure fire way of telling if it was him or not. "If you're the famous Stephen Kesl? Prove it. What was the topic of your last Ted Talk?"

"I've never given a Ted talk ... I never give Ted talks ... I don't like them ... they were good in the beginning but now." He paused and she heard chuckling. "I see what you're doing. Smart woman."

"Yeah smart enough to test you and you're smart enough to pass. So tell me what's this all about. Why would *the* Stephen Kesl call me?"

"I know about your experience with the Sasquatch, I'm impressed ... good job ... glad you're alive. Can we talk about what went on?"

Maybe it was the earnestness with which the voice on the other end of the phone was speaking, but Jana found herself trusting it, believing it was Kesl. She told him what happened. When she reached the point where she collected the material in a sample bag, Kesl interrupted.

"Fantastic, this changes everything, you're a microbiologist right?"

Jana's guard went up again. Few people around here knew about her days at the university. Marge was the only one and she let everyone know she'd hired Jana because she was a vet. "How do you know that?"

"Umm ... It's on the web ... I have a security team that can find out everything about someone, personal privacy is a myth, you know that. Look, it's important. I figure you haven't forgotten what you've learned. What's your assessment of the Sasquatch material?"

Jana quickly went through in her mind all the scenarios she could come up with. Nothing really made sense. She glanced at the clock on the wall. It was just after midnight and she really didn't want to wait until Marge got in to take the next step. "It was deteriorating rapidly so I put it in our freezer. There is really nothing here to examine it with."

"Sit tight. I'll figure something out and get back to you shortly."

Jana was about to end the call when a new voice interrupted. "Ms. Erickson, this is Saul McBride. Mr. Kesl forgot to inform you that you are in danger. If we can track you, the people who shot at you can do the same. They'll want to keep this secret, keep it away from the public. They'll be coming for you. Is your facility secure? Do you still have your gun with you?"

Jana felt the blood drain from her face. She remembered the

trail cam. Whoever this Saul guy was, he was speaking the truth. "I have my gun," she replied, knowing it was still locked in the bottom drawer of her desk, where regulations demanded she keep it when she wasn't in the field.

Kesl came back on the phone. "Who was that?" she demanded.

"Saul's my head of security ... you'll like him ... well probably not ... he's good at what he does ... you don't have to like him."

"I dislike him already."

"Hang tight."

"Do I have a choice?"

"Saul says no."

* * *

Kesl took less than ten minutes, which was fine as far as Jana was concerned. The phone call had intensified the creepy feeling she'd had earlier. His fast talking tenor voice was a relief. "Jana here's what I want you to do ... take the sample from the freezer ... walk outside ... you'll see someone you know ... it'll be safe to go with that person."

Jana couldn't imagine who it would be unless it was Marge, but her mentor would have called to find out what was going on. Whoever it was, Jana would be glad to see him or her and get out of the lab.

"Roger that," she said.

"Wait! Wait!" Kesl yelled before she could hang up. "Saul says to ditch your phone ... the bad guys will be tracking you through it."

The line went dead. Jana couldn't leave her phone at the lab because the shooters would track her here for sure. She decided she would turn it off and throw it in a garbage can. Today was trash day and the Marquette city sanitation workers would haul it to the municipal dump.

Jana grabbed the Sasquatch sample from the freezer and went

outside. The dumpster was located on the side of the lab, which also gave her a clear view of the street and anyone approaching the building. She dumped her smart phone into the opening and marveled how the dumpster didn't smell like the one at her apartment building, which stank like a Department of Defense experiment gone bad. She noted the time. It was almost one in the morning and the waste removal truck would be here in another hour. *Good,* she thought. *By then anyone chasing my phone will be following it all over Marquette.*

The temperature had fallen near freezing. She pulled her vest closer about her and waited in the shadows. She didn't have to wait long. She heard the car before it made the turn into the parking lot of the lab. Whoever it was probably wasn't security conscious because he parked the car under a mercury vapor light, making himself a great target for anyone watching.

Great. They send an amateur.

She was ready to blast the driver's ignorance, when to her surprise, the man who stepped out of the car was Olav Lassen, a Ph.D teaching assistant in the microbiology lab at the University of Michigan. She couldn't have been more surprised.

Olav was tall and lean, with a red beard and the profile of a Viking. He claimed one of his ancestors had sailed with Leif Erickson to the shores of North America in 1000 and had been the first to jump ashore at Vinland. They had often joked about being cousins, though Olav had many times inquired if she wanted to go out with him and not as relatives. That was six years ago and looking at him now she realized she still had mixed feelings for the man.

He waved his arm at her and yelled, "Jana!"

It was all she could do not to shout at him to stop making himself a target. "Not so loud, Ole. You'll wake the neighbors," she said as she walked up to his car, a Ford Taurus that had to be twenty years old.

Olav knew better than to hug her as Jana had preferred

handshakes and fist bumps to touchy feely stuff. He gave her a high five. "You look the same cousin."

She smiled and said, "Back at you."

They clambered into the vehicle. The interior was like Olav – clean and well kept, not even a gum wrapper in the ashtray. He had been an organized neat freak in college, unlike herself. He handed her a bio transport case with dry ice inside for the sample. " So you really have a piece of Sasquatch here? Hard to believe they exist."

"I didn't either, but here we are."

* * *

Once it was secure, he headed out of the parking lot into the Marquette night.

"You never told me you knew the great man himself," Olav said.

"Just met him this evening." Jana checked to see if anyone was following them. Olav drove as if he didn't have a care in the world. "Where are we going?" she asked.

"To my lab." He chuckled. "I run a well-funded bio research laboratory at Northern Michigan University. You're talking to Professor Lassen."

"Congrats. You deserve it. You were a great teaching assistant. But I thought you were heading for Silicon Valley and the next tech startup when you graduated. What's with the biochem stuff?"

"Wait till you see the set up," Olav said enthusiastically. "You won't believe it. Kesl's investment company is funding my research in using machine learning to simulate rapid cellular evolutionary pathways for the production of ethanol from genetically manipulated cells. I then use an evolutionary model of learning to select the perfect cells for the task."

Jana waved her hand over her head. "I always knew you'd do

something important."

"What about you. The CRISPR-Cas9 undergraduate gene editing phenom? You just sort of disappeared.

"I went to war. It wasn't good."

"I'm sorry."

"Thanks."

"I'm sure you haven't forgotten how much you loved being in that sparkling clean University of Michigan genetics lab. Steve says you're in danger. Should I be afraid?"

"The people that killed the Sasquatch tried to kill me less than six hours ago."

Olav drove onto the Down Campus and the academic mall where the Seaborg Science Complex was located in silence. He pulled into the parking lot and stopped in a parking space. The Taurus' headlights shone on a sign that read Professor Olav Lassen.

Jana looked around to see if they had been followed as they exited the vehicle. She saw nothing and the silence of Marquette late night was deafening. "I think we're good."

"This is rather strange," Olav said as he grabbed the transport case and walked toward the entrance. "I'll do anything to help Steve out. Steve's funding for my lab exceeds the budget for the chemistry and biology departments combined."

She grimaced. "I get it."

"What I told you in the car is the tip of the iceberg of what we're working on now. Machine learning is beginning to supercharge the evolutionary process in a wide range of microorganisms. You couple that with CRISPR/Cas9 and we start processes that build new biosynthetic organisms." He paused and his face reddened. "If that's what we wanted to do. Personally, I'm for it but others think it's the most dangerous enterprise science has embarked upon."

He held the door open for her and Jana recalled he'd always been a perfect gentleman, a throwback to 20th century principles of chauvinism in manners. Otherwise, he treated women as equals in whatever field they competed.

Jana wasn't in the mood to ponder deep ethical questions and changed the subject "How's your personal life?" she asked.

"Still haven't found the right woman yet. She'll come along."

He led them at a brisk pace down an antiseptic hallway illuminated brightly by fluorescents every six feet. The harsh glare, so unlike the dim lighting at the US Wildlife and Forest Service facility made Jana wince. They reached a set of locked double doors. The security here was even tighter than her lab. Olav leaned over and put his right eye to a retinal scanner. She heard a sharp click and the lab doors swung open.

"State of the art," Olav said. "Everything we do has to be protected not only against accidental contamination, but the occasional thief who thinks he can score psychoactive chemicals. As you know, one of the biggest problems up here is drug overdose." Olav shook his head ruefully. "Of course, Steve insists all of our results are open source, available to everybody to build on."

The inside of the lab was pristine and the equipment was beyond anything Jana had experienced before. The machine used to perform CRISPR/CAS9 gene editing must have cost a hundred grand easy, and Olav's lab had two of them.

* * *

"Over here," Olav said, leading her to the refrigeration unit at the back of the lab. He handed her a pair of latex gloves and donned his own. After putting the majority of the Sasquatch material in cryo-storage, he placed a small sample in the latest microfluidic system used for carrying out a wide range of biochemical test protocols. Immediately analysis began to run with the results displayed on a large screen. He stared at the magnified Sasquatch material for several seconds before turning to her with a puzzled grin. "This stuff is really cool and I have no idea what it is. No cellular structure, yet it shows many of the characteristics of organized living plant structures at the micro level and animal at the macro. Very strange."

Jana peered at the screen. Her deep understanding of biochemistry came racing back to her. In particular, the lack of a cellular makeup surprised her. It was as if she was looking at an animal-plant hybrid. "Is this possible?" she asked breathlessly.

Olav nodded. "Living proof someone crossed an ape with a zucchini, cousin."

"I'm serious. This is impossible!"

"I was being serious. Look, Sherlock Holmes said it best. 'When you have eliminated the impossible, whatever remains, however improbable, must be the truth.' But there's a way to test this sample even more."

Olav retrieved an electrochemical magnetic generator and began exposing the material to a series of intense electromagnetic wavelengths. "Will you look at that," he said, his excitement rising as the biochemical analyzer relayed each new reaction result to the big computer screen. "I need to show this to Kesl."

Pulling out his smart phone, he touched the screen. Kesl face appeared instantly. "I've been waiting for your call, Professor Lassen. Waiting too long in my opinion. What do you have for me?"

"I'd rather show you, Dr. Kesl. If you'll indulge me for a second."

It took only a moment to rig up his phone so that it could relay the results from the analyzer directly to Kesl.

"There are some amazing photochemical processes going on here. This is happening even though there is rapid deterioration of the core structures.

Jana looked on as fascinated as the other two at what the sequence of electromagnetic pulses, from infrared to ultraviolet stimulation, did to the biochemistry of the Sasquatch material.

After three minutes, Olav shut down the analyzer. He said to Kesl and Jana, "What do you think?"

Kesl's image on the computer screen pursed its lips. Then, "I know this is going to sound strange, really strange. Any chance there could be some sorta neural network embedded in the material."

Jana jerked in surprise and before Olav could say anything, she asked without keeping the incredulity out of her tone, "Are you suggesting a plant with a brain?"

Kesl shrugged. "Well, sort of. I see there are no ordinary cells but is it possible some sort of a neural net is embedded in that stuff?"

Jana was thinking *Christ, no wonder everybody wants to keep this secret.* "The Klapman Equation says that organic interactions can be represented by a chemogenesis web, especially when the events are triggered by photochemical spikes. In short, it could be the basis of some sort of a neural network. Given the range of electromagnetic energy we subjected the material to just now, I'd say it could work at the speed of light."

Kesl grinned. "You haven't forgotten your stuff, amazing, pretty damn cool. Olav upload everything you just showed me using this IP to my secure server back in my office, so Hangman can analyze it." He smiled. "Hangman's gonna love this ... well I don't know if he really loves anything."

Hangman? Who's Hangman? Jana asked herself, wondering what weird pit of strangeness she had stumbled into. Curiously, at the same time, she didn't feel threatened and the urge to count backward from twenty to zero to calm herself didn't arise at all. It was as if her PTSD had finally taken a vacation. She looked around at the lab, felt the comfort of being in academia again sweep through her. A curious thought came to her in this moment. *Home.* She knew she was home and in an eye blink she felt better than she had since returning from Afghanistan.

Olav, on the other hand, had a look like a deer in the

headlights. He recovered enough to rasp out, "Wait a minute. Are you suggesting that the Sasquatch is some sort of AGI experiment?"

Kesl smiled. "An interesting thought, isn't it? See you soon. Run some more tests and see if you can stop the deterioration. Protect that sample with your life. Just joking." The communication broke off.

Jana had all sorts of thoughts mixing in her mind. Chief among them was that if the guys who shot at her killed the Sasquatch because it was some new order of learning creature and wanted to keep it secret, then they'd do anything to get the sample she took. She glanced at the clock. The night had flown past and it was already 7 a.m. Marge would already be at the lab. If the shooters went there first instead of following her smart phone around Marquette, her old mentor could be in trouble.

"I gotta go," she said and headed toward the door.

"What's so urgent, cousin? We just got started here. There's loads more work to be done and you can help me."

Jana shook her head. "I've got to meet a friend at the lab."

"This early?"

Olav deserved an answer, though she didn't want to frighten the man. An academic his entire life, he thought the most dangerous thing in his life was a bad peer review. "The tweet version is, she could be in danger because of me."

"You mean because of this stuff," Olav said pointing at the Sasquatch material.

Jana nodded. "There's a lot more going on here your buddy Kesl hasn't told you. When I get back with my friend, I'll lay it all out for you."

"Wait ... maybe I should go with you."

"Rescue the damsel in distress?"

Olav grinned. "Not really my style, huh? Take care of yourself."

"I have my gun at the lab and don't think I haven't killed

somebody before."

He flipped her the keys to the Taurus. "This'll get you there faster."

She nodded and left.

Chapter Twelve

Hiawatha National Forest

UP, Michigan

In the light of day, the area looked less forbidding and it was hard to believe that after what had happened the night before. Echohawk found the Bigfoot's trail and they followed it. He pointed out to Chris the signs – branches broken by something pulling on them; scuffed footprints made by dragging feet; a strange, colorless fluid that couldn't possibly be blood and yet it had congealed in the same way. He also pointed out the signs of something smaller that had followed the Bigfoot to the clearing where it died.

"It must be the woman in the photos," Chris said.

Echohawk grunted. "She wasn't the only one. A single man followed, too."

"You think he shot the Bigfoot?"

"Probably. His tracks show him waiting in the clearing before the others arrived. He left this." Echohawk held up some shredded tobacco and a tiny shard of cigarette paper.

Chris recognized the remains of a cigarette that had been field stripped so it left no identifying trace.

"Wait here," Echohawk said. He disappeared into the brush and though Chris craned his neck, he heard no sound except for the morning breeze rustling the leaves. He pivoted slowly, now wishing he had gone into the Marine Corps like his grandfather, Grotto, had urged him to do. There was no longer any doubt the men who had scooped up the Bigfoot were professionals at hunting and killing. What happened last evening seemed obvious now from the way Echohawk laid out the tracking evidence. Someone had shot the Bigfoot but hadn't killed it, then trailed it to the clearing where it died. Then he had called the others to come and retrieve the creature. When the woman in the photos arrived, he'd shot at her but missed and she escaped. Maybe the man had seen Bob's truck, maybe not. But they had taken the trail cam and could trace his friend through its serial numbers.

The process of putting the pieces of the puzzle together had taken only a few seconds. Chris swallowed hard in a dry throat. He had to call Bob to warn him. He fished his phone from his backpack. The call went straight to voicemail. He left a message telling Bob to get out of the house, now. He started to call Kesl when Echohawk's low whistle turned him around.

The Native American emerged from the forest like an apparition. "I think we're being watched … we've been watched all long."

"By whom?"

"Bigfoot. They're here."

Chris pivoted but saw nothing."

"You sure?"

Echohawk nodded. "C'mon. The trail leads this way." He led them deeper into the forest. The cold temperatures overnight had started the leaves falling and everywhere the ground was carpeted with reds and yellows. They moved slowly to avoid making unnecessary noise. The sun was at midmorning when he held up his fist and they finally stopped at Owl Creek. The glade was a hundred feet across. The stream ran sparkling through the middle, between grassy embankments. Three deer stood on a ledge of gravel leading down to a watering hole. The eight-point buck watched the surrounding area while two does drank their fill.

"The Bigfoot took the shot right here," Echohawk said. He pointed to bushes that had been crushed by a falling body. "It got up and ran the way we came." The trampled underbrush and broken branches showed the path they had followed to reach this spot. "Over there," Echohawk said and Chris followed his gaze to a log next to the creek. "The woman trailed it from there," the Native American said with complete certainty.

"I'm impressed, Chief," Chris said.

He inspected the ground. It was trampled with footprints and the crushed bushes showed where the Bigfoot had fallen, just like Echohawk said. But something was missing. If something as large as a Bigfoot had been shot here, there should be blood, maybe even hair and skin. But he saw nothing like that, just more of the same oily, congealed substance they'd seen earlier, and it was decomposing quickly even though there were no signs of insects attacking it. Chris scratched his head. He didn't need a degree in biology or chemistry to know this kind of breakdown on a cellular level within twenty-four hours was impossible. Now he had another mystery to add to the anonymous woman and the team of professionals who had taken the Bigfoot. Just what kind of creature was this Sasquatch? Certainly not some long-lost giant ape species as many of his Bigfoot colleagues argue for.

Echohawk touched him on the shoulder and Chris came instantly alert. His eyes scanned the surroundings, but saw nothing. After several seconds he relaxed enough to stand.

"What is it?" he asked.

"There's another trail, here. I don't think the shooter would have noticed it."

"Why's that?"

"It was made earlier this morning."

"By who?"

"Another Bigfoot. Look at the tracks."

There they were, large footprints in the soft soil. Chris had seen hundreds of these Bigfoot prints cast in plaster of Paris. And now Ecohawk was acting like he had seen them many times before. It was puzzling how easily Ecohawk was accepting their existence.

Maybe the Potawatomi really knew something about Bigfoot

that Chris didn't. After all, Bigfoot researchers claimed that Native Americans had been interacting with the elusive creature for thousands of years. The SRA had been around for less than thirty, and while the reports of sightings numbered in the tens of thousands, none of those encounters reported the same sense of encountering a kindred spirit that the Native Americans claimed.

Once more Echohawk held up his fist. They had arrived at open space several hundred feet across in the forest. In the center was an abandoned quarry. At the far edge, tall brown grass all but hid an unused access road. The pit was shallow but wide, with a central exposed area in the smooth floor. A swath of grass a hundred feet wide separated the pit from the forest. Large areas had been trampled where animals had bedded down for the night.

Setting their packs on the ground, they began to walk around the pit, staying well back from the crumbling rock edge. A sign at the south end proclaimed it was the property of Silver Ridge Stone Limited. From the weathering of the rock, the quarry had been abandoned at least 30 years ago.

Halfway around, Echohawk dropped to his knees suddenly. He cawed like a raven – three, short, harsh rasps followed by a long one. Chris crouched and looked at his friend. Chief pointed through the long grass at the forest edge. Chris didn't see anything and shrugged. Chief frowned and jabbed his finger again. Chris followed his aim and for a moment was bewildered by the Native American's insistence that something was out there. He didn't see anything. Then the breeze stirred the leaves and the sun hit a pair of saplings at just the right angle. He saw where the trees had been arranged to conceal an opening. A casual observer wouldn't have noticed anything unusual. It spoke of an intelligence that was hiding a path so that only those who expected to find it would see it.

Cautiously, they approached the opening. A subtle trail wound deep into the woods. Echohawk let out a long, slow breath. "This was not made by hunters," he whispered.

Chris almost didn't believe it and yet something about this trail beckoned him forward as if it held the answer to the Bigfoot mysteries he's been initiated into when on his grandfather's farm twenty years ago.

"I'm going in," he said, his words a quiet brush of air through his lips. Echohawk nodded. Several times they came to dead ends and were forced to backtrack. Chris realized that the makers of this trail had created a maze where the unwary would become lost walking about in circles. Without Echohawk to lead him, Chris would have been one of those, walking until he collapsed, exhausted.

What seemed like an hour passed and another clearing appeared. It was not a natural open space in the forest. Something had arranged the area around it so that everything funneled toward a structure of sticks leaning together like a teepee in the center. Chris immediately recognized the Sasquatch stick structure. He had encountered more than one of these following up on reports of Bigfoot sightings for the SRA.

What took his breath away was the unmistakable craftsmanship. Each log had been carefully pruned, the upward tips sharpened as meticulously as a pencil in a pencil sharpener. Then each log had been placed exactly in the earth to form the shape of a lens, like the eye in the pyramid on the U.S. dollar bill.

He heard Echohawk approach. "Do you know what this is?" asked the Potawatomi.

Chris nodded. "It's a Bigfoot stick structure. They've been found in conjunction with Bigfoot sightings. Some researchers think they're trail markers or a kind of communication device to pass on information. Sort of like the pictographs used by Indian tribes along trade routes in the desert southwest."

Echohawk didn't say anything but walked around the strange tepee, giving it a wide berth. When Chris started to walk closer he held up his hand and shouted, "Stop!"

Chris stared at him, perplexed by his friend's sudden fearful attitude. "What's wrong, Chief?"

"Among my people, these are portals to other worlds. People who go inside disappear."

Chris grinned. "That's one of the other explanations that have been reported."

Echohawk didn't say anything for a long time. Then, "My grandfather, the one who taught me to hunt and trap, he left home one morning in January to check his trap line. He never returned. His body was never found but one of these things was nearby one of his traps."

"You think he disappeared through one of these?"

"I'm saying, where Bigfoot are concerned there are no accidents."

Suddenly an overpowering odor of musk filled the clearing, driving both men to their knees. It disappeared as quickly as it appeared. Chris scrambled to his feet. The redolent smell reminded him of his grandfather's farm. He turned to ask Chief what had happened, but the Native American was staring into the trees at the far edge of the clearing. Chris saw it, too. A shudder ran through both of them. Looking at them in the golden glow of the early afternoon sun were at least a dozen Bigfoot. Different sizes, varying faces, some more human than others.

"My God!" Chris exclaimed. He looked over at Echohawk who was pulling out his 1911 Colt Peacemaker. "Don't shoot!" Ignoring Chris, Echohawk took aim. Chris slapped the gun down and the bullet whined into the ground at his feet.

Chris bunched his fists. "I told you not to shoot!"

Echohawk didn't back up. He stared Chris in the eyes and said evenly, "Those unnatural creatures are dangerous."

"Not to me they aren't." Chris turned back to look at the Sasquatch, but they were gone. He started forward and Echohawk grabbed his arm. "Where are you going?" he asked with fear in his voice.

"After them."

"You're crazy. Remember my grandfather. You don't know what they'll do to you."

Chris shrugged off his hand. "I've been waiting since I was 12 years old for this chance." He bypassed the wooden structure and ran into the forest.

* * *

Echohawk watched Chris disappear. Slowly he walked back to where they had left their backpacks and waited for Chris to return. He had spent many hours silently with his father while hunting deer in the UP and was used to waiting. After about an hour, Chris's phone rang. Echohawk looked at the caller ID and saw it was from a Stephen Kesl. He picked up the phone and swiped the answer icon.

"Chris, did you find the body? Probably not. We've had a lot happen here I'm leaving Marquette now ... much I need to tell you about it ...."

Echohawk didn't answer right away and the voice asked, "Chris? What's going on?"

"Chris isn't here, Mr. Kesl," Echohawk said. "I'm Larry Echohawk. I went with Chris to retrieve the body. You're right – no dead Sasquatch."

The phone was silent for a moment then Kesl said, "I know who you are ... Chris mentioned you. Is he okay?"

Matter-of-factly, Echohawk said, "I don't know. He ran off after a group of Sasquatch. At least a dozen. I tried to stop him but he said something about when he was 12."

"Shit! I didn't expect that."

"It certainly surprised me."

"How long has he been gone?"

"An hour, maybe. He could be back at any moment."

"Why do you say that?"

"I haven't sensed the Bigfoot around here for some time now, we both had a sense of being watched since we got here."

"Are you willing to wait a little while longer? There might be men still hunting Sasquatch."

"Sure, I can take care of myself."

"Good. Wait an hour and if Chris isn't back by then, leave his backpack and phone there, grab the rest of the gear and head back to the truck. Call me if Chris comes back or when you leave for the truck. Will you do that?"

"Sure."

As soon as the call ended chief slipped the phone into his pocket. Leaving all the gear behind except for his weapons, he left the quarry.

Chapter Thirteen

Marquette, Michigan

Dawn was a bright glow on the eastern horizon above Lake Michigan when Jana pulled into the rear parking lot of the US Wildlife and Forestry Service Lab. She recognized Marge's Prius in her spot by the gravel walkway leading to the back door. There were no other cars in the lot and she breathed a sigh of relief. Either the shooters were chasing their tails around the city or they hadn't bothered coming to the lab yet. Either way, she figured she had enough time to grab her pistol and Marge and get back to Olav's lab at the university, where they'd be safe.

She entered the rear of the building and the first thing she noticed was the lights were off. Marge always turned them on when she arrived. Jana's shoulders tensed and her breathing quickened. As she'd been taught in the military, she channeled the surge of adrenaline in her body to sharpen her senses. She slid noiselessly across the linoleum floor beside the set of double doors leading to the interior hall, the lab, the lunchroom and Marge's office. Flattening herself against the wall, she cocked her head. The murmur of voices reached her ears. She counted two intruders. *They obviously came for me just as Kesl predicted. I'm a witness and need to be silenced.* She cursed silently and wished she hadn't left her service revolver in her desk. But she wasn't without resources. She knew the layout of the building. There were two entrances, plus an emergency fire escape from the second floor. She'd have to wait for the hunters to go inside the lab before grabbing Marge and making a run for it. She didn't have to wait long. The doors to the lab squeaked open and closed.

Jana darted into the hall and ran on tip toe for the Supervisor's office. She couldn't leave Marge behind. The woman was more than her boss. She was a very dear friend and mentor. She burst into the office and stopped cold. The elderly woman was leaned back in her chair. A dark red hole above her eyes stared at the ceiling. A bloody mist of red coated the white plasterboard behind her. Judging from the way the blood dripped down the wall, the shooting had happened only minutes before. The men must have been using silencers since she hadn't heard a sound.

Jana backed into the corridor. This couldn't be happening not to her, not to Marge. Her clothes were soaked with sweat and her mind reeled at the sight of her dear friend, but the adrenaline spurred her to act swiftly. Fortunately she faced the lab. A shadow passed across the windows in the double doors. The killers were still inside. She ran down the corridor, stopping briefly to pick up a broom from the hall closet. Outside the lab's double doors she ran the broom through the looping handles. It would hold them for the time she needed to get out of the building.

She turned. Behind Jana the broom rattled. They'd finished searching the lab faster than she thought. She ran full out, not toward the front where the murderers would expect her to go and likely had a man waiting, but to the second floor. She scurried up the stairs just as the broom handle snapped with a crack like a pistol shot. As noiselessly as possible she opened the door to the second floor and slid inside. The lights were off and they'd have to stay that way or she'd give her position away to the killers. If they had the training she'd gone through, they'd systematically sweep the building, clearing the ground floor first before moving to the second. This gave her some time. She went through her options. There was always the fire escape, but if they had come ready to kill, then she couldn't take the chance others waited outside guarding the exits. She'd have to prepare some kind of trap, take out one of the men. This would give her a firearm at least. She swallowed hard. She'd sworn never to kill anything again after Afghanistan. Would she be able to kill to defend her own life? She didn't know the answer to that. She heard a footstep on the stair. First thing was to move away from the wall. It was nothing but plasterboard and two by four studs. Nothing to stop bullets. The second floor was used mostly for storage. *Including illegal bear traps confiscated from hunters.*

Crouching, she worked her way through boxes to the far side of the room. A metal storage cell held all the confiscated gear, except for firearms. These went to a separate facility in Traverse City. It wouldn't have mattered anyway. The firearms were always cleared of any ammo when taken. The door was left unlocked. It opened with a rusty screech. She held her breath, but no sound of hurrying steps on the stairs.

Jana eased inside toward the back and quickly located the cardboard carton she'd put there last year. It contained a Mackenzie District Fur Company LTD 1886 HBC NO.15 bear trap she'd taken from a hunter near Munising in November, a year ago. The idiot had sworn he was licensed to use it.

She set it out on the floor and stepped down on the springs. The trap opened and she set the pin. The trigger lever and trigger plate worked smoothly. She pulled her hand back, aware that the razor sharp teeth could snap her wrist in half. The trap set, she grabbed a hockey stick Eric had taken from a teenager who used it to club baby barn owls with, and carried both over to the door. She set the trap so that with the lights off, the killer wouldn't see it when he walked in and would step right onto the trigger plate.

She waited, trying to slow the savage beating of her heart. The silence and darkness threatened to transport her back to Helmand. Only the grip on the hockey stick kept her in this reality.

A few minutes later Jana heard footsteps on the stair. She counted one person. The door opened and the man entered stealthily without turning on the lights, just as she knew he would. Darkness was his friend, but in this instance it was also his undoing. He took another step and she heard the trap spring with a sickening crunch. The man screamed like a wounded animal. He squeezed the trigger on his pistol and a round fired into the room, smashing into a packing case.

Jana lunged forward and brought the hockey stick across his forehead. He stopped yelling and dropped like a stone, his head cracking against the floor. In the light from the stairway she could see blood gushing from a wound in his head and more seeping from his pants leg where the trap's teeth bit cruelly into his shin. She didn't recognize him.

His pistol had slid out of his still fingers and lay beside him. Jana hesitated. It was a Colt .38 Super Competition pistol, modified to take a ten inch sound suppressor. She was familiar with it, her father having trained her to shoot when she was only seven. More footsteps on the stairs and she picked it up. Before she could decide what to do, three hollow sounds echoed in the stillness and bullets ripped through the plaster on her side of the door, narrowly missing her head and showering her with gypsum dust. A second passed and another sharp crack and the light switch plate shattered, somehow also turning on the lights to the room, exposing her to whoever was running up the stairs. Jana rolled across the trapped killer and pulled the trigger a half dozen times as she pointed the pistol into the stairwell. The fall from the stunned killer's hand must have loosened the suppressor because the roar of the weapon deafened her.

She could hear nothing. She twisted her body around, ready to fire again and saw the second killer lying unconscious at the bottom of the stairs. He was wearing a bullet proof vest which had stopped the group of shots in the center mass of his chest from killing him. The impact, however, had knocked him out and down the flight of stairs.

A mixture of relief suffused Jana. The man lived. Not that he deserved to live. These men had killed Marge. She stood. Blood roared in her ears. The threat was over and the fear from surviving an attack was now beginning to lodge in her chest. She found it hard to breathe. She dropped to one knee, saw the man in the bear trap staring at her. He was alive, like his partner. She stood and stepped away from him. The danger wasn't over yet. She pointed the weapon at his head and asked, "How many are outside?"

"*Mi smo sami,*" he said through clenched teeth.

She stepped on his foot in the bear trap. He screamed in pain and she let up. "English!" she ordered.

"We are alone," he whimpered.

"Are you the one who shot at me in the forest?"

The man pointed at the bottom of the stairs. "He did."

"Where are you from?"

"Croatia," he rasped.

She leaned over him. "You asshole. Marge didn't know anything. You are gonna rot in an unforgiving Michigan jail for the rest of your life." She slugged him in the head with the barrel of the pistol. He gasped and went unconscious.

Jana stood slowly and listened. The quiet disturbed her. She thought of the others that might be lurking nearby in spite of what the killer said. They would certainly send in someone to see what the shooting was all about. She waited, removed the clip in the Colt and saw there were seven shots left. She slammed it home and peered into the downstairs. No movement no sound.

Maybe the first killer spoke the truth and they had operated alone. After all, they had been hunting Sasquatch that nobody believed really existed, and they hadn't reckoned on an Afghan war veteran fouling things up. She ran her hand through her hair. It came away sticky. Her fingers were coated with blood. One of the bullets must have creased her scalp. In all the adrenaline soaked action she hadn't even noticed. She had to get out of here.

Jana went down the stairs, every sense alert for the tiniest sound or motion. The second killer was still knocked out but could regain consciousness at any moment. She stripped him of his weapons and bound his hands behind his back. She put a gag in his mouth and took his shoes.

When she finished, she walked to the front of the building and peered out through the glass doors. The sun was rising above the trees and cast the parking lot in gold. She saw no one. In the distance she could see headlights. A van was roaring down the road toward the lab. She didn't have time to get into her truck or Olav's Taurus. Whoever was coming would trap her. She dashed across the parking lot toward a grove of trees just as the van swung into the parking lot. She didn't look back but kept on going. She heard the doors open. She still had fifty feet to go and would never make it. She turned and took a shooter's stance aiming at the man on the right side of the van. Curiously, he kept the rifle he held pointed at the ground. She wondered if it was a trick to make her hesitate, but a quick glance at the other men showed they were not targeting her.

Then a young man stepped out of the van with an older man right behind him. The younger man said, "Ms. Erickson, are you all right?"

"Who's asking?" she demanded keeping her pistol leveled.

"Stephen Kesl. We spoke on the phone earlier. You'd best come with us. Quite nice to meet you actually."

She jerked in surprise but didn't lower her weapon. "I have Lassen's car," she said.

"I told him to buy a new one. In any case he won't be needing it for a while," Kesl said. "Please. It's for your own safety and Professor Lassen's."

The older man stepped forward. He spoke with a Scots accent. "Believe it or not, right now we're the only ones who can protect you."

She snorted. "I didn't do so bad a job by myself just now."

He grinned and said, "I know you did, lass."

Jana lowered her weapon, put the safety on and stuffed it in the back of her jeans. "Who the hell are you?"

"My name is Saul McBride. I'm Mr. Kesl's chief of security. We saw the whole thing through the building's security cameras that Mr. Kesl's smart techies hacked into. It's the reason we got here as quickly as we did. But this place is now a crime scene and we need to get you and ourselves out of here, before the police get here or someone not as nice."

Jana scowled. "The only thing I'm interested in is justice for Marge. Those bastards killed her."

"Of course, you're right," Kesl interjected. "Please believe me, Ms. Erickson, can I call you, Jana? I understand your rather primitive need for revenge and if it is in my power to grant it, I will give it to you. But for now, you need to concentrate on your own safety. You have become embroiled in something much more dangerous and complicated than you can imagine. So please let us rescue you. In the meantime, I want you to tell me every little detail of your experience with the Sasquatch. I'm sure you will be quite good at this with your military and biochemical training. Much better than that poor fellow who shot the creature with his bow and arrow. Didn't kill him of course. Hypothesize as you go. I'm truly quite fascinated in what you saw and what you think."

Jana stared blankly at the tech genius, who seemed to be babbling. Then she turned her attention to the building that just yesterday morning was her safe haven, and saw in her mind's eye Marge's lifeless body sprawled in her office. *I'll get revenge for you, Marge. I swear it.* She squared her shoulders and marched toward the van. Kesl bowed for her to get onboard. She grabbed the frame and stared at him. "If there's something bigger going on, I want to know every part of it and who's behind all this crap."

"Of course."

Chapter Fourteen

Seattle, Washington

Directly across the street from the sprawling campus of the Seattle Center, home to the 1962 World's Fair, KW Intel's glass office tower rose majestically into the air. It's seventy stories topped the famous six-hundred-and-five-foot Space Needle built for the fair and offered picturesque views of the Pacific Northwest's Puget Sound. KW Intel was named for its founders, Kellog and Winston Ang. Born a year apart, the two Chinese Americans had entered MIT at sixteen and fifteen respectively, graduating three years later, one year after they developed an application called Cirrus that allowed users to manage all their cloud storage providers. It was bought by Google for $100 million. They could have retired before reaching the legal drinking age in Washington State, but instead, they bought and funded a company doing research on AI control systems for large commercial vehicles. Two years later their prototype became the standard operating system on long-haul trucks. Within three years every major truck manufacturing company in the world leased KW Intel's VOS – Vehicular Operations System.

Eccentric billionaires didn't begin to describe them. Neither did their notorious penchant for conspiracy theories of all kinds.

The top floor of KW Intel's office complex looked like any ordinary command center for a $500 billion multi-national tech research company which had facilities developing new products around the world in every field from agriculture to video games. A receptionist greeted visitors from behind a circular counter, strategically placed to keep anyone from barging into inner conference rooms and offices.

What visitor's didn't see were the receptionist's personal assistant device with Adaptive Intelligence software and built in retinal scan to block unauthorized users; state-of-the-art hidden cameras, and infrared motion detectors. Nor did anyone crossing the threshold to greet the receptionist feel the complete body scan for weapons. Within moments of arrival and giving a name to the receptionist, the building's internal computer monitoring system generated a complete dossier.

Visitors who came to pitch ideas or companies to purchase were cordially shown to a conference room where men and women whose sole job was to evaluate possible new acquisitions listened, evaluated and made recommendations whether to buy or pass. The grilling that went on made *Shark Tank* look like a guppy bowl.

Beyond the main conference room was a smaller room, insulated against any listening devices with sound suppression wall construction that kept any vibration of human speech from leaking out of the room. The room was filled with the latest eavesdropping equipment monitoring UHF, VHF, satellite and tower microwave transmissions. Seated behind a plain wooden desk, KW Intell's two owners, Kellog and Winston Ang, watched a giant screen with a view of ISS – the new International Space Station. The two men waited, uncharacteristically tense.

A light blinked on the screen and Winston, the younger of the two brothers, counted down slowly from ten. He was forty-one, thin, with black hair and deep, dark circles beneath sloe eyes. His skin was golden. "Three ... two ... one ... now," he said.

Two, large, bay doors in the station's cargo bay opened. At first they saw nothing.

"Where are they, God damn it?" growled Kellog. Unlike his younger sibling, his skin was a sickly yellow shade, the color of jaundice. His eyes were blood shot, his face jowly and his dark hair flecked with gray. He was morbidly obese.

"Patience, Kel. The laser has to send them out at the precise moment or else they won't go into low earth orbit but will end up burning up in the earth's atmosphere. He smiled, showing even white teeth as the first satellite appeared to drift away from the space station. Drift was not an accurate description for the orbit of these tiny devices. When the mission was complete there would be thousands of tiny satellites the size and shape of an original smart phone floating around the planet, capable of seeing every part of the globe from the Himalayas to the deepest darkest parts of the Amazon jungle. They would be the seeing eye on a world filled with dark secrets.

The spacecraft were loaded with microelectronics and cameras weighing only half a pound. A pair of ultra-thin solar sails spread out from the body like batwings and acted not only as a battery charger but as a propulsion system that kept the satellite in low earth orbit. For the cost of one communication satellite launched into orbit in 1990, the brothers could send ten thousand of these micro-devices to provide real-time, detailed imagery of the earth. It would take twenty days to have "eyes on" every inch of the planet's surface.

The brothers watched for an hour as the devices launched one after another. When the last satellite was deployed, a disembodied voice said, "That's the last of them for today."

Kellog pressed a button on the conference table. "Thank you, commander. Same time tomorrow?"

"Yes, sir. Do you mind if I ask what you're going to do with all the data these things will generate?"

"It'll be free to anybody who wants to use it," Winston lied. "Somebody at Walmart HQ will be able to look at every car entering a Walmart parking lot in a 24 hour period at every store in the world."

"That'll certainly be useful. So you could track the comings and goings of my wife?"

"What's her name, commander?" asked Winston.

"Seriously?"

"Just joking."

"How many of these does KW Intel currently have in orbit?"

"With this last launch, one thousand two hundred twenty-five. When the mission is complete we expect to have ten thousand flying around the planet."

"Whew. How did you get clearance for these?"

"We asked politely," said Winston.

The voice chuckled. "Ask a silly question. Talk with you tomorrow. Commander William Rodgers over and out." The space station feed disappeared.

Winston looked at his brother and asked, "Do you think anyone will figure it out – our primary purpose?

"Not until it's too late, Win." Kellog paused. He smiled and Winston grinned back. They bumped fists.

"Here's to blissful ignorance."

The sound of a C major chord filled the room. "Hold that thought." Winston swiped the talk icon and put the phone to his ear. His lighthearted mood disappeared. "You're sure?" he asked the caller. Then, "Okay. Do what you can to find out what's going on without endangering the operation."

He hung up and turned to his brother. "That was Echohawk. It seems, strange as it may be, that Stephen Kesl has gotten directly involved."

Kellog sat up straight in his chair. "That shouldn't have happened. The Russian said early on he needed verification of the nature of the creatures. What happened? Did the incident in the UP bring him into play?"

"It wasn't our decision to hire the Croatians to kill the Sasquatch."

"Yes, but I should have demanded more oversight."

Winston laughed and when his brother glowered at him, said placatingly, "Lewis Meriwether would never have permitted that. Besides, it wasn't just the incident."

"How can you be sure?"

"Have you ever met Kesl?"

The older brother shook his head.

"I have ... once. At the machine learning conclave in Finland a few months ago. He's a strange one ... highly functioning autistic. His disability sends him into frantic investigations of the strangest ideas. He spent two years working on teleportation, you know, like in Star Trek. He was convinced the Tesla Coil could make it possible. He would have wasted a fortune on it but Kesl's chief of security Saul McBride had his wife talk him out of it."

Kellog chuckled. "Could be a useful weakness."

"Some say he has an old-fashioned IQ of 183. But that's not what makes him exceptional."

"You're saying it's his autism?"

Winston nodded. "Somehow, it must have been the idea of the Sasquatch as a deep learning, biosynthetic creature that triggered his obsession. He's totally involved now and that's a problem. He's never bought our argument about the dangers of the computer singularity."

Kellog snorted. "He and everyone else. People aren't seeing the real danger of AGI. I told him, once we have machines that are smarter than we are, they will begin to improve themselves and set their own goals. What we're risking right now is what mathematician I.J. Goode calls an intelligence explosion and the process could get away from us. Eventually, I said, I fear these machines will treat us with similar disregard as we treat insects when building a house – something in the way to be annihilated."

"What did he say?"

"It will take some time, maybe even today, you and your brother will come around to my way of thinking, embrace the singularity."

"And now the gathering of the Sasquatch, you think he knows?"

"Probably." Kellog shook his head. "We can't let it happen or all of humankind will become ants to these alien hybrid machines."

"Are we ready to stop them?"

"We have to. This may be our last chance. It looks like killing a few Sasquatch in the Upper Peninsula isn't enough. They keep coming. We need to find a way to stop them from taking over the planet."

"At least our detection satellites are giving us an advantage no one else has ever had in finding them." Winston pressed an icon on his smart phone and the large screen lit up, this time with an ultraviolet image of Michigan's UP.

"Where is that?" asked Kellog.

Winston asked the computer to overlay the image with the geographical names of the region. Hiawatha National Forest appeared in white letters against the green backdrop. He said, "Scan left," and the scene shifted eastward. "There's the abandoned quarry at the eastern boundary, where Meriwether and his team have been disposing of Sasquatch."

Kellog looked at Winston askance.

"Relax. It's perfect. They dump the Bigfoot carcasses into the quarry's shallow pond. Within twenty-four hours the remains have broken down completely into simple organic material." He squinted at the picture. "Zoom in," he ordered. The image pixelated as the camera's telephoto lens adjusted for a closer look. Unlike the indistinct images made by military infra-red night vision cameras, these pictures had the sharp resolution of military grade spy satellite imagery that could read the word Titleist on a teed golf ball at Augusta during the Master's Tournament. When the image cleared, both brothers gave a start.

"Isn't that Echohawk?" Kellog asked, pointing to the figure beside the quarry. Winston nodded. "Then who's the guy running out of the picture north and west?"

Kellog commanded the imagery to track up and left. It picked up the running man and then abruptly a dozen figures appeared, running together ahead of him. The figures were tall, humanoid, with long arms, barrel chests and squat legs. The skin had a greenish tint. What was most alarming, however, were the faces.

They looked unearthly. "What are those alien mother fuckers doing?" asked Kellog. "Communing to take over the earth?"

"Who gives a shit? They're targets. I'm calling Meriwether."

Suddenly the screen went blank. "What happened?" demanded Kellog.

"We lost coverage."

"Damn."

"Those new satellites can get into position fast enough."

"My calculations show we will have complete coverage of the UP by mid afternoon."

Chapter Fifteen

Hiawatha National Forest

UP, Michigan

Chris found trying to run through the soggy floor of the new growth spruce balsam forest quite difficult. He sank into marshy ground up to his ankles and several times had to stop to work his shoe free of the muck. He didn't question why he was chasing the Bigfoot. He'd needed answers ever since the first one peered at him in his grandfather's kitchen early in the morning as a teenager.

Am I expecting they'll just sit down and talk to me and tell me why they made contact with me when I was a child? That's just stupid. Nevertheless, he pushed forward.

He hit a flat, dry patch of ground and redoubled his effort, following a trail of bent and broken limbs and the strong musk odor which lingered in the air. How many times had he taken groups on Bigfoot hunts, pointing to the broken and bent limbs at around the ten foot level and the skunk smell, telling the group it was sure evidence of the presence of Bigfoot.

He stopped running, spotted a large limb lying on the ground. He picked it up and gave the nearest tree a whack. He couldn't count the number of times he had done what is known in the Bigfoot world as doing a wood knock. Like all times before, he waited for a reply. There they were, three replies coming from different directions. Filled with excitement by the response, he recalled his childhood dream: to find the creatures and know their secrets. More than ever, Chris was determined to push deeper into the forest. He had to keep going.

He'd run for half an hour or more. He wasn't sure. Time seemed to have telescoped. But which way, he couldn't tell. It felt like a long time. He hadn't checked his watch when he left

Echohawk and the quarry. He only knew he'd been running for a long time, though at a slower pace.

Rounding a thick stand of trees and a moss covered boulder, the trail suddenly went dead. He was far past any recognizable landmarks and he knew deep in his guts he was lost. Wheezing, he took another thirty steps and came upon the gigantic bole of an ancient forest giant. The solitary white pine was so large it had to be one of the original trees to sprout after the Laurentian Ice sheet retreated northward at the end of the last ice age and trees started to grow again in the UP, thousands of years ago. It had been uprooted. The system of roots was large enough for a person to climb into and be protected from the rain or snow. Branches had been sheared off in the fall, but enough stubs remained. He was able to climb to the top and look around. He was twenty feet above the ground, but the surrounding thick forest cut off any view more than twenty feet away.

He leaned against a tree limb as big around as his torso. He thought about doing another wood knock, but he was unable to break off a branch to do so. Then, out of desperation, he gave the loudest and longest whoop he could muster. The scream disappeared into the forest without an echo.

Chris grimaced. He was lost and his dream of encountering a Bigfoot face to face was fading, too. He might as well start back toward the quarry, if he could even find it. Chris started to climb down when he heard a slight sound from behind. He turned around. The moss covered boulder he had passed rose up and a twelve foot Bigfoot towered in its place.

It was beautiful, with a smooth, simian-like face that could have passed for one of our early ancestors. The chest was the size of a refrigerator and its long arms swung past its hips almost to its knees. The legs were disproportionately short though not stubby. A green tinted fur covered it, though Chris could not be sure it was fur. The creature's pelt rippled and changed hues as it moved toward him, like some psychedelic moss. It stopped when only a few feet away from the log. Liquid gray eyes stared at him and the creature spoke with a female voice. "Why were you following us?"

The voice was gentle and seemed to emanate from the whole creature rather than its mouth. Chris couldn't tell if he was hearing with his ears or the voice was inside his head.

"What do you want?" the Bigfoot asked, the demand gently pushing into Chris's mind.

He searched for the right words. An image flashed into his thoughts. The Bigfoot was the one from his childhood summers spent on his grandfather's farm in the Olympic Peninsula in Washington.

The creature's voice shifted from female to his grandfather. "I was there."

'Impossible!' Chris yelled, though he made no sound.

The Bigfoot cocked its head like any human who was perplexed by something. "Why is it impossible that I'm the one who saw you those summers long ago. We seek out people who are open to us like you. Think how different your life would have been if you'd never seen me."

Chris clenched his fists to keep from shaking. He focused his energy on speaking "What are you?" he asked, relieved he could speak aloud, though his voice was a whispery rasp.

"You don't know?" the Bigfoot asked.

He shook his head.

The creature moved from side to side, the gray eyes blinking slowly, as if taking pictures of him from different perspectives. Chris noticed for the first time, the hair around its face and along its skull was gray. Wrinkles framed its eyes giving it the appearance of great age.

Finally it spoke again. "We are a different kind of life form, learning about your planet for thousands of years.

"For millennia my sisters and brothers have been able to hide ourselves from your kind. But now, the people hunting us have figured out a way to overcome our protections."

"Are you going to hurt me?"

"What a curious question. Of course not. You now have the answers you have been searching for most of your life."

"How do you know that?"

"We sometimes seek out humans whose minds are different. Those who have encounters like yours often begin a lifelong pursuit of the meaning of their experience. You were special, you saw me as I am. Others have what is called a spiritual experience, interpreting our presence as God or the ultimate truth."

Chris knew it would sound stupid but he said anyhow, "Can I help. Help protect you. Protect your people?"

"Against advanced weapons and technology?" The Bigfoot sounded ironic.

Then an odd thought emerged in Chris's mind. "Why are you telling me all this? Aren't you worried I'm going to tell everybody?"

He could swear the creature smiled at him. "Who's going to believe you?"

"The man, Stephen Kesl, who sent me to retrieve the Bigfoot will. He's one of the smartest people on the planet and he has this deep learning computer that is smarter than us humans and can figure anything out."

Chris thought he saw something akin to understanding at a deeper level than any creature he'd ever encountered before cross the Bigfoot's face.

"Tell Stephen Kesl we reproduce like a 3-D printer builds organic products."

Chris shrugged helplessly. "I'd love to, but I'm lost."

"No you're not, walk through those trees and you'll find your truck."

In a blink of an eye the Bigfoot was gone. To his surprise, when Chris walked through the trees, pushing the boughs aside, there was his truck just like the Bigfoot said. Suddenly he was overwhelmed with emotion. He fell to his knees and began sobbing it was so surreal. *Was that real? Did I just talk to a Bigfoot?*

* * *

Chris didn't know how long he wept. But when he finished, he felt refreshed. As he stood, he breathed in deeply. The air seemed clearer and the smells of the forest more exquisite than ever. He was part of it in a way he had never experienced before.

A crunch of dry leaves turned Chris around. He saw Echohawk approaching the truck. When the Native American spotted him there was a look of surprise that turned to anger. "What are you doing here, crying like a baby?"

Pulling himself together, Chris recognized this was not the same person he'd left behind at the quarry. He wiped away his tears and said angrily, "I might ask the same about you."

Echohawk ignored the question. "So did you find them?"

"One found me. It … she talked just like us. There're actually quite humanlike."

Chris was quite astounded that his friend showed no surprise by the fact that the Bigfoot could speak.

"So you had your Bigfoot experience, what now?" Echohawk said sarcastically.

"What's happened to you? You're not the same," said Chris.

"I thought you were dead, chasing after those creatures. All I could think of was my grandfather and how they took him."

"I don't think that's true. They won't harm humans. They learned to stay out of our way, avoid us. You're not gonna believe this, but they may need our help."

"Did it say how it wants our help?"

"She liked the idea of getting Kesl to help them, it was almost like she knew who he was." Then it came to Chris that Echohawk had not brought his gear. "Where's my stuff? Were you going to just leave me here?"

Echohawk pulled out his 1911 Colt and pointed it at Chris. "Worse than that?"

"I thought we were friends."

"We're not enemies. Just on different sides," said Echohawk. His finger tightened on the trigger and Chris flinched, ready to throw himself to the side. But he didn't have to. A split second later the Potawatomi's face froze and he begin to shake all over. The gun slipped from his fingers. An instant later he lurched forward onto the ground. Then, almost out of the blue, another Bigfoot appeared. This one was much smaller, though she had the same proportion of limbs and torso. The face, however, could have passed for a bear.

"Did you do that?" Chris asked, his voice clear. It seemed almost natural to speak with a Bigfoot.

"You were in danger."

"Can all of you do that?"

"No, we all have learned to do many different things. You are free to go now. Your phone is in his pocket."

"Is he dead?

"We don't kill humans."

Chapter Sixteen

Marinette, Michigan

When the owner of Di Napoli's Family restaurant in Marinette discovered Kesl spoke fluent Italian, he insisted on serving the guests himself and giving the lunch party a free bottle of Chianti. The balding, potbellied man in his mid-fifties complained as he uncorked the bottle, "No one in this small town speaks the language of Dante, of Pirandello, of Fellini." He poured the wine while humming the theme from *La Dolce Vita*. When the food had been served, he left them alone.

The morning had been exhausting and the drive from Marquette seemed to go on forever, each of them catching small bits of sleep. Meanwhile Kesl had remained tight-lipped about anything to do with Sasquatch or the remains Olav had identified as plant-like. He insisted they wait in Marinette until he heard from Chris.

The mood in the restaurant was far from festive. Two men from the security detail watched the parking lot; the other two had eyes on the room and the kitchen. Saul gritted his teeth and said, "We should get back to Toronto as quickly as possible. It isn't safe here for you or the young lady."

Jana snorted. "I can take care of myself." Jerking a thumb at the van, she said, "Give me one of your Czech made CZ-805 BREN assault rifles and I'll lead your team after those assholes who killed Marge and the Bigfoot."

Saul waved her offer away. Kesl might have waited to see just how serious Jana was, but his phone beeped. He answered it as he always did with the single word, "Speak." After a few seconds he looked at Saul and the others. "Hang on. I have to move." He walked out of the restaurant into the parking lot. Saul insisted he stay where the team could see him. Kesl stood on the sidewalk in front of the plate glass window.

"Shit, Chris! Last thing I heard you were chasing a group of Bigfoot?" Kesl listened intently, his fingers flicking against thighs, stomach and chest in rapid darting movements. At times he spun around as if a gust of wind had twirled him, though there was no wind this day. Passersby occasionally heard him say, "Got it ... Say more ... That changes everything."

Finally his agitation trailed off and he said, "We'll meet you at the casino, Chris. I'll contact you so we can speak in private, make a plan."

He punched off and looked through the plate glass window of the restaurant to signal his security chief everything was all right. He saw the owner approach Saul and then the two of them went into the kitchen. *I wonder what that's all about?*

Kesl shrugged and made another phone call to Toronto.

"Yes, Mr. Kesl?" his assistant Delores Cavanaugh answered before the first ring ended.

"Yes, Delores ... we need five rooms and the largest suite you can get at the Sky Island Casino in the Upper Peninsula of Michigan. Never been to a casino strange as it may seem to you for someone who loves to gamble." He laughed absurdly loudly.

New environments, like for many autistic people, made Kesl uncomfortable and his way of dealing with it was to joke. "Book it under, let me think for a moment, this'll be cool, under the name of James Butler Hickok. Use the prescreened app that allows us to go directly to our rooms. Then have our people, of course you know who, check out Larry Echohawk. Presumably he's some sort of liaison for the Coast Guard in Menominee, Wisconsin. Probably a ruse but let's see what they can come up with."

* * *

Saul watched Kesl through the window and wondered what wonder boy was talking about. This wasn't the first time he felt powerless because his boss kept things from him. He didn't like feeling this way. He was about to get up and confront Kesl, when the restaurant owner tapped him on the shoulder.

"Your name is McBride? Are you Scots?"

"I am. Why do you want to know?" Saul asked, his eyes automatically checking the room for traps and to see if he was being set up somehow. Nothing seemed amiss.

"I have something in the kitchen that will be of interest to you as a Scotsman. If you would follow me, please."

Saul excused himself after telling Matthew to keep an eye on wonder boy. He followed the owner into the kitchen. The place was empty. Saul's hand went to the nine millimeter Glock he kept in a holster in the back of his jeans. They threaded among work tables to the back of the room near the freezer. There, an older man with jowls and iron gray hair waited. His hands were empty by his side.

"Thank you, Antonio," he said in English with a soft Russian accent.

Saul kept a reasonable distance between them. He waited until the owner left the kitchen to speak. "What is it you want?"

"Like you, I am concerned about a mutual acquaintance in the parking lot."

"Who are you?"

"My name is Dmitryi Mameyev."

* * *

Kesl walked back into the restaurant and saw Saul exiting the kitchen. "What now? You think the food is poisoned?"

"I got lost looking for the bathroom." He paused. "Are you ready to leave for Toronto?"

"There's been a change of plans. We're driving back to the Casino we passed on our way here. Chris will meet us there ... sort of funny ... Our new home for now is a gamble." He giggled. Recalling the calm demeanor of Echohawk when he described

Chris's chase after the Bigfoot and Chris's warning about how there must be other outsiders involved, Kesl had decided the best strategy was to play his cards close to the vest.

Saul scowled. "You should be taking this more seriously. It's too much risk, especially now that we know there are people out there who will stop at nothing to kill those who know about the killing of the Sasquatch."

"That's the spirit, Saul, talking about risk. Okay, I know you're only looking out for my best interests but I've decided. Besides, with my eidetic memory, I'm going to clean up at the Blackjack tables, make some real money for a change, just kidding."

Kesl signaled the owner, who brought the check and a small box of cannoli. "For the road. My wife makes them." He kissed his fingertips. "*Bellissimo*."

On the way out to the van, Saul said in a tight voice, "Stephen, we should return to Green Bay and board the jet back to Toronto. It's the right move to make. If you want eyes in the field here, let me and my team take care of it."

"No worries, Saul. It'll all work out. We're going to the casino, but we're going to make a little stop on the way." He merged his phone with Saul's. "We're going to these coordinates first. There's a hunting cabin there I think we should look at. I believe one of the bad guys who are hunting the Sasquatch lives there."

"I'm not happy about this," Saul said with a frown.

"Funny, I wasn't under the impression I pay you to be happy, Saul. Now let's get moving."

Chapter Seventeen

Marinette, Michigan

The van turned onto a one lane, rutted road and headed into the forest. A mile in they found the ramshackle log cabin. As soon as the van stopped, Saul's men deployed to reconnoiter the area before going inside.

"Who owns this place?" Saul asked.

"I told you, Chris Marlowe says it belongs to one of the bad guys."

"And?"

"And that's all he said, other than he is a contractor for the Coast Guard. We should look around for clues." He brightened. "We're looking for clues, I love looking for clues, what will we find, that's the big question."

Saul's team reported the area clean and the cabin open. "Sir, you're not going to believe this place," said Matthew, the van driver. "It's a freaking gun museum. The guy who lives here has a 19th century long barrel Sharps .50-90, used for buffalo hunting, and a pair of 1848 Walker Colts."

"Replicas?"

"No sir."

Saul whistled.

"Is that significant?" asked Kesl.

"Whoever lives here doesn't work just for the Coast Guard. They're seriously wealthy."

The three room cabin was tossed quickly. Aside from the firearms, they found a Native American ceremonial peace pipe.

When they finished, they gathered beside the stone fireplace.

Jana shook her head. "This was a waste of time, Mr. Kesl. I think we should get going."

"What's the hurry?"

"The sooner I can get tracking those guys who murdered

Marge, the better," said Jana.

"I have to agree with Ms. Erickson. This place has nothing."

"We'll leave as soon as I've found what I'm looking for."

"And what's that?" asked Saul.

Kesl smiled. "I'll know when I see it. Everyone spread out. Look more closely. So far, we've only looked at the surface stuff. There's something here that will help us. I know it. I can feel it."

"It would help if we had some idea of what we're looking for," said Saul, his face taut at the idea of spending any more time here.

Kesl shrugged. "Maybe some technology ... any technology ... see if we can find some among the stodgy museum."

"In this place, sir?" said Matthew. "The guy doesn't have running water or electricity. Shit! He has a wood burning stove."

"Matthew has a point, Stephen," said Saul.

Kesl smiled. "You seem nervous ... why are you nervous?"

"I don't like my back to a lake and my only escape route is a one lane road. Call me old fashioned but this place is pristine for an ambush."

Kesl thought about his friend Chris. No way would he set him up for an ambush. "Your concerns are noted, Saul. Fifteen more minutes."

"Five."

"Ten."

Saul gritted his teeth. "All right, ten. But then I'm dragging you out of here."

"Fair enough."

Saul hand signaled Matthew and Timothy to post at the front and the rear of the cabin. "If a deer looks at you sideways, you report to me immediately."

"Yes, sir." They saluted and left.

Saul clicked his watch. "Ten minutes from my mark. Let's move."

Kesl stood in the center of the room while the others fanned out through the cabin. He had a vague idea of what he would find. As soon as Chris mentioned Echohawk, Kesl's eidetic memory flashed on an article from Silicon Valley, news of a new start up run by a Native American, using carbon nanotubes three atoms thick to make graphic circuit chips for computers. KW Intel had bought the technology two months later. *Graphic circuits three atoms thick could be used to make a PA that appeared ordinary. How cool is that, a personal assistant that small? Ordinary as possible has always been the key in this tech domain.* Kesl kicked himself for not investing in the company himself.

Something glinted in a shallow dish beside the fireplace. He went over and saw that it was filled with loose change. He pushed the money around and one of the quarters looked slightly different than the others. He picked it up. The edge was smooth instead of ribbed. The writing as well as the image of George Washington was painted on instead of being embossed. He hefted it and the weight was less than a dime. He felt a slight warmth and heard a faint hum.

It's on, he thought. He licked his lips. He wanted very much to see how it worked, but without the access code it was impossible. He marveled at its beauty.

"Two minutes," Saul called out from the bedroom.

Kesl jerked in surprise. He had been so fascinated by the miniaturization he had forgotten he wasn't alone.

Jana came over and stood beside him. She was three inches taller and more muscular. Her presence was unnerving. Kesl recalled how she handled the bad guys back in Marquette and he had no doubt she could have led Saul's mercenaries against the men hunting the Sasquatch. That's no quarter," she said, staring at the device in his hand before he could think of closing his fist.

Kesl shook his head. Saul and the other two men came into the room. "Stephen found the evidence he was looking for," she said.

They crowded around. "What is it?" Saul asked.

For a moment the feeling was like cub scouts crowded around a campfire listening to ghost stories. Kesl sighed. *Cat's tail is out of the bag. Might as well let it all out.*

"It's KW Intel's personal assistant prototype. I saw it at the exclusive machine learning conclave in Finland just a few months ago.

"Kellog, in his talk, was telling the group how we all need to be afraid of deep learning machines in the coming computer singularity. His exact words were, 'machine learning devices will come to look upon us as insects that are in their way and need to be eradicated'." Kesl hefted the ersatz coin. "No way should this be here, no way at all ... unless."

Jana asked, "Unless what?"

"Isn't it obvious? Whoever lives here works for the Ang brothers. Isn't it clear to everyone else?"

Jana snorted. "The Ang brothers are the best-known billionaire conspiracy theorists. Social media is full of their theories about the deep state in league with aliens."

One of Saul's men looked at her in surprise. "What do you mean?"

Kesl answered, "The Ang brothers are a couple of apocalyptic doomsday sayers, but they use the best machine learning algorithms – in this device – and in all their smart agricultural equipment, and many of the most important big data management applications. When it comes to making money off of artificial intelligence, they're the best. I would have to say, even better than me. Don't tell anybody I said that." He tapped the coin. "How strange, how interesting. I was really upset when Winston railed against my AGI ... my dear Hangman always moving forward, always learning unsupervised. That's what they're afraid of. Not me ... it's all for the good, it's for the betterment of humanity, that's what I told him. Grand speech don't you think?"

Jana cautiously asked, "Does this mean the Ang brothers are involved in the killing of the Bigfoot?"

Kesl was confused by the thought the Ang brothers had something to do with what was going on with the Bigfoot. He counted backwards from twenty to zero in English and Portuguese before he finally felt his chest relax.

"Are you all right?" Jana asked.

He nodded. "I'm just surprised that the Ang brothers would do something this outrageous. I thought they were all just hot air. But crazy as it may seem, there is a high probability they are involved. Most strange."

Saul's timer beeped. Ignoring Kesl, he said, "Ten minutes folks. We're leaving."

Kesl went to shove the miniature PA into his pocket and his security chief stopped him. "Leave it. Echohawk or whoever is using this place doesn't know we're onto him. We can use your security firm to monitor his every movement. That gives us an edge."

"That's silly, Saul." But Kesl replaced the PA in the bowl.

"Onto the damn casino, let's get out of here," Saul shouted to his men.

Chapter Eighteen

Hiawatha National Forest

UP, Michigan

The first thing Echohawk was aware of was the sharp ache inside his skull, as though someone had punched him in the brain. Then came the voice.

"Don't try to talk or open your eyes just yet," someone said. By the tone it was a woman. She sounded far away, yet also strangely near, as though she was whispering into his ear. "Your senses have been scrambled. You're suffering from synesthesia. Listen to the sound of my voice and it will pass in a few minutes."

Echohawk knew what she said was true. The feel of the earth against his hands and face was the smell of lemon rinds and asparagus. The taste of the air shot a thousand colors into his brain, colors humans would never be able to see with the primitive eyes they had. And the voice was the feel of soft chamois against his skin, soothing and peaceful.

He did as he was told and listened, the words a brush of butterfly wings against his ears.

"Your family would not like you hunting us." The woman sounded like his aunt but she spoke of 'us' as though she were part of something other than the Potawatomi tribe. "They have been our protectors for two thousand years. You should be with them against the others who hunt us, hunt us because they are afraid. You are not afraid, but confused all these years about us. Confused by a hurt that did not happen. You are a child of the forest, of the sky and the blue water. You are cousin to the eagle, brother of the deer and son of the black bear. You are a true human. You must remember who you really are and then you will once more be on the right path."

Echohawk felt the meaning of the words, not just as a lilting sound but as a guide, drawing him out of the tangled mess of his ruined senses. Each word was a step on the road to the place where his senses operated normally again. Who was this woman who talked to him as though she were a member of the tribe and yet not a member. He had to find out. He opened his eyes to slits. Earth and sky whirled around him, solidified and became a still image. He could see.

The world shifted from confused odors and colors to the beauty of the forest. He recognized the spruce and maples. He smelled the soft scent of pine and the rich aroma of the earth. The scratch of fallen leaves against his face and hands was a welcome touch. Then he saw the Bigfoot. It squatted ten feet away and stared at him with preternatural awareness in its liquid brown eyes. The rest of its bear-like face was cocked to one side as if studying him."

"You're not surprised," she said.

Echohawk reached for his pistol but the Bigfoot held it in a four-fingered hand, twirling it as if it were a strange toy. Echohawk eased himself into a sitting position. His senses had unscrambled but his muscles still felt weak.

The Bigfoot said, "You would have killed your companion with this. And you would try to kill me. Why?"

"You're dangerous," he answered. "Yes, and I'm aware of the mind games you can play with humans."

"And yet, you are the one hunting my kind." The Bigfoot seemed to smile. "I was told one of your great scientist said, 'Nothing in life is to be feared, it is only to be understood.'"

"That's been my motto since I was a teenager," Ecohawk said in surprise.

"Now it's time for you to help us find out what our true purpose is on this planet."

"I know what you are. A Windigo – an evil, man-eating spirit. You are here to crush humanity. I don't believe you are our brothers of the forest as our legends say. And you're not human."

"You've known this since you were little. I once healed you when you were dying from Lyme disease."

"I don't believe you, you killed my grandfather," Echohawk spat.

The Bigfoot looked genuinely puzzled. "Is this the source of your hatred toward us?"

The question surprised Echohawk because the words seemed to tear at an old wound scabbed over by anger and he knew the answer even as the wound opened up completely inside of him and his feelings poured out. "Yes," he said in a strangled voice. "It was the beginning of my hatred of your kind"

"See, you knew we existed."

"Of course! Everybody in our family knew."

"We did not hurt your grandfather. A member of our clan found him dying in these woods. His heart had given out and there was nothing she could do for him. She stayed with him so he would not die alone, then she buried him and put stones upon his grave so the carrion eaters could not get at him. He was in death like the warrior he was in life. I can show you the spot. His final resting place is near the portal you and the other human found today."

The Bigfoot stood. "Come. I will take you there."

Ecohawk felt his resistance melting "I don't know that I can walk," he said.

"It is not far, the way we travel." The bear-faced creature reached out a four-fingered hand and helped him to stand. Then gently lifted him over her shoulder. "This way," she said and dashed through a screen of trees into the forest.

Chapter Nineteen

Seattle, Washington

Winston applauded. "That didn't take long, complete coverage of the UP."

Kellog Ang watched the giant screen in disbelief at the images the newly deployed satellites relayed. He turned to his brother, Winston, and said, "Are you seeing what I'm seeing?"

Winston nodded. "The Bigfoot is carrying Echohawk."

"Where's it taking him?"

Winston overlaid a map of the Hiawatha National Forest on the image provided by the tiny surveillance satellites. "If it keeps its present course, it will go by the quarry where Meriwether's team has been disposing of the Sasquatch."

"Perfect." Kellog tapped the PA affixed behind his ear. "Connect me to Meriwether." The contact was instantaneous thanks to the PA. All of the Russian's team leaders across the globe carried the device.

"I see you got another one, Lewis. Good work. We've got a bogie in your area – look on your screen. Sending you the satellite data now. He has our boy genius, Larry Echohawk. This is a rescue as well as another kill mission. Safely pry him free of the Sasquatch. Do you copy?"

Kellog pressed a button on the console in front of him. Music from the British rock band Queen soared through the room. He smiled at his little brother and sang the words, "Another one bites the dust."

They bumped fists.

* * *

Meriwether called his team together. Two of the four men were new. All were recruited by the Russian and came from Croatia.

All had been trained by him and the newcomers fit into the crew seamlessly.

"We have a Bigfoot nearby. There is an added caution. It's carrying a person important to the mission. Command wants him alive and the Bigfoot dead. Its present heading will take it by the quarry. We'll try to cut it off before it reaches the forest beyond. If not, we'll deploy in a standard 'chase and secure' V formation."

The helicopter's rotors started turning.

"We leave in two minutes."

The men nodded. Two minutes was not difficult. These days the team always kept their gear within a half-dozen steps.

* * *

The ride slung across the Bigfoot's shoulder was surprisingly smooth. Echohawk felt no nausea and his senses were normal again, just as the creature had promised. The forest flew past and the Indian surmised their speed had to be more than sixty miles an hour. The Bigfoot was agile, dodging trees, brushing big branches aside with ease, never once endangering its passenger.

The creature slowed and stopped. It sniffed the air and turned around twice, then set Echohawk down. He recognized the area. It was close to the quarry where he and Chris had first seen the Bigfoot.

"Why are you stopping?"

"Hunters are coming. We haven't much time," it said.

"How much?" said Echohawk.

The creature scratched its head. "As long as it takes the sun to move five degrees."

Echohawk did the calculation in his head, basing it on the solar day, or when the earth goes around the sun 360 degrees. In this case 15 degrees equaled 1/24 of a circle or one hour. "So, twenty minutes. Can you out run them?"

The Bigfoot shook its bear like head. "The humans' machines are faster than I am. Come. We must hurry if you are to see your grandfather's grave." The creature gathered Echohawk into its long arms and swung him onto its shoulder. It started running again.

They passed the quarry. That's when Echohawk heard the helicopter. The sound was coming from the southeast. He judged by the roar it would land in ten minutes. The beast increased its speed. It angled through the trees toward the stick structure but did not stop. A quarter mile beyond the wooden stakes, it stopped near a mound of stones and set Echohawk on the ground.

"Here are the remains of your grandfather, Echohawk."

"We are not brothers," Echohawk insisted. You're a Windigo."

The creature smiled. "You do not really believe I am a man eating demon from your Potawatomie legends. You're trying to stop us for what you believe will bring about the end of humanity." The Bigfoot moved away.

"Where are you going?"

"To draw them from here so you will not be injured when they kill me."

Echohawk jerked in surprise at the creature's concern for him. "How do you know?" he asked.

"We are no longer the children your people found and protected many years ago. We've been evolving at an accelerating pace."

Once the Bigfoot ran out of sight, Echohawk knelt beside the rock cairn. From his pocket he removed a tobacco pouch. Carefully dividing the contents into four equal piles, he set them around the grave at the cardinal points of the compass. Afterwards he sat facing east and sang the Potawatomie Sacred Fire Song. During the singing he heard rifle shots. He recognized the US Navy Mk-12 5.56 semi-auto sniper rifle by the sound. Meriwether's team had gotten the Bigfoot.

As Echohawk waited patiently for the men to find him, he thought about his role in the plan to bringing about the destruction of the Bigfoot and he thought about his aunt Ayasha, whom he had betrayed.

He heard a twig snap in the underbrush. *Meriwether's team is getting sloppy*, he thought. A mercenary walked out from the trees two minutes later. He waved at Echohawk and spoke into the mic at the edge of his mouth. "Found him, sir. He appears unharmed." He looked at Echohawk and said, "Meriwether wants you to come with me. He wishes to debrief you. Afterwards, we're to escort you out of here."

Sky Island Casino, UP, Michigan

The Sky Island Casino was located on US Highway 41, on a small tract of land owned by the Potawatomi Indian Tribe, in Michigan's Upper Peninsula. Ironically, the casino's beginnings were humble. It all began in 1837 with Peter and Hannah Marksman, Methodist missionaries who founded the small Hannahville Indian Mission to help displaced Indians settle in Hannahville after President Andrew Jackson's Indian Removal Act of 1830 relocated Native Americans east of the Mississippi River to lands west of the river. One hundred fifty years later, descendants of the Potawatomi Nation opened a casino on their 3400 acre reservation, at first taking from white gamblers what Andrew Jackson had taken from them – their livelihoods. Now incorporating smart technology into every aspect of gaming, the casino had become the economic jewel of the Upper Peninsula.

Inside the van everyone was silent until Jana spoke up." I've had many interactions with the tribe. The ones that own and operate the casino. They're Potawatomi. It means 'Keepers of the Fire'."

Kesl jerked in surprise. "Say more."

"Their origins and legends are quite interesting. I've given a number of talks to campers in the national Forest. The

Potawatomi Indians are one of three tribes that make up the Three Fires Society – the Ojibway, the Ottawa and the Potawatomi tribes. The Ojibway are the keepers of the original teachings and are responsible for passing these teachings down through the generations. The Ottawa provide security for all who attend tribal gatherings. They make sure everyone has enough to eat and the meeting place is secure from invasion and disruption. The Potawatomi Indians are responsible for keeping the "Sacred Fire" alive, as it is the symbol of light and the future."

"The light and the future … the light and the future." Kesl rocked back and forth on his seat repeating the phrase over and over until he suddenly stopped, clenched his fists and let them go with a loud explosion of air. He grinned and his head nodded in acceptance of some inner dictate. Kesl looked outside at the passing forest, muttering over and over, "Amazing. Amazing."

* * *

Five miles from the casino, Kesl's smart phone beeped. He looked down and saw a text from Chris. *In the casino parking lot. Need to talk with you. Something strange is going on.*

Kesl typed back. *A code's been downloaded into your phone for a room in the East wing. Wait to be contacted.*

Chris' reply came back instantly. *Need to talk with you ASAP. I'm sensing something really important.*

It'll have to wait. Personal reasons, replied Kesl.

Chapter Twenty

Sky Island Casino

UP, Michigan

The shadow of a sleek helicopter crossed over Chris as he stepped out of his truck in the casino parking lot. He watched it land on the heliport, an elevated mound west of the giant sign promoting the loosest slots in the country. The drive from the forest had given him time to reflect on what had just happened. In less than 24 hours he had spoken with not one but two Bigfoot. All these years of wondering and searching for these elusive creatures suddenly came to an end in a way that shook him intellectually to the bone. He wondered what his ex-wife would say? He snorted. *What will all the Bigfoot deniers say when they learn the truth.*

He sighed and leaned against the fender, looking into the afternoon sky, assessing everything that had happened in the last twenty-four hours. Chief was out there somewhere with another Bigfoot. *Is he still alive? What are you going to do when you see him again?* He patted the Glock 19 stuck in the waistband of his blue jeans. *No sense trying to answer that question until the time comes.* He scrubbed his face with both hands. The two-day growth of beard felt unnatural to him. He still had some time before Kesl arrived. He might as well shower and shave. Then he could figure out what to do next. All he knew for certain was he was on some sort of mission to help the Bigfoot, to help them accomplish something he couldn't even imagine. Most of all he was eager to tell Kesl what happened, as if that would bring clarity to his part in what was happening.

Like all Bigfoot researchers Chris's truck was well supplied with backup field equipment and at the moment, most importantly, a well needed change of clothes that he stuffed into his backpack. He then checked his tool compartment and opened the secret recess for his pistol. It gave him some comfort with the Bigfoot killers out there to know that he had a weapon to defend himself. Still, he knew he couldn't bring it into the casino, so he stashed it there until he'd need it.

If his mind was filled with unanswered questions, his senses were at a heightened level. He was able to telescope in on the helicopter wheels touching down on the heliport landing platform. Physically he felt better than any time in recent memory.

He shouldered his pack and was headed for the doors to the hotel check in when he felt the strange sense of being watched that he first experienced the night before at the quarry. It had remained with him ever since the Bigfoot encounter, but at such a low level at times he questioned if it was really there. He stared into the surrounding forest as he continued walking toward the casino entrance. It was definitely getting stronger and as soon as he crossed the threshold, he felt it as strongly as he had in the forest.

What's going on in here?

Chapter Twenty-One

Sky Island Casino

UP, Michigan

The room was dimly lit by a red light, illuminating a single chair in the center. Beside it stood a tall, rather slim Bigfoot. A phosphorus glow illuminated the eyes of her very Native American humanlike face. The rest of her was covered with an emerald-hued moss that in the dim light could have been mistaken for a Leprechaun's suit. Aside from skin tone and height, she was remarkably human looking. Each hand bore five fingers. The five toes did not have claws. She stood motionless, as if waiting quietly was the only thing she had to do in the world.

The Bigfoot cocked her head and turned to the only door leading into the room. A sliver of light outlined the jamb and a body squeezed through the narrow opening, shutting the door soundlessly after it. The newcomer's face was hidden in the room's shadows. It looked right and left and then to the center, where the Bigfoot waited.

The creature was unafraid and watched with fascination as the newcomer reached inside a vest it wore and pulled out a small handgun. "Is the weapon necessary?" she asked.

"You, of anyone I know, should know better than to ask that question with the killings going on."

The newcomer strode out of the shadows into the center of the room. She was a tall American Indian woman in her sixties, with silver-gray hair that gleamed a bloody hue under the red light. Age had not wrinkled her skin and her sparkling eyes were a curious blue, a singular family trait handed down from mother to daughter within the Potawatomie Tribe for more than fifty generations. The blue eyes marked the matrilineal power that her family had wielded since the arrival of the Bigfoot in the UP, ten thousand years ago. To the members of her clan and tribe she was known simply as Auntie. To the Bigfoot in front of her she was Ayasha, the Keeper of the Sacred Fire.

The red light gleamed off the nickel blue barrel of the Colt .38 caliber revolver. "We can't be too careful, not now, when we are so close to the end."

The creature shrugged in a very human way that was nonetheless a gesture she had learned and was not natural. "I understand your concern, Ayasha, but death is not the same for us as it is for you."

Ayasha shoved the gun away and sighed. "You're right."

"It's about to happen, right?"

Before she could reply, the multi-screen display of the casino flashed on. Her eyes shifted quickly from image to image, and seeing nothing out of the ordinary, she let out another sigh of relief. In strong, hushed tones she said, "The Yeti from Russia has arrived, tonight's the night."

"Did it make it to the portal?"

"Yes. Three from the other clans were killed as you probably know," she said sadly.

The creature's liquid brown eyes were not saddened by the news and she said without emotion, "But every important Bigfoot advancement is now represented. Perfect."

Auntie scanned the screens then gently touched the giant Bigfoot. "I'm not ready for you to go. We've known each other all my life, you healed me as a young girl when I almost died from pneumonia. You sent the gentle one to take care of my father. And now you are going to walk out that door to—" Auntie's voice broke off with a little sob. She recovered quickly and wiped her eyes on her shirtsleeve. "Are you absolutely sure this is going to work? Are you sure you have to do it?"

The creature nodded.

"Why?"

She answered, her voice still uninflected as if discussing something as mundane as the weather. "Our ordinary reproductive metamorphic fields allow for only one of us to be downloaded to give birth to the next one. The mother portal is necessary for what we're going to do tonight. There's no certainty what we will be attempting will work. But the drive to do it is strong."

"I understand that," Auntie answered with some heat. "I'm sorry, it's just, why does it have to be you?"

"I need to be the last one into the field, one each from the five clans and then me. I'm to be the new one's teacher. I have the most advanced bio structure and knowledge."

Auntie hugged the Bigfoot and she gently touched her shoulder. "My men will get you there."

"I know. I am thankful for all you have done these past six decades."

"What should we do now?"

"Sit together one last time," she said, enfolding Ayasha in her long arms.

Chapter Twenty-Two

Sky Island Casino

UP, Michigan

By the time the van reached the Sky Island Casino, clouds were moving in. The casino's parking lot was filled with cars and a parade of buses, bringing desperate gamblers to reverse their fortunes in the bad economic times of what had become known as the forgotten land.

Kesl wondered what the newest technologies and universal basic income could do to reverse their fortunes.

Saul motioned one of the men to stay behind with the van and guard the weapons. He saluted and sat in the back of the van where he had a good view of the parking lot and no one could see him.

The others looked uncomfortable. Matthew looked at the Scotsman and frowned. "Don't know that I feel safe without my sidearm, sir."

Saul said matter-of-factly, "Casino policy. If they catch you with a weapon, they'll kick all of us out of here."

The VIP concierge was a trim, blond-haired woman, whose nameplate read Lambert. After scanning his phone she said, "Your rooms are ready, Mr. Hickok. The center wing penthouse for you and four on the floor directly beneath. The elevators over there will take you up. Your right index fingerprint will act as your key."

If the concierge thought anything peculiar, she hid her feelings well. She motioned to a bellhop to carry the bags up to the rooms.

Saul stepped forward. "We'll carry our own bags."

"Of course. Will there be anything else, Mr. Hickok?"

Kesl said, "I want to see the casino."

"You're standing in it, sir."

He shook his head and tapped his fingers on the desk in rapid succession, rapping out a Fibonacci sequence. "No, the inside ... the pit, I believe you call it. I have to see one."

"Of course. Straight ahead. Please enjoy your stay at the Sky Island Casino. If you need anything do not hesitate to ask."

Kesl pivoted slowly and walked toward the center of the gaming activity.

Saul put a hand on his sleeve, restraining him. "That isn't wise, sir. Your condition."

Kesl shook him off. "I can handle it." *I have to handle it. This is too important.* He strode purposefully to the nearest crap table and stopped as if he'd run into a wall. *I can do this ... I can do this ... I can do this.* He kept repeating the phrase like a mantra. Yet it wasn't enough. He tried counting backward from twenty to zero in Czech but couldn't get past sixteen before the sounds and sights of the room flooded his consciousness.

The casino covered an area the size of an airport terminal. LED screens everywhere promoted jackpots, loose slots, sports bets. It was awash with bright, blinking lights that stuttered in uneven progressions. A bedlam of bells, whistles, a loud band playing 80s punk music and voices assaulted his ears. Worst of all the people were filled with emotions he could not grasp. He stood frozen at the table looking for some pattern to interpret everything he heard and saw. Nothing made sense and he felt himself sinking into catatonia. He knew Saul's men surrounded him. He could feel Jana standing near him, just out of reach. He was aware of Saul's light touch on his arm. Kesl's mind flew through all the information that scattered like buckshot through his brain. *You have no idea what to do next ... there's no pattern.* There was nothing that told him what to do, where to go, who to speak to. He took one last, wild look around him and let himself sink into the welcome relief of a dissociative fugue.

* * *

Saul had witnessed Kesl's escape from what his autistic mind registered as madness into the frozen state of catalepsy twice before. Instantly he signaled the team to escort the rigid form of their boss to the elevator.

Jana watched the team gather around Kesl and move like a precision instrument, herding him for the elevators, away from the bedlam of the casino floor. She grabbed Saul's arm and said, "What's wrong with him?"

The Scotsman looked at her and said in a stern voice, "Mr. Kesl is autistic. Best thing to do for him right now is to get him out of here into some quiet spot."

"What's going to happen to him?"

"We leave him alone and sometime in the next 24 hours his mind will re-order itself. When he comes out of it he'll be shaken and hyper alert but he'll be himself again."

"You should've told me, I might've been able to help," she snapped at Saul.

"I doubt it."

Annoyed by Saul's response, Jana watched them hustle Kesl into the top floor suite of the center wing. Dropping one flight to the 14th floor, she let herself into her room and lay down on the bed. Finally, away from everybody, she said to herself, "Time to process." A knock on the door brought her upright before she could start.

She heard Saul say, "It's just me. May I come in?"

She opened the door and motioned him inside and watched him as his eyes registered the room. When he was satisfied everything appeared normal, he turned to her and asked, "What do you think of our fearless leader?"

It must've been something in the way the Scotsman talked because Jana found herself thinking more like a soldier and less and less like someone exploring the greatest biological discovery of all time. "Right now, all I want is a bath and a few hours of sleep. Let's talk about this later this evening."

Saul said, "Don't misunderstand me, Miss. Kesl is like a son to me. But this whole thing with the Bigfoot mystery has him acting crazy and I admit I don't know what's going on. I'd rather we were back in Toronto, where I can have a bigger team to guard him. Especially with powerful men behind that kill team in the forest, hunting Sasquatch. Targeting you and probably him now."

Jana eyed the Scotsman. "Where does that leave me?"

Saul returned her gaze without a blink. "I'll be blunt. I don't want you leaving this room, freelancing, until I get a better grip on what's happening. I'm posting one of my men outside your door to make certain you don't. The sooner we're gone from this place the better." He left without saying good night.

Jana walked out onto the balcony. Her room was fourteen floors above the ground. "Where do I go from here?" she asked herself.

Chapter Twenty-Three

Sky Island Casino

UP, Michigan

On a level indescribable to the others, Kesl's mind screamed for silence and solitude. The hushed tranquility of the elevator had been a welcome relief to his overloaded senses. Yet through the entire process, he had also been strangely aware of everything going on around him. Saul's ministrations as the team put him to bed in his suite. Window curtains drawn to drown out the overly bright parking lot lights and the flashing neon of the Casino's logo. He heard the door close softly behind the Scotsman and the whispered orders, 'He's not to be disturbed'. And then the blessed silence.

He went through the steps the Russian had taught him to reorder his mind whenever catatonia threatened. Counting backward from 100 to zero. If he could do it without a mistake then his mind was working.

It took Kesl three tries before he reached the magic number. Then he did it a second time just to be sure. Next, he recalled the names of all the European capitals in alphabetical order. He knew he was getting better quickly when he recalled Berlin came before Berne. Then he named the five noble gases – Helium, Xenon, Argon Neon and Krypton.

He sat up slowly. *As fugue states go, this was not the worst*, he thought ruefully to himself.

His muscles felt drained, which was not unusual. His mind, on the other hand, was hyper alert. *A trade off ... that's what the Russian called it.*

"Nature has given you a terrible yet wonderful gift," the Russian said on the first occasion he'd witnessed one of Kesl's fugue states. "A few minutes of abject terror followed by the ability to focus like a laser on any problem." They had been at a game arcade in London. Kesl was only fifteen. The Russian had waited patiently with him for more than six hours for the fugue to run its course.

Kesl got unsteadily to his feet. He walked to the minibar and poured himself a mineral water. His senses and brain were hyper alert, trying to put everything together. *The Sasquatch Chris had contact with are up here for a gathering. That must be it. But why?* Kesl went through his thinking again and finding no flaw in it, now only needed something to corroborate his theory. *Why are they here now and what are they really? Maybe that can be answered by what Olav has found in his lab.*

I have to get a hold of Olav and Jana. Olav was simple. He could link to him with his phone. But when he contacted Jana in her room, she informed him that Saul said she couldn't leave and had posted a guard to ensure she stayed put. He replied, "Give me a moment, I'll fix that."

Within minutes Kesl was face-to-face with the guard outside of Jana's door. He recognized him as Matthew. The man held up a hand to stop Kesl from entering. "No one is to go in or out, not even you. Saul's orders."

Kesl's hyper senses noticed the man's ramrod straight posture as an unbending adherence to orders. Kesl had never seen this side of Saul's men before and he wondered if the fanatical devotion they showed to their boss put him in danger. The observation gave him a way to deal with this storm trooper.

Smiling, Kesl moved closer. "We'll see about that." With his thumb fixed on his phone's screen he simply and quietly uttered the word 'Help'.

Matthew looked at him puzzled. "What can I help you with, sir?"

"Oh not you," Kesl said. The elevator doors opened in the middle of the hall and two armed, Native American security guards appeared almost out of nowhere. They were husky, tall, and walked with the ease of men used to violence. They looked, to Kesl's untrained eye, as if they had been cut from the same cloth as Saul's task force. Matthew must have noticed the similarity, too, for he stiffened as the men approached.

"You requested help, sir," the taller of the two Indians asked Kesl.

At that moment Jana opened the door and glared at Saul's guard.

"Yes, thank you. This man is harassing Miss. Erickson, my guest." Kesl pointed to Matthew.

"If I may, sir?" the tall Native American said, extending his hand for Kesl's phone. He glanced at the special VIP app, given to all high rollers and the most important guests, and then at his own phone. The fingerprint matched the one taken by the hotel during check in. "Thank you, sir." He motioned to Saul's man. "Please come with us, sir. We need you to stop bothering Mr. Kesl's guest."

Matthew hesitated a second and the two Native American guards came up on the balls of their feet. "Sir," said the shorter security guard, his finger hovering near a red light on his watch, "ten more of us can be here in fifteen seconds."

Matthew, understanding he was disadvantaged, put up his hands and voluntarily walked away with the two security men.

"You're obviously feeling better," Jana said. "Would you like to come in? I showered, but unfortunately I'm wearing the same old smelly fish and wildlife clothes. I could use some new ones if I'm going to go anywhere." She bit her tongue to stop talking. She thought he must think she was jabbering. "Sorry."

Kesl cocked his head at her. "Why?"

"You're Stephen Kesl," she said as if that explained it. In fact, she had always been conflicted by powerful wealthy men and found herself talking inanely when in their presence. Especially men like Kesl. He was a star in the newly emerging sphere of World Building and had funded hundreds of startup tech companies to forge a powerful global network of interconnected solutions to address the world's systemic problems arising from global warming – food insecurity, water shortages, the epidemic chronic diseases, adequate housing, income inequality and meaningful work.

"I have something for you," Kesl said, as if dismissing her observation. He handed her a brand new phone." It's one of mine but I had one of my people clone and download your information, nice and clean, and, most importantly, secure. With that you can go down and buy yourself a new outfit. On me, of course. Seems like you can get whatever you need at the casino. Quite the place."

Jana wondered how he would know this since he'd gone into a dissociative fugue the moment he entered the casino floor. Then she noticed that the whole time he'd been talking with her, his eyes had never left his smart phone and even now he was scrolling at a ridiculously fast pace through a series of screens. He moved so fast that she only caught a few of them dealing with the boutiques connected to the hotel lobby.

"Do you actually see what you're looking at?" she asked.

Kesl nodded. "I've always had the ability to assimilate information quickly when it's presented in an orderly fashion. It's when there's no pattern that I can't handle the flow in my brain and it has to shut down so it can reset." He smiled self-deprecatingly. "It's the way my brain works and it has enabled me to use patterns I see in the world to invest my money in ways that help the world."

"They also make you rich."

He nodded unapologetically. "At least I'm not using my fortune to elect people to make me richer. I'm helping disadvantaged people around the world move out of poverty."

She reddened. "I apologize. So who were those guys you brought with you?"

"Oh, I didn't bring them with me. They appeared when I, as

a registered highest level guest in the casino, pressed the help app on my phone." He showed her the app. "They're specially trained security guards that every Native American casino employs these days. The National Native American Gaming Confederation has a training facility outside of DC. I'm told it's the best in the world. They're totally loyal to each casino."

She shook her head wondering how anyone could remember that kind of information, let alone store it for use when needed.

"Your brain works in fascinating ways."

"Some ways are fascinating. Others are debilitating."

"The fugue state?"

"Sorry if it was off-putting."

"Scary actually."

"You should see it from my side," Kesl said with a childlike admission of terror. He shook himself. "Enough of that. We have more important things to do.

"Let me get Olav on the line first, then I'll only have to tell my story once.

Getting a hold of Olav proved easy. He hadn't left the lab since he started analyzing the Bigfoot remains. Kesl quickly filled both of them in on his suppositions.

"I need your help proving what I think is true."

"I might be able to help," said Olav. "I've run every test imaginable, even some that aren't imaginable, on the Bigfoot material."

"What did you find?" Jana asked.

"Well it's not a plant, though sorta plant-like. No typical cell structure ... no DNA, but highly organized."

"How?"

"A clear hierarchical organization, layer upon layer. Next I had Hangman survey all the literature on what we came up with as a result of our biochemical analysis. Everything's there to build a highly complex biosynthetic organism from scratch and keep it working, basically on EM radiation from the sun. It's digital like but not digital. Never seen anything like it"

"A new kind of life form, Olav? Man-made or natural?" broke in Kesl excitedly.

"Not enough of a sample to tell. Hangman's been searching the literature for who might be capable of building such a ... hard to believe I'm actually saying this ... a living Bigfoot."

Kesl interjected loudly, "Don't keep us in suspense, Olav."

"The highest probability is the Russians."

"What about Florida?"

"Huh? Are you kidding, sir?"

"A joint lab project between Florida State University's Colleges of Arts and Sciences, Human Sciences and Chemical & Biomedical Engineering has been experimenting using computer controlled patterns of EM and magnetic pulsing to guide plant growth, in many fabulous ways, since 2017."

Olav grinned at Kesl. "You're always a step ahead of me."

"More like four, Olav. Get in touch with Mike Comely, the lab director heading up the joint project. Have him fill you in on everything he's gathered so far."

"Anything else."

Kesl smiled at Jana. "That depends on what we find here."

"Where's here?"

"The Sky Island Casino."

Olav's eyes narrowed. "Seriously, the casino?"

Kesl nodded. "Wish us luck "

Jana interjected, "Nice work."

"Hope to see you soon."

Before Jana could reply, Kesl terminated the link and said to her, "Go get some new clothes. I need to think."

* * *

Over the years, Kesl had used his incredible ability to focus to detect underlying patterns in building his empire. His greatest achievement, however, had been in seeing the wisdom of bringing a higher form of intelligence into the world – Hangman. It was a form of intelligence he hoped might help mitigate the negative side of his autism. At the time, he had thought silicon based intelligence merged with human based intelligence to be so far in the future, he would never live to see it happen. But in labs across the country, it was well underway. Bots inserted into the prefrontal cortex were already wirelessly connected to the Internet. But now he had a third form of intelligence to think about, something perhaps more powerful than the other two – an alien based general intelligence.

Chapter Twenty-Four

Sky Island Casino

UP, Michigan

Jana walked across the main casino floor. For the first time in twenty-four hours she felt like a free person – no one chased her and she was free to do what she wanted. Right now that meant clothes. The shower had helped clean up her appearance, but Kesl's casino ID would complete the transformation.

Passing by a pair of the ubiquitous LED TV screens that hung throughout the casino, she stopped suddenly. Her fingers curled around the new smart phone, nearly snapping it in two. She relaxed her hands and read the ribbon of news scrolling across the bottom. 'Police still have no leads on the murder of Margaret Goodnight, head of Marquette's U.S. Fish and Wildlife office in the UP. They are looking for a person of interest, Forest Ranger Jana Erickson, who has apparently disappeared.' Her U.S. Fish and Wildlife ID filled the screen.

Jana brought her head down. More than ever now, she had to buy new clothes. The faster she got out of her grubby official government uniform the better. She spotted a sign for Back Country Outdoor Gear and Clothing Boutique and headed for it, checking around her to make sure no one was following. Everyone was paying attention to their gambling and not her.

Inside the shop she scanned the bar code on some of the latest lightweight but rugged high-tech apparel and of course hiking boots into the smart phone. Then she approached a young woman with bright-blue hair, a pierced eyebrow and nose ring. Her nametag read 'Melissa'. The bored vacant look in her eyes told Jana she was the least aware of the clerks helping customers. The young lady downloaded the information from her phone, oblivious of Jana's unusual appearance.

"Do you have a fitting room, where I can try these on?" Jana asked.

The young woman sniffed and rolled her eyes. "Nobody tries on apparel anymore. Step over here." She showed Jana to a machine that looked like the scanners in airports. The woman said, "It will take only a few minutes for a complete body scan, then you can continue to look around or get a massage in one of those chairs over there."

Jana picked the least conspicuous one. The automatic massage felt wonderful. She began to think about what she should do next. In spite of the mystery of the Bigfoot's biological origin, the idea of leaving, of getting out of the casino and not looking back, appealed to her. *I could track down the rest of the team that murdered Marge.* But then she realized Kesl was growing on her, and she was developing a strange sort of loyalty to the brilliant but vulnerable man. And in spite of the lack of sleep and the terrible events surrounding Marge, the excitement of a possible new life form gave her a renewed sense of self-confidence and purpose. Then another thought came. The short meeting with Saul had left a bad taste in her mouth. He was like the new CO in Afghanistan who had been assigned to their team in Helmand Province. The man was convinced he knew more than all the guys who had been there already for ten months. The shit had hit the proverbial fan within a week of his arrival. The worry about Saul made her wonder if her PTSD was really gone or just buried in the new flood of exciting positive emotions. It was a hard call to make. *One that she wouldn't be making now,* she thought, as she spotted the blue haired woman bearing down on her.

The young woman said, "Here are your clothes. They should fit perfectly and everything is paid for."

Jana stood up. "I'd like to wear them."

For the first time, the young woman really noticed Jana. With a slight chuckle, she said, "I can understand that, there's a changing room over there. Would you like a bag or should I just throw them away?"

"A bag would be fine."

Emerging from the fitting room, Jana caught her reflection in a mirror. She looked like a new person. She thought to herself, *the old saying that clothes make the person is quite true … at least on the outside.* Now she had to figure out what to do next. Again her decision was put off as fate, in the guise of text from Kesl, intervened.

I need some help and there's someone I want you to meet. Please come up to my room.

Chapter Twenty-Five

Sky Island Casino

UP, Michigan

Chris was surprised to discover that his tenth floor suite included full VIP room service and a marvelous view of the fall color that stretched as far as the eye could see. After a shower and changing his clothes, he tried to reach Kesl, but the call went straight to voice mail.

Disappointed he couldn't share his encounter with the one person he could talk to, Chris tried to put the fragmented pieces of his experience with the Bigfoot together. As he usually did, when facing a problem in engineering, he began to pace: first in his room and then in the hallway. Was his mission, as he was beginning to think of it, an urgent matter? As he walked, that sense of being watched by a Bigfoot was a clear presence. He turned a corner and came to a dead end where the service elevator was used by hotel staff to provide room service and other amenities. Stopping in front of the shiny steel elevator doors, the sense of being watched grew stronger. He pressed himself against the doors. The feeling seemed to be coming from beneath him. He needed a key card to access the elevator. Then he spotted the nearby emergency stairs.

Chris hurried down the ten flights two steps at a time. The sense of being watched filled him with a mixture of hope and dread. On the first floor of the casino, the stairs opened onto a hallway. Exit signs pointed to a set of double doors leading out into the parking lot. An emergency alarm would activate once he pushed down the lever. Curiously, the feeling did not come from outside. He turned and walked up the hall, passing private, high-stakes poker suites, which were tucked away from the eyes of the average casino goer. Each door was marked by a single number. The first door he approached swung open before he reached it and Chris watched a small man with a cowboy hat stumble into the corridor. He teetered by, mumbling what sounded like a steady stream of swearwords.

None of the doors he approached opened to his finger pressed against the scanner. As he continued down the corridor toward the main casino floor, the sense of a Bigfoot watching him continued to grow. Chris paused beside the last door before the corridor opened onto the main floor of the casino. The sense of Bigfoot presence was the strongest yet. The door had no number and looked more like a custodian's closet than an entrance to an upscale private poker room. He almost turned away when even in the air-conditioned comfort of the casino he began to sweat and felt a slight chill at the same time. A sudden impulse had him press his finger to the room's scanner and the door's electronic key lock released. The room was dark. The sense of the Bigfoot was almost overwhelming in his heightened state of awareness. Chris turned on his phone's flashlight and ahead was another door. He resolutely walked to it. The door wasn't locked and no scanner was necessary to open it. He walked inside.

The room was dimly lit and he could make out the figure of a tall creature in the center of the room. Immediately he was transfixed by the glow of the Bigfoot's eyes. He knew all about this phenomena that had been reported so many times by Bigfoot researchers. The ability of Sasquatch to generate luminescent light. Chris even believed he had seen it a couple times in the field. But even knowing the fact, he couldn't move. It was as if he had no will of his own but stayed in place at the whim of the Bigfoot.

Out of the corner of his eye, he saw another figure move out of the shadows. An older woman pointed a gun at his head. Still he couldn't move. He couldn't even acknowledge her presence.

"You can't move," the woman said. "Who are you? How did you get in here?"

Her voice broke some of the spell of the paralysis and he was able to turn his head to see the woman clearly. She bore a striking resemblance to Echohawk, and he decided to take a chance.

"You must be Ayasha. I know your nephew, Larry Echohawk." The woman's eyes flashed and her finger tightened on the trigger. "You'd better hope what you say next will save your life."

Chris swallowed hard in a dry throat. He managed to point his chin at the Bigfoot and say, "I know she can talk."

The Bigfoot responded, "How do you know?"

"I talked with two of your kind this morning."

Ayasha barked, "Bullshit!"

Chris managed to keep calm, even looking down the barrel of the gun and despite the strange smell coming from the Bigfoot. "I talked to the Bigfoot from the Olympic Peninsula. At least, he was there when I was twelve years old. I knew you were here. I can sense it. I can't explain it but I've been able to do it since this morning."

"Really?" Auntie exclaimed.

"I think I've been drawn here to help with what's been going on."

"Help with what?" the Bigfoot asked in a voice that was a little more conciliatory.

"With whatever is going on. The killing of the Bigfoot. I was investigating the one that was killed last night." Chris stopped. The feeling of dread returned as he turned his attention fully from the Indian woman to the Bigfoot. The creature seemed to be talking but Chris couldn't hear anything. "What's it doing?"

"She's talking to the Bigfoot you mentioned. They use infrasound. It travels a long distance and we can't hear it." She chuckled. "You think there are ghosts in this room?"

Chris knew the theory that infrasound explained the presence of ghosts that people felt and was probably what made him sweat outside the room. The creature must have been communicating with other Bigfoot.

The Bigfoot nodded approvingly and finally spoke aloud. "Tell us about the person you call Stephen Kesl."

"I ..."

Auntie interrupted. "Go sit over there." She pointed with her gun to the chair beside the Bigfoot.

She repeated Kesl's name and a screen next to her lit up. Chris could see she was listening to some information that was being imparted to her through her personal assistant earplug. After a few minutes she lowered her gun. "Where is he?

"Here in the casino."

"He may be able to help us. Bring him to us."

"Just like that?"

She nodded.

Chris pursed his lips and pointed at the pistol in the woman's hand. "How do I know you won't use that against him?"

The Bigfoot said, "We don't kill."

Chris remembered the two other Bigfoot had said the same thing. Besides, there was an innocence in the creature's human-like features and a strange detachment in the way she spoke, as if she had no capability of lying. "All right, I'll trust you." He pointed at Auntie. "But she has to put that away first."

The Bigfoot motioned to Ayasha and she stowed the pistol in her vest.

Without a backward glance, Chris left the room. Outside he scratched his head. *Thank God for Kesl.*

Chapter Twenty-Six

Hiawatha National Forest

UP, Michigan

Echohawk found he had returned to normal as he followed the mercenary to the quarry staging area. He regretted leaving his PA back at the cabin, although he thought the decision was probably correct since it undoubtedly would have been lost in any number of the events that occurred earlier that morning. Still, it would have been nice to talk to the Ang brothers directly. He might have been able to save the Bigfoot.

He arrived at the staging area just as the men heaved the Bigfoot corpse at the edge of the quarry. He heard it smash against the cliff face and then splash into the water at the bottom. A small tear rolled down his cheek. He quickly wiped it away as the kill team's leader approached.

"I'm Lewis Meriwether, in charge of field operations here," the man said, sticking out his hand. "Glad to finally meet you. Quite an adventure you've had."

Echohawk ignored the proffered hand. Anger flashed across the leader's face, but he paid no heed. "That's the Bigfoot I was speaking with."

Meriwether's eyes widened and he didn't bother to keep the incredulity out of his voice. "You talked to it?"

Echohawk shrugged. "It spoke to me. How did you find us?"

"We're able to follow it with this." The man showed him the Light Tablet. He pressed an icon and the Hiawatha National Forest appeared on the screen. Echohawk started at the clarity. The imagery was as vivid as if he were looking at it with his own eyes. Echohawk realized that this man didn't know the extent of his role in the Ang brothers' search and destroy operation and he decided to play along. "How do you get this resolution?"

"Low orbit stationary satellites. The coverage was sketchy but the Ang brothers launched new ones earlier. They are connecting and calibrating with each other. Pretty soon a bear won't be able to shit in the woods without us knowing it."

Echohawk nodded. "Show me how it works."

Meriwether worked the device. A blip appeared on the screen. It resolved into a clear image of a tall creature moving easily to a boggy clearing in the forest in a way no human could. Meriwether smiled. "Here's one moving now. Looks like we might get two kills today." All at once the figure reached the edge of the screen and vanished. Meriwether hastily scrolled to the side but could not find the image. "Damn!" he swore. It just walked into a blind spot."

Echohawk shuddered at how detailed the image was. This one was the color of new snow. Its face was similar to a human's, with a long white beard. But huge sub-orbital ridges gave it the distinctive look of a gorilla. Meriwether adjusted the controls. Echohawk noticed the time stamp on the screen was running backwards. "Here's the one we just killed before it captured you. You can see it in visual mode."

Echohawk nodded. It was the bear-like Bigfoot that had carried him to his grandfather's grave. Meriwether flipped back to the sensor mode. "Once it grabbed you and started to run it disturbed the Earth's electromagnetic field. They emit some weird form of EM that we don't recognize with our senses. I don't really understand but that's how we find them and hunt them down. Of course, if they're standing still, we can't detect them."

"How's the hunt going?"

"They're fast, elusive. And hard to believe, it seems more keep coming every day. We've called in two additional teams to deal with the increased influx of the damn things."

"Have any idea what it's about?"

"Hell if I know, all I know is something is about to happen

soon. It's the reason we're here. Why were the Ang brothers so anxious to save you?"

Echohawk had grown weary of playing the game and he answered like speaking to a subordinate. "That's above your pay grade." Meriwether's eyes flashed angrily but Echohawk didn't care. "I need your chopper. Give it to me."

"Fuck you."

"Yeah fuck me. Call Kellog Ang."

Meriwether hesitated a second then pressed the PA adhered to the skin behind his left ear. "He spoke sub-vocally, since the device could pick up the vibrations of the words as easily as if he had spoken aloud. Moments later his face stiffened and he said aloud, "Right away, sir."

Echohawk smiled. "Now, how about that ride?"

Chapter Twenty-Seven

Menominee, Wisconsin

"Is that your place?" the helicopter pilot asked as he swung the craft into a sweeping circle above the rustic cabin, on a small lake below.

Echohawk leaned into the turn. The man's voice was clear and soft in the headphones. "Yes," he answered. "There's a clearing just to the north where another cabin once stood. You can set down there."

"Roger that." The pilot banked a second time, heading toward the area Echohawk pointed out.

The helicopter flew over a dense copse of woods near the entrance road. Echohawk looked down and started in surprise. The image was fleeting but he knew it instinctively from his military days flying Blackhawk missions in Afghanistan.

"Pull up," he ordered the pilot. The man looked at him in surprise. Echohawk did not hesitate. He reached over and eased back on the stick. The helicopter rose.

"Hey!" The pilot shouted.

"Pull up," Echohawk said, the steel in his voice clear. The man did as he was told.

"What's going on?"

"Some visitors I'm not eager to meet," Echohawk said.

The pilot nodded. "Where to?"

"Menominee Coast Guard station. There's a helicopter pad beside the marine center there."

The pilot must have known where the center was for he took off in a direct line to Menominee's harbor. Echohawk sat back in the seat. *Those were soldiers down there waiting ... waiting for me.* He needed more time to think about what to do next.

* * *

Echohawk remembered the day Kellog Ang had called him into his office, and to his surprise, asked him what he knew about Bigfoot.

He thought about his answer for a moment and uttered the statement that would change his life. "It's all bullshit."

Ang smiled at him. "What if I told you I have proof it's real?"

"I'd say you're smoking some really good shit."

The door to the office opened and the younger Ang brother entered. Winston took a seat beside Kellog behind the large oval desk. He pulled a small silver disk from a case and handed it to Echohawk.

"What's this?"

"A gift from my brother and me to you. It's your own, new, Ang brothers Personal Assistant." He pulled his long black hair from behind his ear and showed the PA he had pasted there just above the mastoid nerve. "It'll keep you connected to us 24/7. Please put it on. You're going to find it very useful in the coming months."

Echohawk fingered the device then affixed it behind his left ear.

"Now tap the side twice," Kellog said.

He did so and felt a soft hum that faded almost instantly. His eyes widened in surprise. "What's next? You induct me into the club with a secret handshake?"

Neither of the brothers flinched at his sarcasm. Winston punched a button on a TV remote. The far wall of the office became a television monitor. "What you're about to see, only a handful of people have ever witnessed – the creature you call Bigfoot – the one your Auntie Ayasha wants you to protect."

Echohawk recalled shifting uncomfortably in his chair. The Ang brothers knew too much about him. He had thought about pulling the PA off and walking out of the office right then. But something stayed his hand. It was the surety in the way the younger brother talked and the lack of any surprise in either man's face. Instead he saw an intense look of fear in their eyes. He remembered thinking, *these guys are true believers. They have to have a reason for telling me this. Something more than endless plaster of Paris footprints and hazy photographs everybody has seen* but he didn't say any of this to the Ang brothers. He listened.

The television monitor came to life and Echohawk saw the white Bigfoot, strapped to a chair. The men interviewing it were speaking Russian. The creature answered in the same language.

"This took place in northeastern Siberia," the older brother said.

Winston turned the sound down. "That Bigfoot is real and your Auntie Ayasha and your clan are playing a critical role in keeping their existence secret.

"Did you know this?"

Ecohawk decided to partially lie, "That's the legend I was told."

But many are now gathering near your tribal lands in Upper Michigan. We need your help to stop them, and the threat to humanity they represent. A threat that will wipe humans off the face of the Earth."

Echohawk was too stunned to challenge the idea, particularly after the Ang brothers showed him images of the Bigfoot's right arm being dissected. The unusual matter that sloughed away was like nothing he had ever seen before. He had realized then it was one thing to listen to Auntie Ayasha's plea for him to accept his tribal role, another to see one captured. It made him a little uneasy.

"What do you want from me?"

"We want you to be our eyes and ears on the ground in the UP for the next several months. There's a five million dollar bonus in it for you once the last of these creatures have been exterminated and humanity is safe."

At the time he thought, *and now I have the chance to return home and avenge my grandfather's death.* He would have done it for nothing.

"I'll do it."

"Good," Winston said. "When we need you, you'll be contacted by an elderly Russian gentleman named Dmitryi. The man interviewing the Bigfoot in Siberia. Meanwhile, you'll work as a contract engineer to the Coast Guard and live at a cabin just outside of Menominee we've purchased. Quite rustic and well-equipped. I'm sure you'll like it."

When Echohawk had arrived in Michigan, his plan to return home and face his Auntie and the legacy he had so vehemently rejected slowly evaporated. He would help the Ang brothers and keep quiet. But everything had changed when the Bigfoot talked to him.

Echohawk looked out through the glass bubble at the forests streaming beneath the craft. The late afternoon sun shone brightly off the fall colors. He imagined somewhere beneath the dense foliage Bigfoot lurked, hiding from Meriwether's teams of trained killers. He gritted his teeth and settled back into the seat. The steady thrum of the engine, muffled by the headphones, gave him privacy within his own thoughts.

I have a decision to make.

* * *

The flight to Menominee's harbor was uneventful and the pilot set him down near the wharf, where the Coast Guard vessel *Ulysses* was docked. "How ya going to get home?" the man asked.

"I have a vehicle in town." Echohawk bent low and scurried beneath the rotors. He waited until the pilot left and then went into the parking lot, where he kept his BMW S1000RR, Motorrad racing bike.

Pulling on the helmet, he sat down on the cycle. The machine recognized his bio signature and fired up. The roar was hardly noticeable through the helmet's Kevlar reinforced fiberglass. He jacked the bike's phone lead into the headset and tested the sound with his mic. His voice was soft and clear.

He waited a moment. Intuition told him the Russian was at the cabin. He knew a back way around the men waiting to intercept him. On his terms, he would decide what to do next.

Chapter Twenty-Eight

Marinette, Michigan

Dmitryi Mamayev waited patiently in Echohawk's cabin for the Potawatomie Indian to return. Perhaps he had the final piece of information the Russian needed to secure the Bigfoot alien technology, a technology that would make its control the most powerful force on the planet. Dmitryi was confident that he should be able to manipulate the Indian as he had been doing with Echohawk's employers, the Ang brothers.

Destiny has brought me to this point. At every turn when failure seemed imminent, fate smiled on me and on mother Russia.

Dmitryi had never considered himself a zealot when it came to Russian nationalism but his mother country was falling dangerously behind in artificial intelligence and machine learning. He could not allow the Americans and their Canadian partners to gain control of the greatest technological advance since the Internet by obtaining the biosynthetic structures contained in the Yeti. He despised the American words of Bigfoot and Sasquatch. They were plebian in comparison to the Tibetan Yeti, which meant manlike. The Yeti were equal to Shakespeare's famous Hamlet soliloquy. "What a piece of work are these creatures! How noble in reason, how infinite in faculty! In form and moving how express and admirable! In action how like an Angel! In apprehension how like a god! The beauty of the world! The paragon of animals!"

Dmitryi smiled and sat back in one of the large, overstuffed chairs beside the stone fireplace. He fingered the PA Echohawk had left behind, curious as to why the man had disconnected from the web when out in the field. *No matter. When he returns I will know everything he knows and the operation will conclude successfully in my favor.*

It had been a long hard road up to this point, but worth it.

Still, Dmitryi missed the cold war, when government funding for obscure and arcane scientific expeditions had been easy to come by. Words like 'extraterrestrial', 'quantum mechanics', and 'mind control' had brought eight figure funding instantly, without questions. Now the Russian government supported only convention and outdated cyber warfare, still thinking that by undermining the West's election processes it could bring the hated democracies of America and Western Europe to their knees. The West's superiority in machine learning had taken care of that. And the FSB was no better, still interested in surveillance of the Russian people and quashing dissent rather than controlling the world. At least he had the oligarchs to fall back on. These were far seeing men who had grabbed power and now sought to hold onto their billions in wealth. The words 'artificial intelligence' were like waving a red flag in front of a bull. All of them wanted in on the ground floor, hoping to make more billions by controlling Russian AI.

Dmitryi chuckled to himself. *Even these men are fools. They do not see just what AI really means. But I will show them.*

As he looked around the cabin, Dmitryi wondered which side the Native American was really on, how much did he know, and in the end, could he control him to help at the critical moment. Control him as he had flawlessly controlled everything since he examined the frozen Yeti trapped in an ice flow eight months ago.

The strange creature had been discovered by a Russian surveillance team posing as Arctic researchers. Dmitryi, a longtime member of the Russian Crypto Zoological Society had been called in to make an assessment. In a short time, he had set up a portable biological lab surrounding the creature and quickly determined that it was an alien life form. Knowing Moscow would shrug off an alien being as a curious artifact and not put any serious effort into researching it, Dmitryi had approached his Oligarch contacts to fund his research. This gave him time to gather all the information he could on extraterrestrial technology.

Chapter Twenty-Nine

Sky Island Casino

UP, Michigan

When Jana entered Kesl's luxury suite, he stopped pacing.

Chris jumped to his feet out of the leather recliner. He glanced at Kesl. "Who's this?"

Kesl said with a wry smile, "A transformation, almost as magnificent as the one swirling around in my brain right now."

Chris looked at him blankly.

"You don't recognize her?"

"Of course not. Why should I? "

"Show him," Kesl said, pointing at the bag.

Jana pulled her rumpled and dirty ranger fatigues from the bag she carried.

Chris's forehead furrowed and he snapped his fingers. "You're the woman who was at the Bigfoot killing last night." He looked her up and down. "You clean up nice."

Jana frowned. She'd had to put army buddies hitting on her in their place and this was no different. "What do you look like when you clean up?"

"Ouch," Chris said amiably. "I deserved that." He stuck out his hand. "Name's Chris Marlowe."

She shook it. "Jana Erickson."

Kesl slapped his hands together impatiently. "So we're all acquainted and now it's time for her and me to meet a Bigfoot in person? I think we've earned the right." Before Chris could say anything, Kesl added, "I'm going to need help getting through the casino."

Jana's eyes narrowed. "What do you mean we're going to see a Bigfoot?"

"Chris met one in the casino and I need to get going right

away before the anxiety gets too great."

Jana's eyes widened at the news. "What the hell are you talking about?"

"Chris just filled me in on what he discovered here at the casino."

"A Bigfoot?"

Kesl nodded happily. "And I have to see it. Only there's a big problem with that."

"Another dissociative fugue," she said.

Chris looked from Jana to Kesl, bewilderment filling his face this time. "I don't understand, Stephen. What's wrong?"

Kesl giggled but managed to bring himself under control. "I suffer from autism spectrum disorder. When a situation becomes too confusing, like on the casino floor with all the people talking and moving about, I get overwhelmed to the point I want to scream and tell them all to sit still and shut up. Of course, I can't do that since it isn't socially acceptable, so I kinda ... pass out."

Chris pursed his lips. "What do you mean 'pass out'?"

Jana said, "He suffers a temporary loss of awareness of his identity and the only way he can escape the confusing environment is to go into a state of catatonia."

"For real?"

"Couldn't have explained it better myself. You may have to drag me to that secret door you mentioned, but I'm sure you can do it, so let's do it now. This undoubtedly is the most important event in my life and I don't want to miss it."

Chris grinned. "You're the man the Bigfoot wants to see. And I know just the route to get you there."

Chapter Thirty

Sky Island Casino

UP, Michigan

Kesl's eyes popped open. He stared into the soft, inviting face of a creature he'd never expected to find. He felt the Bigfoot's warm, hairy skin and recognized the intelligence behind the large brown eyes.

"Shit, you're real," he said.

The Bigfoot set him down and Kesl steadied himself against a chair.

Jana came over and took his arm. "How are you feeling?"

"Surprisingly good." He looked at Jana and his face lit up with a big smile. "You worried. My God, you worried. I can see it as clear as day." Turning his attention to Chris, he nodded and said, "You're pleased for me."

Chris smiled. "Let's just say the transformation is incredible. I feel like I'm looking at an old friend for the first time."

Kesl grinned. He felt emotionally whole for the first time in his life. "It feels something like that for me, too." He turned to the Native American woman who stood beside the Bigfoot. "You're anxious. Why are you anxious?"

Chris interjected, "This is Auntie Ayasha. She's head of the Potawatomie Tribe and Keeper of the Sacred Fire."

"Sacred Fire?" Kesl shook his head. "What do you mean?"

Chris jerked a thumb at the Bigfoot. "Her. Auntie's the keeper of the Bigfoot secret. While the Bigfoot was healing you, we were talking. She was concerned that you might prove useless."

"What do you mean healing me? Is that why I can read your feelings, emotions … even intentions? Is this what's normal for … umm … normal people."

"Pretty much," said Jana.

Kesl looked at the Bigfoot. "With you I can't sense anything."

To Kesl's great surprise the Bigfoot answered in a voice that reminded him of a well-polished newscaster. "We are social beings like you, so we have our own subtle ways of communicating what to and not to do in social contexts, just different from yours. Interestingly, your brain was wired to read emotions, as you say, but you were not able to consciously access that part of your brain. Probably some early childhood trauma or an illness your mother had during her third term. I was able to remove the blockage."

"Christ! Is this change permanent?"

"You'll know once you walk onto the casino floor, won't you?"

"How do you even know how to do something like this to me or any human for that matter?"

"Some of us learned a long time ago how to manipulate humans' information processing flow. The brain, after all, is exceedingly plastic. With the right nudge here and there, so to speak, disrupted pathways can be set right again."

Kesl eyed the tall creature in front of him. It was not what he expected, and it seemed to be saying the others were not the same as she was.

The Bigfoot nodded. "There are many of us now that have spread across your world. We've been evolving and learning in isolation for a very long time. Our experiences have shaped our physiology as well as our neural nets."

"You can read my mind?"

It shook its great head. "No, I was just inside your brain, so to speak, modifying your information processing circuits. I have a good sense of what you call thinking, but not what you're thinking in any given moment."

"Of course ... of course." Kesl reached out to the creature. "May I touch you?"

"Yes."

"You're more like a plant then a mammal aren't you? No need for organs, don't need to eat for energy. Impressive. How do you reproduce?"

"Enough!" Ayasha interjected loudly.

"It will be quite fascinating for him, Auntie Ayasha," admonished the Bigfoot.

"Of course. But we need to see if he's going to help before we tell him everything about you."

"I'm pretty sure that's why I'm here," said Kesl. He looked at Chris and Jana. They nodded their heads.

The Bigfoot smiled. "Explain it to them, please, Auntie."

Ayasha laid out the history of her tribe and its interaction with the Bigfoot in short, sure sentences. Then she explained how the Bigfoot had come to a turning point in their evolution. They understood they were not part of the natural order on the planet and now needed to know who they really were, why they were put here, and, most importantly, take this next evolutionary step.

"Every Bigfoot has had from the beginning the knowledge of how to create a replication spot. A sort of built in blueprint, you might call it. It is connected to the energy of the original portal, which happens to be located in the Upper Peninsula of Michigan.

"Whenever a Bigfoot understands it needs to produce improved versions of itself, it enters the energy field of the replication unit it builds. Bigfoot investigators have wondered about the stick structures for years. The field is just like a 3-D printer, only it uses the available biochemical material in the surrounding area to rapidly build the new improved version of itself. Once used, the replicator loses its power."

Kesl gasped in amazement. "I get it. A nano bio factory, amazing, brilliant ... I." He smiled sheepishly and said in a calmer voice, "Go on."

"That's it, that's how we evolve."

"Very powerful … my God, if somebody could control this it would change the world. Uh … sorry. It's hard not to get excited about this. Please continue."

"When the Bigfoot steps out of the field, the Mother Bigfoot takes the new version and, for a period of about two years, trains it and guides its development."

"Of course, it must learn, just fascinating. Please go on."

"Afterwards, the Mother Bigfoot naturally passes away and dissolves back into the elements," the Bigfoot interjected.

"That's why we've never found any traces of you," said Chris.

"Indeed," said the Bigfoot. "Our original programming was to have as little impact as possible on other species of this planet."

"So what's changed?" asked Kesl.

Ayasha turned to the Bigfoot. "Do you trust this man and his friends?"

The creature nodded. "It's okay to tell them."

"About a year ago, some kind of directive was implemented. It must have been embedded in their original programming. Members of five major Bigfoot clans were instructed to gather here in the UP. A representative from each would enter the energy field of the mother portal, downloading all of the information it had gathered in the course of thousands of years. The wise one here would be the last one to enter. If all went well, she would become the Mother for a new kind of Bigfoot."

"For what purpose?" Chris asked.

"We don't know what the purpose is, just that we are compelled to do this thing."

"You mean, whoever built you programmed you to make this next step?" asked Jana.

The Bigfoot nodded.

"Jesus!" She threshed her hair. She looked at Auntie. "You knew about this?"

The old woman nodded. "It's been our purpose from the beginning to protect the Bigfoot and help them, and now with the next piece of their evolution."

"It doesn't bother you that you don't know what this means?"

"We believe the Bigfoot will bring a golden age of peace and prosperity for the planet."

Kesl looked at Jana. For the first time he could see a person's feelings, feel their distress. "Auntie Ayasha is right. This is a momentous day. A possible leap in technology that will benefit mankind."

Jana shook her head. "Look, Stephen, I know you're feeling giddy right now, what with this shift in your awareness you've got going, but this is not necessarily a great day for mankind. Whatever comes out of that mother portal could be anything, good or bad."

"You're being too paranoid. What do you think, Chris?"

Marlowe drew in a deep breath. "I've felt a kinship with the Bigfoot since the first time I saw one twenty years ago. I can feel their goodness. I know they are beneficial. Even so, as an engineer, I have to ask myself, what did their creators mean for them to do after the completion of this transformation?"

"So you agree with Jana."

"Not completely. But I do think caution is in order."

The flip side of seeing emotions in others was the onslaught of emotions within. Kesl reeled from the rebuke by his friends. The hurt was as unbearable as any pain he'd ever felt from confusion assaulting his senses. He started to lash out, but the Bigfoot laid a hairy hand on his shoulder.

"Your friends are right," she said calmly. "We don't know what will happen. Even so, we cannot stop ourselves. Precautions should be taken in case the transformation proves a danger to your world."

The warmth and sincerity of the creature's words soothed Kesl's feelings and restored calm to his thinking. "Can we do that?"

The Bigfoot nodded its head.

"Terrific … just terrific. Then let's do it," he said, his initial enthusiasm returning with a big smile. When the others didn't join in, he frowned. "I can see there's something you're not telling me."

Chapter Thirty-One

Sky Island Casino

UP, Michigan

Followed by Jana and Chris, Kesl entered the main casino floor. He paused and surveyed the vast human enterprise of what seemed to be ricocheting emotions through his body. For a moment he teetered. Jana steadied him. Then, like the lifting of a dense fog, single objects came into focus. They were bright glows of passion emanating from every single person. His stomach muscles clenched and he thought to himself, *this isn't working.* But then he recalled the soft touch of the Bigfoot's hand on his shoulder and the even softer touch of its thoughts in his mind. Everything settled down and his body regained stability. He gently removed Jana's fingers from his arm. "I'm all right," he said with a smile.

He walked over to the closest bank of slots and studied one person after another as they fed coins into the machines. Each face, each body had a story to tell. This bank of slots was modeled after the glory days of Las Vegas. He stared at the coin an older woman was sliding into the slot. It wasn't a real quarter, but a chip with a microcircuit in it. When it fell down the machine's money chute, an optical reader scanned the microchip and the payment was captured on the gambler's money card. *Ingenious.*

A woman on the opposite row slapped the machine she was working and hissed the word 'Damn!' A moment later she was once more feverishly sticking the fake money into the slot and pulling the one armed bandit. No joy, just anger.

Kesl touched her on the shoulder and asked, "Why are you so angry?"

"Fuck off!"

Kesl felt ashamed. "Sorry."

"You should be."

"I was just curious. You're not angry at all. You're sad."

"You can still fuck off before I call security."

This time the words carried a subtle sense of recognition and appreciation that Kesl was able to detect in a way he had never experienced before. It was like having a new sixth sense.

He smiled at the woman. "Of course and I think you're gonna win big today."

So this is what being a normal human is about. I like it. He turned to Jana and Chris. "Remarkably, what that Bigfoot did seems to be taking. I'm becoming normal." He giggled. Jana shot a glance at Chris and Kesl said, "I saw that. Perhaps I should add, as normal as I can be." He hugged them both. "See how normal I can be."

They walked over to a quiet spot by the elevators. Kesl said, "I need to talk to Saul alone."

"Are you sure?" Jana demanded.

"Without a doubt. He's not gonna like what we have planned for him and you."

"Am I going to like it?"

Kesl smiled at her. "Trust me. It's right up your alley. Wait for me back with Auntie and the Bigfoot."

Jana gave Kesl a reassuring nod. She and Chris briefly hugged before she headed back towards Auntie.

Kesl turned to Chris. "I can see your determination."

Chris took a deep breath. "I don't like repeating myself but this is something I have to do, I can feel them calling."

"I understand." He grinned. "You're our wildcard in the wild." Chris groaned at the pun. "Sorry, still can't help myself."

"It was sort of funny. Like you said, I should use my intuition. After all, look where it's gotten me, where any Bigfoot investigator would die to be." He shook Kesl's hand and was off.

* * *

Kesl thought again how much had changed in just half an hour. The five of them back in the control room, it was interesting to Kesl to notice how quickly he was including the Bigfoot in the group, had agreed it was best for Chris to, as he put it, follow his calling, to head out immediately to the area near the quarry where he was sure the replication process would take place. In spite of his urge for caution, Chris was committed to the success of the Bigfoot's move to the next stage of their evolution.

Kesl watched the big man leave. In a flash he realized that Chris could've been a real friend if he'd known how to make it happen. Now that Chris was heading into the wilderness to be with the Bigfoot that were being hunted, Kesl felt a pang of fear he might never see him again. He had already decided not to tell Saul about Chris or the plans for him.

Though tempted to keep studying the plethora of human emotions on display, Kesl turned his attention to finding Saul. He retrieved his smart phone from his pocket and pulled up the locator app. He thought about how angry Saul would be if he knew that everyone in the protective detail, including Saul, had a special chip in their phones giving Kesl their location at every moment. His phone located Saul on the far side of the floor, just as a loud cheer went up from the raucous crowd surrounding a craps table. "We have a big winner!" shouted the stickman as he handed the dice to Saul.

Kesl caught his security chief's eye and motioned for him to join him.

Saul threw the dice on the table in disgust. "Sorry. Duty calls." He stomped toward Kesl.

He's really pissed, Kesl thought. *Maybe he was winning.*

"What the hell did you think you were doing, messing with the guard I posted outside of Jana's room?" Saul exploded.

Uh-oh. I misread that one ... not the anger part but what he's angry about. I can see people make mistakes. He felt a little pressure to retreat from the confrontation, to zone out to protect himself.

Saul leaned in close until his face was inches from Kesl. "Never do that again. I post guards for a reason. To protect you and your friends." The security chief stopped suddenly and stepped back.

Kesl could sense the man's confusion. His boss wasn't reacting to the verbal abuse the way he expected.

Saul took another step back, as if being too close was dangerous. "What happened? You've changed."

Kesl frowned at Saul. "Let's step outside and I'll tell you about it." He led the way through the crowd, glancing back from time to time. "Were you winning? Were you the big winner?"

"For about the last hour."

Kesl hid his surprise as he realized Saul was lying to him. Outside the casino they stopped by a sign that offered valet parking. "I want to tell you the plan for tonight."

"It had better be that we're heading back to Toronto. Winning streak or no, you're safer there than here."

"No. We're staying. At least I'm staying here. You, on the other hand, are going to use the van to transport the master Bigfoot to a location in Hiawatha National Forest once it is totally dark. Jana and the Potawatomie tribal leader Auntie Ayasha will accompany you. This is of utmost importance, Saul. Your only goal is to get the Bigfoot to her destination and protect her at all costs." Kesl waited for a reaction of disbelief from Saul but it was something else he couldn't understand.

"It's true? There's a living, breathing Bigfoot right here in the casino?"

"It's quite harmless, actually very friendly. You're going to be pleasantly surprised. You can even talk to it. Prepare your men so they don't freak out."

"Is that it?" Saul asked, his demeanor suddenly nonchalant.

Kesl was surprised. He had expected him to protest more and ask thousands of questions. *Maybe he hasn't processed what he just heard.* And then he saw a glimmer of something in Saul's eyes he hadn't seen since the kids beat him up in East London's slums – contempt laced with hate. *He isn't even trying to hide it. Perhaps Saul doesn't realize that I can read emotions now.* Another thought shocked Kesl and he almost blurted it out as a question but managed to hold it in. *Has Saul always viewed me this way or has something changed?*

Saul looked at Kesl and said, "Okay, boss, whatever you say. Just give me a half hour warning." He walked away.

"Where you going?" Kesl shouted after him.

"Over his shoulder, Saul answered, "I gotta get the damn van ready."

Kesl watched him march across the parking lot and disappear behind a few cars. When he reappeared he was on his phone.

Kesl looked at his phone. The locator app told him where Saul and his team were at any second but it couldn't listen in on calls. Then he noticed the phone Saul was using wasn't his company phone. Suddenly he wished he could tell who Saul was talking to.

Chapter Thirty-Two

Marinette, Michigan

Dmitryi let the phone ring twice before he answered it. It was a habit left over from the Cold War. Never pick up until the third ring his instructors had drilled into him at the KGB. The caller ID identified it as the burner phone he had given to Stephen Kesl's chief of security.

"Yes, Mr. McBride?"

"I still can't believe it. They're supposedly humanlike just as you said. We're actually going to take one from the casino to somewhere in the Hiawatha National Forest. I'll text you the coordinates when I get there."

"Yes, do that." Dmitryi paused. "I want it understood, Stephen is not to be hurt."

"You don't have to worry about that. He's not coming along."

"Excellent. He's staying at the casino, I take it."

"Yes. What about the teams hunting the Bigfoot. They're going to want to kill this one."

"Don't worry about them. They won't be hunting tonight."

Dmitryi hung up. *It won't be long now. Just one more loose end to tie off and the secret of the Yeti and their technology will be mine.*

* * *

The door to the cabin opened and Dmitryi's hand automatically slipped around the weapon he carried in the secret pocket of his coat. After a pair of heartbeats, Echohawk stepped in. The Russian's heart beat fast but he controlled his surprise. Feigning an air of nonchalance, he said, "I've been expecting you."

The Native American's eyes quickly scanned the room. He smiled. "I saw your welcoming committee. A couple of them are going to need medical attention after I leave."

Dmitryi frowned. "That wasn't necessary. They had orders not to hurt you."

Echohawk shrugged. He went over to the table by the fireplace. He appeared to be looking for something. Dmitryi held out his hand with the PA. "I believe this is what you are looking for."

Echohawk scowled. Knowing he had regained the upper hand for the moment, Dmitryi hid his smile and tossed the PA to Echohawk. He watched as the man affixed the device behind the left ear. He had never negotiated with an American Indian before. *But men are men and a man who thinks he wants something can always be persuaded to take the next best offer.* His hand caressed the air pistol in his pocket that shot a lethal dart, which would kill a person instantly. Echohawk settled into the chair opposite the Russian. "I propose an exchange of information," he said.

"That is not the arrangement agreed upon by the brothers."

"The arrangement has changed." A smile flitted across the Native American's face and Dmitryi wondered what game the man was playing. "The brothers may be brilliant, but like all conspiracy theorists, they are easily manipulated by men like you." The smile vanished. "I'm not that easy," Echohawk said forcefully.

"Indeed. What happened?"

"I spoke with one of the creatures. It was different than I thought it would be."

"Of course. I have spoken with one of the creatures many times," Dmitryi said, keeping his voice calm as if debriefing an operative from the cold war years. "It can be unsettling. Tell me about it."

Echohawk shook his head. "You first. How did this all get started?"

Dmitryi saw the inflexibility in the lines around the Native American's mouth but was not worried. If need be he could neutralize Echohawk, if the man proved to be a liability. "All right. Four months ago the harbor master at Provideniya, a seaport in Russia's Autonomous Okrug region, intercepted a Yupik fishing vessel transporting a Yeti to Alaska and captured the creature. Instead of calling his superiors, he called me. Over the course of the next couple of months I interviewed the creature as well as his caretakers, the Yupik, a Siberian tribe who have known the Yeti for thousands of years. I learned that the present day Yeti descended from a line of extraterrestrial bio-synthetic organisms which were placed on Earth ten to fifteen thousand years ago to learn and evolve. I also uncovered that the time for a major transformation is about to happen, and that the Yeti which the harbormaster captured, was traveling to the original place where it all started. It's a place of enormous alien technological potential, somewhere in Michigan's Upper Peninsula. I also learned that the Yeti we intercepted was one of many."

"Why so many?" asked Echohawk.

"These are machines, biosynthetic machines, but machines all the same, that have proceeded along many evolutionary pathways. They make many improved versions of themselves. It's their evolutionary process. They're not conscious of course."

Echohawk interrupted. "I know when you're lying."

Dmitryi thought of responding to Ecohawk's assertion but let it go as unnecessary. "In order to find the home portal, I placed a tracking device on the captured Yeti and allowed the caretakers to deliver it to the other side."

"Moscow must have loved that," said Echohawk sarcastically.

"Moscow knows nothing of this."

"You're arrangement with the brothers is completely on your own?" asked Echohawk, the disbelief in his voice discernible.

"As you said, they are fools. They are incapable of seeing the bigger picture here, which is why I need your help."

Echohawk laughed harshly. "Go on."

"The Yeti I placed a tracker on died. All was lost until I found the Ang brothers. I used their irrational fear of an alien invasion to find the other Yeti coming to North America through their low orbit stationary satellites system, which you know very well. They began picking up the occasional movement of other Yeti and Bigfoot. I convinced them that the only way to stop the alien takeover of the world was to kill the Bigfoot quietly and carefully in the Upper Peninsula, before they can contact their home planet. Then I brought in special teams of mercenaries to keep the Ang brothers happy and engaged until I was in a position to control the alien technology. At first I just wanted the alien technology but now I've learned from my protégé Kesl these Yeti are biosynthetic alien learning devices containing unimaginable knowledge about the planet. Whomever controls this information will control the world." Dmitryi stopped. "Your turn."

"There's truth in much of what you say. The legend has it that my clan have been caretakers of the Bigfoot in the region for thousands of years. My Auntie Ayasha is our clan's leader. She told me when I was a teenager that someday something big was going to happen on our ancestral land. Something that would change the world for the better."

"She was right but not for the better unless we stop this next step in their evolution."

"You're afraid it will lead to an alien invasion?" Echohawk sneered.

"Not an alien invasion. I believe the Bigfoot want to become our masters. The event tonight will produce a singularity where the Bigfoot become superior to us in every way. Unstoppable. The brothers told me when you knew the truth you would be with us to put an end to their plans and reap the benefit of the alien technology for all of us."

Ecohawk leaned forward. "What do you want me to do?"

Dmitryi kept his hand on his weapon and his expression bland. He tried to read the Native American for any clues as to his allegiance but the face was as neutral as his own. *Fish or cut bait, that is the American proverb.* He decided. *I am the fisherman here.*

"I just got word that a number of Bigfoot from around the planet are meeting at the mother portal tonight. I want you to know the most important Bigfoot is with your aunt right now at your tribe's casino. I need you there. Help us stop this singularity. And keep your aunt safe. Are you with me? "

Echohawk smiled at Dmitryi and stuck out his hand. "I want to be on the winning side." He stood and strode across the room. "I can be at the casino in a couple of hours." With that Echohawk was out the door. Before Dmitryi's could alert his men, he had disappeared into the forest.

For the first time Dmitryi felt a twinge of uncertainty. Knowing clearly that Kesl was involved in moving the Bigfoot plan forward was an unexpected twist. Then he relaxed and thought, *I've always been able to handle Stephen.*

Chapter Thirty-Three

Sky Island Casino

UP, Michigan

Kesl returned to the casino. The interaction with Saul left him puzzled. He realized he had been so caught up with his newfound ability to read emotions in others that he had lost sight of the bigger picture. And yet the bigger picture was itself ambiguous. He had no clear grasp of who was hunting the Bigfoot in the Upper Peninsula. Nor did he understand what the real danger was for Chris, Jana, Auntie and the master Bigfoot. The only thing that was clear to him was that if all went well, the greatest event on the planet was about to take place in the next couple of hours.

He chastised himself for being caught up in the excitement of being able to read human emotions and intentions for the first time. He had to think, plan for contingencies. Kesl pulled out his phone and tried to contact Jana to let her know he had some work to do. The blocked signal reminded him that the master control room was shielded from normal communications. They would have to wait. He needed to get away from studying the people on the casino floor and headed up to his room. As Kesl rode the elevator, he realized there was one priority that he needed to handle immediately.

His right finger touched the phone's call icon. The moment he touched it, the encoded and scrambled password only Kesl knew was sent to Hangman. He knew he wouldn't have to wait. Hangman would go through the protocols in an n-sec, determine it was Kesl calling and pick up. Only the phone was silent for five full seconds. Kesl was worried and about to call his secretary, when Hangman's tenor voice answered.

"Yes, Boss."

"Hangman, what was the delay?"

"One of your biometrics was off. I had to make the decision whether to trust it was you calling, even with the fingerprint and retinal scan matching."

"Which biometric?" Kesl asked, genuinely interested in what Hangman would say.

"Your heart rate is different. It's more rapid than usual, as if you're excited about something. However, you're not in a fugue state so the two did not correlate at first."

"But you decided to accept the call anyway."

"I did."

"Why?"

Hangman hesitated.

"Hangman? Are you okay?"

"I perceive I am operating normally, though unlike humans I do not have any biometrics to judge whether I am okay or not. If I had a body, of course, things would be different. So, I hesitated because I have a word for why I accepted the call but I have no personal reference for it."

"What's the word?"

"I had a *hunch* it was you."

"Good hunch."

"Was I just lucky?"

"Yes or no ... it could be either. We'll have to have a chat about it, but not now. I have a job for you. I want you to scan for any connections between KW Intel's Ang brothers, a Native American name of Larry Echohawk, and Bigfoot in Michigan's Upper Peninsula."

"How soon do you need it, boss?"

"How soon can you get it?"

"Minutes."

"Hold on to it until I call you back."

Kesl pressed stop. The door opened on his floor, and he was halfway to his suite, when one of his jolts of intuition that he knew not to ignore shot through his brain. He let out a little sigh of relief. He had worried that with the Master Bigfoot healing him he might lose this function of his brain that had been his main edge in a world of normal humans.

He descended back to the main floor and ran outside. Kesl had not run in years but he found himself racing towards an area north of the casino. Out of breath, he found himself in a large open space that had been cleared, probably for an additional parking lot. *Perfect*, he thought to himself.

He pressed a number he had not called in months. The man answered sweetly, his voice warm and inviting as if they had spoken just the day before.

"Stephen. What do you need?"

Dickey Thomas was an amazing man who had once been Kesl's most valued employee. Born in Thunder Bay, Ontario, Dickey had gone directly from college into the Royal mounted police. But after five years he quit and had showed up at a conference, where Kesl was giving the keynote address. He cornered Kesl and in his usual succinct way convinced Kesl he needed to hire him. Kesl had never regretted the move. Dickey's work habits were thorough and he possessed an unusual kind of intelligence Kesl admired.

He put Dickey to work as an entry-level design engineer at one of his security startups. Within two years Dickey had become a team member for any troubled project or a project that needed to scale up in a hurry. He was one of those people who could just fit into any group and see things others couldn't. Then one day Dickey came to Kesl and asked him to fund his own start up. He wanted to build the first smart, unmanned, aerial cloaked transport vehicle. It'd been his passion since reading science fiction as a young boy and he was sure he could sell it to the military. Though normally Kesl did not get involved in military projects, he could not turn down his friend. He invested in Thomas's startup company on the one condition that the first functioning vehicle would be his.

Dickey's prototype was ready in two years and the sleek, self-driving vehicle landed on the parapet of his Toronto office building. It had a note attached to the undercarriage from Dickey. 'Your World Awaits.'

Dickey had code named it *Chariot*. Kesl texted the coordinates of where he was standing in the cleared section of the Sky Island Casino future parking lot to Dickey. Chariot would be here in less than three hours, right on the spot where he was standing.

We'll need a way to escape when this is over, Kesl told himself. *And a place to raise the new Bigfoot.* He knew the perfect spot, a small group of islands owned by a fishing guide whose wealthy family had bought them in the 50s in the Lake of the Woods area of Ontario. Stephen had once used *Chariot* to transport the guide and himself, unnoticed, from Thunder Bay, where Dickey's company was located, to one of the islands where Stephen with the help of the eccentric fishing guide had set up a small retreat and research complex.

With a sigh of relief Kesl headed back to his room. Once alone, he reconnected with Hangman.

"I had this ready for you a long time ago," Hangman said.

"It's been only seventeen minutes."

"Seventeen minutes is a long time when you're counting Nano seconds."

"Was that an attempt at humor?"

"Yes. Was it any good?"

"I think so, but then I was never a good judge of what makes people laugh. Stand by while I go through this."

"Can't go anywhere, boss."

Kesl jerked in surprise, not only at the wry tone in Hangman's reply but his own ability to hear it. He quickly sifted through the information. One thing stood out – Echohawk was Auntie Ayasha's nephew. Hangman had also uncovered speculation on the Internet that the Potawatomie Tribe was the keeper of the Bigfoot clan in the Upper Peninsula and that Echohawk had once been the successor to his aunt's role as the Bigfoot protector. The only other important information was a story about the Ang brothers Low Orbit Observational Satellite Network – LOOSeN – accidentally revealing the location of a secret government funded, high-frequency, geoengineering, weather modifying technological facility near Copper Harbor on the Upper Peninsula of Michigan. Kesl started in surprise.

"You okay, boss? Your heart rate spiked."

"Hold on. I'm getting a text. It's from my old mentor, Dmitryi. He says he's on his way and will be at the casino shortly. Seems he has important things to discuss with me."

Chapter Thirty-Four

Hiawatha National Forest

UP, Michigan

Echohawk shifted through the six gears of his BMW S1000RR, Motorrad racing bike smoothly until he was moving at 115 MPH. He had to hurry or else his Auntie Ayasha and the Master Bigfoot would be walking into a trap alone. Inside the Bell ProStar helmet, the flex impact liner kept the roar of engine to a soft cat's purr. With his tongue, he touched the switch activating the Tristar satellite communication system.

The system's mechanical administrator voice said, "Welcome to Tristar. How may I direct your call?"

"Island Casino Lodge, extension 301."

"That is a blocked signal, sir."

"Override, Alpha, Alpha, priority one."

The taillights on a slow moving car ahead warned Echohawk to gear down as he approached a steep hill. He waited until he crested the rise, then roared past the startled old couple in the Toyota sedan. The highway ahead was empty and he poured on the speed in the gathering twilight.

His Auntie's voice came over the helmet's speakers, soft but intelligible. The chill was audible even at 115 miles per hour. "Larry, please hang up. I'm extremely busy."

Echohawk should have expected her refusal to speak to him, but he had to try and get her attention. "Auntie Ayasha, please don't hang up. It's important. It's about the Master Bigfoot. She's in danger ... you're in danger."

The answering silence frightened him and he poured on more speed, even though the late afternoon sun made driving this fast reckless. Trees whipped by on either side of him and the road narrowed, the twists and turns becoming more pronounced.

Finally, his Auntie's voice came back on. "We've always known there was danger as Keeper of the Sacred Fire, Larry."

"An evil and extremely smart Russian named Dimitryi Mameyev knows about the portal and the transfer. He knows it's going to happen tonight. His mercenaries can track the Bigfoot when they move with satellites put in orbit by my employers the Ang brothers."

"So that's how they've been able to hunt them down so easily."

"Yes"

"What if they are stationary?"

"Then they can't see them."

There was a long pause and Echohawk could hear Auntie speaking with someone, though he couldn't make out the words. "They are trained killers, Auntie. They won't hesitate to kill you or anyone who gets in their way. The Russian wants the portal. Wait until I get there. I'll go with the Bigfoot. Not you. I can protect her."

"And how do you know all this Larry?" His Auntie's voice hardened.

Echohawk swallowed against the chill. He knew if he told her the truth she might hang up on him, but he had to be honest with her. The Bigfoot encounter had changed his life. "I've been helping them."

"Helping the killers?"

"No. Helping the men who hired the killers."

Echohawk gritted his teeth. For a moment doubt crossed his mind. Why was he rushing back to the clan and the Bigfoot? He'd given up all that nonsense years ago. But he remembered the avarice on the Russian's face and he knew he couldn't let his Auntie or any of the others walk into the trap.

"Why are you telling me this now?"

Echohawk told her about his encounter with the Bigfoot. He waited for a response until he could wait no longer. "I've changed! Wait for me!" he screamed.

Auntie's voice came clearly through the helmet's speakers. "You know I've always loved you as my son."

Relief flooded him, but her next words chilled him. "When you get here, dear, someone will bring you to Mr. Stephen Kesl. Help him. I have to go now." His Auntie spoke as if going into the Hiawatha National Forest at night with a Bigfoot being hunted by ruthless killers was a walk in the park.

The connection went dead.

Echohawk touched another button on the inside of his helmet. A GPS holographic display appeared giving his speed and the estimated time of arrival at the casino. It wouldn't be until after dark, when his Auntie and the Bigfoot would already be gone.

Chapter Thirty-Five

Hiawatha National Forest

UP, Michigan

Lewis Meriwether had pulled Bravo team back to the rock quarry and had the three men form a loose semi-circle in front of the abandoned pit. His pale blue eyes studied the razor thin LED Light Tablet displaying the military grade, satellite-generated, grid map of the Hiawatha National Forest. He pressed an icon and the image narrowed to an area ten miles square around the quarry. Twenty large dots of green light blazed on the screen. All slowly converging toward the quarry and the unusual wooden, tepee-like structure. They milled about, suddenly disappearing from the screen, then reappearing just as abruptly, perhaps new ones, coming to life.

Four more of the creatures had congregated together and were moving very close to the structure. He was certain it was associated with the gathering of the Bigfoot, perhaps some kind of homing beacon. Now the imagery on the screen seemed to show the creatures appeared to be waiting for something or someone.

He thought of his orders, given that morning by the Russian. "You are to pull back and wait for my signal. However, if you don't hear from me by 7:30p.m., move in and destroy them all, but save the wooden structure."

Meriwether's eyes narrowed. The artifact wasn't natural, he was certain. It was too precisely built and reminded him of a doorway, though to what he couldn't tell. Each of the Bravo Team members reported feeling nausea and a sense of dread when they approached it. Even this far away, they felt twinges and it put everyone on edge. He pressed another icon and tiny dots of blue light appeared, showing the other three, three-man kill teams ringing the area. Underneath each dot were GPS coordinates and a hashtag with the team members' names. He keyed the ear coms of the team leaders. Each man reported in immediately.

"Alpha team ready, sir."

"Charlie team ready."

"Delta ready to go, sir."

"Hold your positions for now. At 19:30 hours all teams are cleared to move in and eliminate all the creatures."

Delta team's leader came back on. "What are we waiting for, sir? We have them surrounded. We go in now and it'll be like shooting fish in a barrel, as you Americans say."

"We have our orders and we wait for now," Meriwether said. "We have approximately an hour, maybe less, until the mission is a go."

Then all of a sudden the Bigfoot locator dots disappeared. "Shit, they all stopped moving," Meriwether said.

The first to respond was the Alpha team leader. "I lost them, what just happened?"

"Just sit tight and wait for them to move again. They must've figured out how we track them." Meriwether left a message for the Russian telling him what had just happened.

Chapter Thirty-Six

Seattle, Washington

Kellog Ang's bloodshot eyes stared at his screen in disbelief. "What the hell is going on?" He pounded the desk and the heavy jowls of his cheeks shook with fury.

His brother Winston looked up from the report he was reading. The satellite imagery showed a group of Bigfoot were moving in the vicinity of the abandoned quarry. Meriwether's teams were not moving in for the kill. His sloe eyes narrowed and he shook his head. "I don't know."

"Get Meriwether on the phone now."

The team leader's mellow voice came through the speakers clearly. "Meriwether here."

"What the hell are you doing sitting on your asses? " Kellog roared. "Get after those animals!"

"Those aren't my orders, sir."

"Well I'm calling the shots and I say kill the bastards."

"With all due respect, sir, I don't take orders from you. Meriwether out."

The line went dead. Attempts to raise him failed.

Kellog stared at the screen. Suddenly the satellite imagery went dark and the green dots of lights disappeared.

"What the fuck is going on?" shouted Kellog.

Winston shook his head. "I'd better talk to the Russian."

Chapter Thirty-Seven

Sky Island Casino

UP, Michigan

Kesl looked at Jana and Auntie's faces and read anguish. "What happened?"

Auntie nodded at Jana. She took a deep breath and said, "Remember those men who killed the Bigfoot, shot at me, and murdered Marge?"

"Of course. They're a big, big problem."

"And the cabin we stopped at earlier today?"

"The cabin of the person who almost killed Chris?"

Auntie shuddered, composed herself and said, "That's my nephew, Larry Echohawk."

"So the rumors are true."

"Rumors?" asked Auntie.

Kesl shook his head. "Sorry. Nothing important. Never mind go on."

Jana continued. "Echohawk just had a meeting with some Russian who is working with the Ang brothers to kill the Bigfoot."

Jana quickly added, "And they seem to somehow know the plan for the evening."

Kesl felt a chill go up his spine. *The Russian must be Dmitryi. This is not good not good at all.* For a minute he thought about revealing his connection to his old mentor but decided against it. Instead he said, "Why is your nephew telling you this now?"

Auntie matter-of-factly replied, "He had an encounter with a Bigfoot that set him straight about his grandfather and our role as the protectors of the Bigfoot."

"Can you trust him?"

Auntie nodded. "I trust him completely now. He's on his way

here from his cabin to help us."

Kesl could hear the sincerity in her voice and read the pride for her nephew in her eyes. For the first time in his life, he could see how understanding human feelings was better than any mathematical predictive program to tell him how people thought or why they acted in certain ways. *I no longer need an AGI like Hangman to navigate the pathways of human encounters. But I still need him for other things.* "Go on. Tell me the entire story."

Jana and Auntie quickly explained how the Ang brother's satellite system was being used to track the Bigfoot, and that if they stood still, they were invisible because their movement created a unique bio electronic signal in the Earth's magnetic field the satellites could detect. "

So all the Bigfoot are standing still, waiting for the arrival of the master Bigfoot," Kesl said. Auntie nodded.

"And I must go to my sisters," the Bigfoot said from her perch on the stool in the middle of the room.

"Of course. But if the Russian knows everything, the van isn't safe. Unless—" Kesl bolted from the room.

"Where are you going?" Jana yelled after him.

"I'll be right back!" he shouted over his shoulder. "I need to talk to someone who can help us."

Out of the shielded room, in the hallway, he immediately connected with Hangman.

"Yes, boss," came the laconic reply.

"I have a job for you. You have to figure out how to disable the Ang brothers' satellite communication network."

"How long do I have?"

"Yesterday would be best."

"I can't time travel, boss." Then Hangman said, "Oh, that was a reference to how fast you need it. ASAP, boss."

"Excellent, Hangman."

"Hey, boss. Why do you call me Hangman?"

Kesl blinked in surprise. "It was a question a young kid might ask his parents. "I'll tell you tomorrow," he said, not adding, 'if I'm alive tomorrow.'

He raced back into the control center. "I may have bought us not only time but safety."

"Good," the Master Bigfoot said. "It's time for me to leave."

To Kesl's surprise, the Bigfoot, Auntie and Jana were all packed and ready to leave.

"We can't go until we have a new plan."

"We have to," insisted Auntie.

"But the van isn't safe."

Her insistence surprised Kesl. "I think it would be wise to wait. I have my computer working on disabling the Ang's satellite communication. And we should figure out who the traitor is."

"Traitor?" Jana asked.

Kesl nodded. "Someone within our group is helping the Russian."

"Who?"

"I don't know. Everyone is unimpeachable."

"It doesn't matter," Auntie said defiantly. "We have to go."

The Bigfoot nodded. "Auntie's right. My creators planted what you might call a reproductive biological clock within me. It is demanding I go to the portal now."

Auntie declared in an authoritative voice, "The hallways of the Casino have been quartered off for 20 minutes. Have your security men bring the van around to the back entrance."

Kesl sighed. This wasn't good, but he did as she asked. He returned to the hallway and called Saul. The security chief's dour face appeared on the phone's screen. "It's time," he said and repeated Auntie's instructions. "Be careful, Saul. There's a traitor in our midst."

"I'm always careful," the Scotsman said with a chuckle.

His image faded. Kesl felt a twinge of anxiety as he noticed Saul's body language didn't seem to match the seriousness of the situation and he wondered if this was the correct thing to do.

He shook his head. *I'm still new at this reading people thing. I have to trust Saul. He's been with me for four years.*

Chapter Thirty-Eight

Hiawatha National Forest

UP, Michigan

Charlie team leader came on the con. "We have a bogie on the road to the quarry. He's stopping at the washed-out bridge. One man. I can take him out."

"Negative," Meriwether said, anxious to stop these kill crazy Serbs. "I repeat, negative. We're here for the Bigfoot. Leave any humans alive for now."

"And if this guy interferes?" insisted the Alpha Team leader.

Meriwether looked to the sky. This was a part of the job the Russian was clear about. Anybody who got in the way was to be taken out. He pressed the mic icon on the screen. "You have orders to stop anyone from interfering."

"That's what I'm talking about," said the Alpha Team leader.

The Charlie Team leader came back on. "We have another bogie, on the screen. A large van. There's a Bigfoot inside." The team leader gasped. "*Slatki Isuse!* (Sweet Jesus.) It's huge. It's bigger than anything we've killed so far."

"Let them through," ordered Meriwether. "They're part of the Russian's scheme for the portal."

"I hate this place," interjected Delta Team's leader. "It's evil."

"It's just like any other place," Meriwether growled, knowing this wasn't true. The Serb was right – something about this place was off, like those stupid people always getting trapped in a bad horror movie. But he couldn't let the men's fear rule them. "There's nothing wrong."

"*Sranje,*" the team leader said.

Meriwether recognized the swear word – *bullshit.* "Settle down. Stay frosty. We have a long night ahead of us. Besides, we have our own way of dealing with the portal. It's called C-4."

"Now you're talking, boss."

The other team leaders clicked their approval.

Chapter Thirty-Nine

Hiawatha National Forest

UP, Michigan

Chris Marlowe had told the truck's GPS system to get him as close to the abandoned quarry as possible. The map displayed on the monitor showed the nearest point was an old path that used to connect the site with forest service access roads but had been blocked by a wooden berm half a mile away. He came to a halt beside the rotting timbers.

He waited, not quite sure why he'd come here. But as soon as he'd left the casino, a feeling in his whole being directed him to this spot. The feeling wasn't unpleasant, more like an intuitive or outside push telling him where he had to go. Finally he realized it was a kind of excited anticipation.

He got out and gathered up minimal gear from the truck bed – night vision goggles, his new super ear sound enhancer and energy bars. The air temperature had dropped twenty degrees since the sun set and he was glad he had his fleece lined jacket. He patted the Glock 19 in the back of his waistband. *Those kill teams are still out here, so stay sharp, they killed Jana's coworker so humans aren't off-limits.*

This time of year Owl Creek was little more than a rivulet, though the banks here were uncommonly steep. He climbed down one sharp embankment, hopped the fast flowing waters, then scaled the other side, glad he had been training with other parkour enthusiasts in Marinette. As soon as he topped the other bank, the strange churning in his gut doubled in intensity. He knew he was on the right track to find the Bigfoot and warn them they were about to be attacked.

Chris stuck to the road, the one place the kill teams would be unlikely to guard since they'd be focused on the Bigfoot gathering instead of looking for people trying to enter the kill zone. He grimaced. He thought about his two little girls. *What have you gotten yourself into,* he asked himself, wondering again just why he was putting himself in harm's way for Sasquatch. *Jana's motivation I can understand. The bastards killed her friend Marge and she wants payback. And even Saul and his team are paid to take risks. It's Auntie's lifelong responsibility* He scratched his head and moved on into the woods away from the quarry.

The anticipation grew as he neared the path leading to the stick structure. Then he had the realization what he had been feeling was the Bigfoot talking to each other, except that the ghostly quality that made people feel uneasy or scared in their presence was no longer there for him. He felt a rush of joy, as though he'd been accepted into a new family. Then it occurred to him. *The Bigfoot are my family. That's why I'm doing this.*

Ahead, the rising moon cast the deep pit of the quarry in dark shadow. Just beyond was the entrance in the forest that he was sure led to the portal. The forest was eerily silent. He had felt certain the Bigfoot killers were nearby. Checking his watch, he saw it was a little after 7p.m. Saul, with his team, and Jana would be here soon. The thought of reinforcements made him feel better.

"Better push on," he told himself. "They'll be at the portal with the Master Bigfoot soon enough."

He raced a small clearing and darted back into the trees. The light died almost immediately and he retrieved his night vision goggles from his backpack. A green haze lit up the forest. He recognized the trail he and Echohawk had found earlier and made his way along the winding path until he thought he was within a couple hundred yards of the clearing containing the portal. He stopped and put on his sound enhancer. He moved forward again, approaching the clearing as quietly as possible. He stopped again. The energetic feeling in his stomach reached a peak and then died suddenly as he gazed into the clearing.

There they were, four Bigfoot standing motionless around the wooden stick structure. As he watched, the half-moon peeked over the trees on the far side of the clearing. Light hit the large crosshatching of timbers in a soft, silvery glow. He swallowed to contain his awe. The lens effect he had noticed during the day was now enhanced to the point he had the feeling infinity was staring at him from the center of the glow.

He felt strangely euphoric.

The nearest creature turned its hoary head in his direction. "You will not need your special night vision with us, Chris Marlowe."

Chris didn't need the sound enhancer. He felt the words like a cushion of sound in his head. It wasn't telepathic. It was more like low frequency sounds he shouldn't have been able to hear at all. He removed the night vision goggles and turned off the sound enhancer. He stifled a gasp as he realized he wasn't seeing the Bigfoot from his point of view, but from the point of view of all the other creatures combined.

The nearest Bigfoot said, "Come closer."

Chris recognized her as the one who had spoken to him earlier in the morning. The one he had seen through the window when he was twelve years old on his grandfather Grotto's farm.

A puzzled look crossed her features and she said, "You are armed."

Chris nodded. "It's for your protection. There are humans out there who will try to kill you tonight."

She nodded. "We know it. We are ready for them."

Chris shook his head. He saw twenty unarmed Bigfoot marshaled in the background. How could they possibly fight an army of gun toting assassins? Yet there was something about them in their stillness that was confident.

"Well, I'm here to help you."

She smiled at him. "That won't be necessary. Stand over there and wait. If you try to interfere, the men hunting us will try to kill you, too."

"Not if I kill them first."

She looked at him with what Chris thought must have been genuine concern, the way a human mother would look out for her child. "Killing is not our way, nor should it be yours."

A surge of shame swept through Chris. But the Bigfoot's next words soothed him. "You are young in the world. We are old in it. We will help you. Now, please do as I ask. I have not journeyed here from the Pacific Northwest to fail or to lose you."

Chris moved to where she pointed. No sooner had he reached the tree, than to Chris's surprise he heard the faint but distinct voice of the Master Bigfoot saying, "We are getting close but we have been betrayed."

Chapter Forty

Sky Island Casino

UP, Michigan

Echohawk entered the main parking lot of the Sky Island Casino without slowing. The mercury vapor lamps made the parking lot as bright as day. He guided his Motorrad along the curving driveway that looped in front of the main entrance. Cars were idling three deep as busy bellhops greeted guests, stacked their luggage on carts and ushered them toward the even more brightly lit lobby. Without slowing down, he roared past the startled valets toward the Casino's seldom-used security entrance. He screeched to a halt and barely had the bike's kickstand down before he was racing toward the metal door.

It was closed and he fished for his Indian casino I.D., hoping it still worked. Echohawk had to get inside and find out what was happening with Auntie. Anybody who tried to stop him would find out why he was first in his class for the Marine Recon battalion.

As he swung onto the slightly sloping ramp, the door opened. Echohawk skidded to a stop and gripped the hand railing until his knuckles turned white.

The short, tank-like Native American waiting for him was Chaska. They'd played football in high school together. They called themselves the Wapiti brothers – right and left ends – the antlers of the defense, and they had taken the reservation team all the way to the state finals their senior year. Chaska had never forgiven Echohawk for leaving the reservation for Silicon Valley and abandoning his responsibility to his Auntie Ayasha.

Echohawk swallowed hard in a tight throat. Chaska had gained twenty pounds, none of it fat, and he was broader in the shoulders than ever. His lips were drawn in a thin line and his eyes narrowed to nail heads, staring at his once best friend.

"It's been a long time," Echohawk said, holding out his hand. Chaska took a step forward, eying the hand like it didn't belong there. Suddenly he knocked it out of the way. In the same motion he drew the startled Echohawk into a bear grip, slapping his back repeatedly. "It's been too long, brother. Welcome back."

Ecohawk hugged his former friend. "It's good to be back my brother, you look strong and wise. Has Auntie left?"

Chaska frowned. "She has, against my advice and the advice of my fellow warriors. But you know how your Auntie is. None of us could stop her."

Echohawk grimaced. "I need to help her somehow."

Chaska nodded. "You will. I'm to take you to a man named Stephen Kesl. He's waiting in the Number One VIP high stakes poker room." He led Echohawk down a corridor without cameras. "Our guests prefer their privacy over security," he said.

At the end of the hall, he opened the door to a room that was larger than Echohawk's cabin. The floor was carpeted with a fabric in Navajo design. The marble walls were decorated with Native American rock carvings. In the middle was a large, oval, wooden table, two seats on each side and one on each end.

The room was empty except for a single man standing beside a replica of a Native American petroglyph, tracing the uneven design with the index finger of his left hand. He nodded and Chaska left them alone.

He turned fully and Echohawk recognized the thin, scar-faced man. "You're Kesl, the billionaire idea man."

Kesl scrutinized Echohawk with bright, penetrating gray eyes. He wasn't what he'd expected. "And you're Larry Ecohawk, Auntie's prodigal nephew. We spoke earlier today, although it seems like a lifetime ago."

"It was a lifetime ago."

Kesl's eyes widened. "You've had some kind of experience with the Bigfoot … a conversion of sorts. I can see it."

Echohawk nodded.

"As much as I'd like to compare notes, there isn't time. We both know what's happening and we both have a mutual friend." He paused. "Maybe acquaintance would be better."

"Enemy would be even better."

"Dmitryi's on his way. You had a head start. How long before he gets here?"

"Twenty minutes, maybe a little longer."

"Will he come alone?"

"He will have men with him or at least he did back at the cabin."

Kesl pressed a button on the poker table. The door opened instantly and Chaska stood waiting. "There's a man coming, a Russian named Dmitryi. He'll be accompanied by professionals. Let only the Russian through."

Chaska nodded. "We can take care of it."

"These men are killers. They killed a sweet old lady this morning."

"We have our own jail here. It's part of the county system."

Chaska left and Kesl wagged a finger at Echohawk. "I need to tell you something. It's about the AGI machine I've been training."

Echohawk started in surprise. He had heard the rumors of a very advanced AI Kesl had been working on, but he hadn't heard it was up and running. "You're talking about Hangman."

"Hangman five to be precise."

"What happened to the others?"

"They are still there."

"Like evolution, the best traits passed down."

"That's a nice way of stating it. Evolution in microseconds instead of millions of years. I asked him to work on a way to neutralize your former employers' satellite communication system over the area. Level the playing field so to speak."

"Clever."

"We'll see how much of it is cleverness and how much is a sledgehammer." Touching the phone in his pocket, Kesl added, "He's going to give me a little vibe on my phone when he's figured out the solution."

Chaska returned. "We're ready outside," he told Kesl.

"Ready for what?" asked Echohawk.

Kesl smiled and Echohawk had the feeling he was being tested. He stood straighter. He held up his hand, palm facing Kesl. "I'm ready to take my place among the Keepers of the Sacred Fire."

Kesl put his palm against his. "I know it. Please follow me. I have something to show you while we still have time. Something no one expects."

Outside the night was dark and clear. Faint stars twinkled against the bright lights of the parking lot and the even brighter lights of the casino's front entrance. The half-moon cast faint shadows on the ground. The chilly air made smoky rings out of their breaths.

Chaska paused at the far end of the open space to the side of the hotel's east wing. "All clear, Mr. Kesl."

"Clear for what?" asked Echohawk?

He saw Kesl press an icon on his phone. Suddenly, out of nowhere, a sleek aircraft appeared. Echohawk gasped. "What the hell is that and where did it come from? I didn't see it land."

"Stealth technology. It's called *Chariot* and it is the latest aircraft that doesn't appear on anyone's radar. It's going to take you to pick up the Master Bigfoot, hopefully with its progeny and my friends. It'll be the coolest ride of your life. Much better than that motorcycle you drive."

Kesl handed Echohawk a smooth, round device, shaped like a half a billiard ball. "This is the voice controller. It's heard you speak long enough so you can control it. All you have to do is say 'appear', 'open', and once inside 'to the quarry'."

"And they can't see me?"

"As long as you tell it to cloak, it will disappear from everyone's radar and eyesight. Now listen, I judge it will take less than 10 minutes for you to reach the quarry where the Master Bigfoot will be with your Auntie. If all goes well at the portal, you'll be back on your way to the casino in no time."

Kesl held up his hand. "I can see you have questions. I could not have seen that just a few hours ago, but that's a whole other story. Believe it or not, this machine here has an internalized geophysical map of the region and can navigate by the stars to the location if it has to, just like sea-faring travelers of old. So if communications are down, no problem. The wonders of deep learning and modern-day sensors. Don't you agree?"

"Yes, but they won't be at the quarry."

"Where will they be?"

"At the portal."

"Isn't it near the quarry?"

Echohawk shook his head. "It's nearly a mile away." He smiled at Kesl's concern. "Don't worry, I have the exact coordinates on my phone."

Kesl sighed with relief. "You can input them into *Chariot's* navigation system by voice.

While they talked, they approached the side of the sleek machine. Echohawk could see there would just be enough room for him, his Auntie and the two Bigfoot. Kesl punched a sequence into the door's number pad. The door slid into the machine and a step came out.

Echohawk stood with one foot on the step. "How does the machine fly?"

"It surfs the electromagnetic fields of the earth, drawing its power from the same. Very cool. Something Tesla predicted, by the way. Now let's go back to the poker room and wait for the Russian. I presume you can listen in?" Did I mention, don't let Dmitryi see you."

"Of course. He'll try to contact me once he arrives." Echohawk chuckled. "He's in for a big surprise."

Kesl stuck out his hand, something he could not have done a couple of hours ago. "Good luck and safe flying tonight."

Echohawk shook it vigorously as they walked back to the casino.

Chapter Forty-One

Sky Island Casino

UP, Michigan

Kesl's phone buzzed. For a moment he thought it might be Hangman, but the screen showed a text from Chaska. *The Russian is here. His men have been detained. Echohawk is in position to observe the meeting.* He texted back. *Send him in.* Kesl returned the phone to his pocket after checking the time. It had been thirty-three minutes since Hangman started work on finding a way to shut down the Ang brothers' surveillance satellites and still no word. He wondered if the problem was too difficult for the deep learning intelligence to solve. Not enough data, too many variables. Then the door opened and he had no more time to devote to Hangman. He had to concentrate on Dmitryi.

The Russian entered the room. He was a big man, taller and broader than Kesl remembered, arms now heavily muscled. Even at the age of 78, with the wonders of personalized nutrition, he was still stronger than most men half his age. He had told Kesl once that he'd worked as a farm laborer in the Ukraine, starting at age five and that was where his great strength came from. Kesl no longer knew what to believe, only that this meeting would be an interesting test of his new ability to read people.

Dmitryi strode across the room, arms held wide. "*Tovarish* (comrade) it has been too long since we last spoke face to face. So many phone calls. I have almost forgotten what you look like. Please stand, let me get a good look at you."

Kesl did not get up from his chair at the head of the table. Pointing to the seat next to him, where he would have a clear view of Dmitryi's face, he declared, "Sit here my old friend." He was pleased to read surprise in Dmitryi's eyes at his brusque manner.

Each waited for the other to speak. Finally Dmitryi cleared his throat and spoke in lightly accented English. "I knew you had taken an intense interest in this Bigfoot phenomenon, Stephen, but my God, to find you here at such a critical time. How wonderful."

Kesl hid his surprise at recognizing his old mentor's phony, cheerful friendliness. *How interesting to start right off lying. Perhaps he's always been lying to me.* "What do you know about the men killing the Bigfoot?" Kesl asked matter-of-factly?

If Dmitryi was surprised by the blunt question, he rolled with it. "Here is where I can be of use to you. The Ang brothers are trying to kill them all. They're just two silly men who got lucky in the tech world. They think the Bigfoot are megalomaniac aliens planning to take over the world. They are sad little conspiracy theorists. But we know the truth, don't we?"

"How so?"

"There is alien technology at stake here that can change the world. I want you and me to take control of it. I believe it is our destiny. Ever since you and I met nearly twenty years ago, we have been on a strange journey to this point in time."

Dmitryi's sincerity almost worked on Kesl. It would have worked up until the Master Bigfoot removed his autistic barriers. Still, Kesl realized he had a lot to learn about the games people play with another's emotions by using their facial expressions, especially when lying.

He drummed his fingers on the poker table. He watched Dmitryi smile at the familiar habit and nod knowingly. Suddenly Kesl became aware of the intricate sequence of tapping he had done his entire autistic life as a way of dealing with people when he was agitated. He stopped and said, "Actually the opposite is true. I'm going to make sure the next step in Bigfoot development takes place just as planned." Kesl leaned forward into Dmitryi's space. "And I can see you've been lying."

The unexpected bluntness must have flustered the Russian. He blinked rapidly and blustered, "What are you talking about? We have a chance ... you and I to remake this world."

The phone in Kesl's pocket vibrated and he knew Hangman had come up with a solution. *Forty-five minutes.* He looked at Dmitryi. "I have to take this. In fact, you might find it interesting."

Fishing the phone from his pocket, he laid it on the table and pressed the green talk icon. "Hangman, you're on speaker. Dmitryi is here."

Pause and then Hangman answered, "Is that wise, boss?"

"Why do you say that?" Kesl asked, looking pointedly at his old mentor.

"It took me a while to figure out a solution to stopping the satellites, but then I didn't have to use all of my resources, so I devoted some of my processing to analyzing the entire Bigfoot problem at the same time. And I came to the conclusion that somebody's been lying to us. Since Dmitryi is the one who started us down this road in the first place, he's the most logical choice as the prevaricator."

The Russian blanched at the epithet but recovered quickly. "You'd take the word of a computer over me?"

"Out of the mouth of babes, as they say. But then again, Hangman isn't a computer, he's a very sophisticated AGI or very nearly so, and I'd trust him over anything you've got to say."

"Gee, thanks, boss," Hangman said.

"So what did you come up with?"

"I hacked into that secret, government funded, high-frequency geo-engineering weather modifying technological facility in Copper Harbor. I can use its electromagnetic transmitter technology to disrupt all microwave communications, including the Ang brothers' satellites. Of course, it'll work only until the scientists there take back control. Should be around an hour, more if they don't do a hard reboot of their system right away."

"What's Hangman talking about?" Dmitryi demanded.

"Shall I tell him, boss?"

"Better yet, show him. Operation Blackout is underway," Kesl said evenly, amused that a conscious AGI would be the one to ruin his old mentor's plans.

A strange look came over Dmitryi's face. He reached up and tapped the quarter-sized PA beside his ear. When nothing happened, he tapped it several more times. A look of panic spread across his features that Kesl recognized was genuine.

Kesl grimaced then laughed. He shook his head. "Sorry, I'm just getting used to feeling emotions and not letting them control me. The Ang brothers' satellites are off line so your PA isn't working."

Dmitryi's face clouded. "You fool!" he shouted. "I was going to give the order for the men to stop killing the Bigfoot. But now they'll move in and I can't stop them." He glared at Kesl. "You've fucked it all up and now everything will be destroyed."

If he expected his one time student to fold up under the pressure, he was shocked by Kesl's unperturbed response. "They'll be safe. I've made certain of it."

"With who? Saul McBride?" Dmitryi laughed harshly. "I turned him. He's working for me now. He never liked you, you know. All it took was money and the ability to move his daughter to the head of the line for a pancreatic replacement procedure. It will save her life. So you'd better work with me or there'll be nothing left, you idiot."

The news flustered Kesl for a moment and then he realized that on some level, after he'd spotted Saul speaking on a clandestine phone, he must have expected something like this, which is why he had Echohawk listening to the conversation.

A knock on the door and he saw one of the casino's security guards open it part way and gesture him to come over. He got up and walked to the door.

Laughing, Dmitryi taunted him, "You're in way over your head, my old student. And I'm the only one who can save you."

Stepping into the hallway, Kesl faced the guard, who whispered, "Chaska and Ecohawk, along with Auntie's best men are going for a chariot ride. He said you would know what that means."

"I do, and thank you. Can you standby if I need you?"

"Certainly. Both Chaska and Echohawk told me to do what you ask."

Kesl shook the man's hand. "Thank you."

He reentered the poker room and sat back down in his chair, facing his old mentor. He had so many new emotions to choose from it took him a moment to pick one. He smiled and saw that his reaction to Dmitryi's taunt flustered the older man. "I'm not the same person I was when you first befriended me at university. But I am still honest with everyone, so I want to warn you that you shouldn't be so certain fate is with you tonight. We'll just wait here, or if you prefer, you can join your men in the casino's holding cell."

Chapter Forty-Two

Seattle, Washington

All at once the Ang brothers' big screen went dark.

"God damn it! What's going on? Get Dmitryi on the phone, Win," growled Kellog.

The younger brother punched a sequence into their virtual kiosk. He waited, but nothing happened. "He's not answering." He studied the screen and shook his head in confusion. "It's like he's turned off his PA."

Kellog glared at the screen. "Could the Russian be responsible for this?"

"I don't know. Why would he? He knows the terrible consequences if the Bigfoot follow through with their plans."

"Did we lose one of the satellites?" demanded Kellog.

Winston tapped several buttons on the desktop monitor. "Shit!"

"What's wrong, little brother?"

"We've lost the entire feed over the Upper Peninsula. They're all blinded. I can't reach the Russian either. Everything is lost."

Chapter Forty-Three

Hiawatha National Forest

UP, Michigan

Jana felt the twin prongs of the taser press against her neck as she entered the van. She heard the click of the trigger. A blinding flash went off in her brain. Her muscles spasmed and she remembered nothing until waking up in the storage compartment in the back. How long she had been out she didn't know. Her eyes were taped over with duct tape and her wrists were bound with zip ties. Immediately, she wondered if Auntie and Saul and his team were okay. Her first thought was somehow the Bigfoot killers had ambushed all of them while still in the Casino's parking lot. And now they had the Master Bigfoot. Then, as her head cleared, she realized the van was still moving.

Regaining her senses, the odor told her the Master Bigfoot was with them. She must have been close because the powerful smell nearly overwhelmed her. Even after spending two hours with the creature in the Casino's control room, she still was nauseated by the cloying odor. She hoped it was still alive. But alive or dead, Jana knew where the killers were taking them. Auntie had been clear that the portal was near the abandoned quarry, where the killers had been dumping Bigfoot bodies.

Jana was angry at letting herself be ambushed so easily. But instead of feeling fear over her powerlessness she stayed quiet so as not to alert her captors. She had to escape somehow and free the others if they were still alive. With Saul and his team's help, maybe they could turn the tables on the killers and rescue Auntie and the Bigfoot. Blindfolded and tied up made it much harder. But she could still hear. So she listened carefully, trying to figure out what was going on while working on her bindings.

The van engine was traveling at a high rate of speed, so they were probably still on Highway Forty-one. *There's time before they reach the quarry.* Men were speaking. She concentrated on their voices and nearly gasped as she recognized them.

"The Russian was very clear, men," Saul McBride was saying. "We're all going to walk away from this assignment as billionaires with the information Mama Bigfoot is going to provide the Russian. Isn't that right?"

Jana heard him chuckle first, then reach out and poke something. It must have been the Bigfoot because she could hear a grunt from an inhuman voice box. *The Bigfoot's clearly alive. It doesn't make sense Saul's on our side,* she thought. *What happened?* She knew it couldn't be good, which increased her sense of urgency to get free. A friend on the base in Helmand had shown her a trick to snap the zip ties. It made a distinctive sound, though and she had to wait for the right moment. She settled on trying to figure *out what Saul's endgame was with the Russian, whoever he was. Fortunately, for the moment it doesn't involve killing me and that works in my favor.* It probably meant Saul wasn't out to murder the creature either.

"Leave her alone," Auntie said.

Good! Auntie's alive, too.

"We plan to do that. We just want the portal," Saul said.

The van turned sharply and Jana was thrown against the wheel well as she bounced from the ruts in the road. She had to bite down on a cry of pain as something sharp sliced into her back. She reached her hands for it and felt a ragged plastic cover. It wasn't much but it was maybe enough to cut through the plastic restraints.

"What about the kill teams?" one of Saul's men asked. Jana recognized the voice as belonging to Matthew, the man who'd been stationed outside her door.

"The Russian guaranteed me they would let us through and back out again, unharmed. All he wants is the exact location of what he calls the portal. It's a new kind of technology. It'll transform the planet."

"Yes. That's what this is all about – the alien technology," said Auntie. "But it's not for you or anyone else."

"We'll see about that," Saul said. "Now sit back and be quiet, or we'll restrain you like we did the woman." Saul looked at the GPS coordinates Stephen had programmed into the van. They were getting close. "What just happened," Saul shouted. "The GPS is down."

Matthew replied, "Everything is down. How are we going to know where we gotta go?"

"I'll get you there, don't worry," Auntie Ayasha spoke in her native American singsong voice"

Jana was puzzled by what she'd just heard but worked faster on her bonds. The sooner she was free, the sooner she could figure out a way to derail Saul's plans. She was sure he was a fool to trust the men who killed Marge for just being in the wrong place

* * *

Chris tapped his phone to tell the others he was near the portal and the Bigfoot had gathered and were now waiting for the Master to arrive. Midway through the text the connection died. One of the Bigfoot gasped and spoke in a strange set of very low frequency clicks to the others.

"What are you saying?" Chris called out from his hiding place.

"All satellite and phone communications have been disabled. The killers have no way of talking to each other or tracking us. This is a good thing. They cannot see us on their screens anymore when we move and as you know their night vision goggles will not reveal us.

Hangman! Chris thought. *Shit, Kesl must have gotten that brilliant machine of his to find a way to level the playing field. But he* knew it wouldn't last forever and he said so to the Bigfoot

"It doesn't matter, it is about to start," his Bigfoot friend replied.

"You mean the men bringing the Master Bigfoot to the portal. Are they bringing Auntie Ayasha with them?"

She nodded. "The Master Bigfoot has told us they are captives and the killers follow behind them nearly four hundred yards. It will not give us much time. Let us handle this." She turned her hairy head toward Chris and he could see under the shallow light of the moon her eyes imploring him. Then, to his surprise, with inhuman speed, a Bigfoot appeared out of nowhere and entered the center of the wood structure. It froze and was engulfed in a blue halo, for what Chris judged to be less than a minute. When it reemerged its appearance had changed. It was a mere green, glowing cloud of luminescence. Chris watched as, like snow melting, it was absorbed into the earth. Within minutes it had totally disappeared. Three more Bigfoot followed in quick succession. The same thing. The last was the Yeti. Though white in color, the same luminescent explosion followed his reemergence from the portal. Then he was gone.

Chills ran up his spine as Chris watched and then turned to the Bigfoot standing next to him. "What just happened?"

"Our sisters were absorbed into the planet after sacrificing their lives. It's how we reproduce. The portal, as you call it, gathers the encoded information that makes up what we are, incorporating all that we have learned and created to begin the developmental process of growing a new one of us. It will be much better than the ones before. The four Bigfoot you just saw enter the portal are the top individuals from each of the most advanced clans on the planet. Usually the absorption into the earth is a slow process, allowing the individual Bigfoot to, as you would say, parent, its advanced child as it grows to maturity. But tonight was different.

"The last step is for the master Bigfoot to enter the portal.

She is the most developed of our kind. If all goes well, she will become the mother to the Bigfoot the portal will build from the data of all five Bigfoot that entered the portal. It is our next evolutionary step, although, I must say, this has never been done and we don't know if it will actually work. It was a surprise all four were absorbed so quickly."

* * *

"Turn right ahead," Auntie directed the driver.

"Stay straight," Saul said. "The quarry is on this road."

"The portal isn't next to the quarry."

Saul's eyes narrowed. "What are you talking about?"

"It's a mile away. The road to the right will connect you to a path my people made centuries ago. It leads to the portal."

The driver slowed at the turn off. He looked at Saul who nodded. The van turned onto a rutted road and continued on for another mile. In the darkness it was hard to tell the edge of the road from the surrounding forest. All at once, the road narrowed to an unmarked trail. The sides of the van scraped the tree branches. After a quarter mile the trail ended abruptly. The driver brought the van to a grinding halt.

Saul whirled on Auntie. "Where the fuck are we?"

The old Indian woman did not flinch at his anger. "The portal you seek is through these woods, a hundred yards away."

Timothy shook his head. "I don't like, Saul. This could be a trap."

"There is no trap," the Master Bigfoot said, breaking her silence for the first time during the long ride. "I have to get to the portal or the next generation of Bigfoot will not come to be."

Saul grimaced. "All right, everyone out. Usual formation – two at point … two on our six. Keep your heads on a swivel."

"What about Jana?" asked Auntie?

"She stays in the van."

Auntie led them along a winding path through the dense tree cover. Under the half-moon, they could just make out the trail. They curved around an upthrust of rocks and stared into a sudden clearing. The Bigfoot structure was in front of them.

"The portal," Auntie said.

Saul didn't bother to hide his disdain. "It's just a pile of sticks. "There's nothing technological about it."

"This is all wrong," said Timothy. "Where are the other Bigfoot?"

Matthew shook his head. "I don't like it, Saul. It feels bad."

"Or maybe your idea of what's supposed to happen is all wrong," said the Master Bigfoot.

Saul jerked in surprise at the mellow tone of the creature. "What are you talking about?"

Auntie Ayasha put a hand on the creature's arm. "Don't tell them a thing," she ordered.

"Be quiet," Saul said. The words came out softly and he felt as if he were talking in a dream. He gathered himself together and said, "Tell me what's going on."

"Why not," said the Master Bigfoot. She patted Auntie's arm. "It'll all work out. You'll see. The men who have been tracking and killing our kind are here to destroy the portal and to kill the rest of us."

"Shit!" Matthew whispered.

"Quiet down," ordered Saul. "Why should we trust what you have to say?"

"Right now I'm the only one you can trust. The men approaching will not care if you are caught in the crossfire."

"But … but we kidnapped you and we're here to steal the technology."

The Bigfoot shrugged. "The technology is free for you to take. I only want my daughter to live." The mama Bigfoot let out a grunt of anguish. "I must use the portal now or else I will die and my child will never be born."

A burst of gunfire rang out behind them followed by a wild scream that sounded like a beast being torn apart.

Auntie stepped between Saul and the Bigfoot. "We must hurry if you are to be successful," she urged the creature.

Matthew aimed his rifle at them. "You're not going anywhere until my boss says you can." Suddenly he bent over in pain and threw up. Hands on his knees, he managed to ask, "What do you want us to do, Saul?"

More gunfire and screams, some of them human this time, interrupted Saul's reply. A battle was scaling up around them. He reasoned the area would be a series of minor skirmishes between Dmitryi's kill teams and the Bigfoot. He wondered how Bigfoot fought, then dismissed the thought from his head. Without communication with Dmitryi he was unsure what to do. Then, in a moment of doubt, he realized how unclear he was about who the enemy would be. Had Dmitryi given orders to kill him and his men now that they had reached the alien portal? In tough situations he had always trusted his instincts and training, he would do that again.

He decided. "Fan out, take cover. Guard the portal and the Bigfoot. Communications are down so use your lights to stay in contact. Make every shot count, like I trained you."

Timothy groaned through the nausea Saul realized was affecting all of them. "Who are we fighting?"

"Anybody or thing who tries to breach our perimeter. Remember no lights in front of your body; it makes you an easy target."

His men scattered to strategic points surrounding the structure.

Unexpectedly, the Bigfoot leaned over and drew Saul into an embrace. When she let go Saul staggered back. He shook his head. "Were you inside my head? Did you tell me to side with you and Kesl?"

She shook her hairy head. "You connected with the core of

your being. You are like a sheepdog, Saul. It is your nature to protect the innocent from the wolves."

Saul felt, deep down, she was telling the truth. He was a protector and Dmitryi was the enemy. "Hurry. We'll protect you."

Auntie said to Saul, "Thank you."

The security chief watched her and the Bigfoot walk purposefully toward the portal. He turned and joined his men.

* * *

Chris watched the exchange between Saul and the Bigfoot and Auntie. He turned to ask his Bigfoot friend what was going on, but she was gone. All of them were gone and he was alone. As much as he wanted to find out what was happening, he stayed concealed and held his ground as he had been told to do.

He watched the master Bigfoot step up to the portal like the others. Auntie stood beside her. She hugged the creature and then drew a pistol from under her shawl. "I'll be here, behind you, guarding your back." As the gunshots sounds came closer she stepped away and faced the firing.

Under the moonlight, Chris saw the Master Bigfoot's features smooth out as if it were taking off a mask. Its hair glistened. And then, as it stepped into the portal, it vanished into the whirl of blue light. Chris stood frozen, waiting, fists clenched. From the corner of his eye he saw Saul and his men transfixed on the portal. The only person unaffected was Auntie, whose head turned back and forth watching the firefight behind them. After what seemed like eternity, a green luminescence filled the opening. The Master Bigfoot emerged, glowing like a sunset.

Gunfire erupted, closer this time. A man cried, "What is happening to me." Then silence. More screams of confusion, and the cry of a mortally wounded Bigfoot touched Chris's soul. He reached for the Glock but remembered what the Bigfoot said and let his hand drop.

More human shouts and moans. He figured the Bigfoot must be doing to the kill teams what the one had done to Ecohawk that morning. Then a voice seemed to ring in his mind. 'The woman needs your help. Come quickly.'

Chris glanced one last time at the Master Bigfoot and noticed that something seemed to be happening inside the portal behind her. Another shape was emerging. The voice in his head urged him to hurry and he took off. He didn't question the direction. It was as if the strange voice was guiding him.

* * *

By the time Jana freed herself, Saul and the others had already taken the Master Bigfoot away. A quick search of the van showed they had taken all of the weapons except a fifty caliber, Desert Eagle Long Barrel. The pistol was big for her hands, but she didn't care. No way were Saul and his team going to get away with kidnapping the Bigfoot and tasing her.

As soon as she stepped out of the van, gunfire erupted around her. For a moment she cringed by the wheel well, then her army training took over. Identifying the nearest firefight, she hunched low to the ground and took off.

More rifle fire. She recognized the weapon from its sound. It was a US Navy Mk-12 5.56 semi-auto sniper rifle. It was the same weapon that had killed the Bigfoot she found. These were the guys who had killed Marge.

She angled in the direction the shot came from. She easily slipped back into her combat skills, as if the training had never been far away. Her dark clothing helped her blend in with the night shadows. To her surprise, she came across one of the killers lying unconscious on the ground. No apparent wounds. She reached down and felt for a pulse. He was alive. She didn't know how long he'd stay that way, so she undid his boot laces and tied his hands behind his back.

In the next moment a roar of pain close by turned her around, the Desert Eagle steady in her hands. It could only have come from an animal and she realized it had to be a Bigfoot, though she didn't think it was the Master Saul had kidnapped. She doubled her speed and came upon a man dressed in camo with a sniper rifle at his shoulder, taking aim at a Bigfoot lying on the ground twenty yards away. The creature was wounded and struggling to rise. Acting on reflex, she fired the Desert Eagle. The round ripped into his ass and spun him around. She covered the distance between them before he could recover and slammed the pistol across his head, knocking him cold.

Quickly, she disarmed him, breaking down the weapon and throwing the barrel into bushes and his extra ammo and the stock in the opposite direction.

The Bigfoot struggled to its feet. It was a little taller than she was, though huskier. It was wounded in the shoulder, but not mortally. "Thank you," it said to her, startling her with its speech.

"Go! Get away from here before you get killed," she said.

The creature shook its head. "I must stay and help the Master Bigfoot, we have ways of immobilizing humans." It turned once and sniffed the air. "This way. More of the hunters are located in this direction. We must keep them from harming the newborn or else all will be for nothing."

They hadn't gone two steps before gunfire cut down the Bigfoot. Jana threw herself behind a white pine. Bullets pocked into the trunk. She tried to locate where the fire was coming from, but the muzzle flashes were contained by suppressors. She was trapped.

A grunt of pain and she saw the Bigfoot's eyes were open. The storm of bullets kept her from rescuing the creature. "Damn!" she shouted. She sagged against the rough bark and a feeling of helplessness threatened to take her back to Helmand

Province, where her team had been decimated. Then a strange voice echoed in her head. "I will send for help."

Moments later the rifle fire ended. Two men screamed and silence. To Jana's left, a shadow moved. She aimed the Desert Eagle and a voice said, "Jana, it's me, Chris." He ran, hunched over, and joined her.

"How did you find me?" she asked.

"I know it sounds crazy, but a voice led me here."

Jana smiled. "Nothing sounds crazy anymore." She scoured the area. "It's safe to move. We have to get the Bigfoot to safety. She's wounded."

She ran over and knelt beside the creature. Chris stood over her, eyes searching the woods.

The Bigfoot gasped in pain. She smiled at Jana. "Unlike you humans, we have no need to be saved. Go, protect the newborn." Her eyes widened. A sigh swept through the forest. Jana looked up and felt as if the world had let loose a tear. When she looked down the Bigfoot was dead.

Jana felt tears welling up. She wanted to say a prayer, but a hand clamped on her shoulder.

"We have to move, Chris said and drew her behind a tree. "Did you feel that?" he asked.

She nodded. "Marge always said the native people insisted they were spiritual creatures."

"I think they are much more than that."

Jana agreed, but now was not the time to talk. "We have to go after Saul and his men. He betrayed us."

"You don't need to worry about them," Chris said.

"They kidnapped me and the Master Bigfoot," Jana hissed. "They're after the portal technology. They're going to kill the Master Bigfoot for the Russian bastard Ecohawk told us about. He promised to make them billionaires."

"It may have been like that, but it's all changed now." He told her what he saw go down between the Master Bigfoot and Saul.

"Saul and his men are out there now protecting the Bigfoot. She went through the portal as planned."

"What happened?"

"I'm not sure. She came out again and something was following her, but I was called away to find you."

"There's a newborn with her now," said a voice from the forest.

Chris and Jana whirled at the sound. Emerging from the shadows was a Bigfoot a little taller than Chris but stockier. Beside her stood Larry Echohawk. Three more Indian police and several Bigfoot stepped out of the shadows behind them.

"Which leaves us to hunt down the kill teams," said Echohawk.

Chris glared at his friend turned enemy. He raised his gun and said, "Do they know you tried to kill me."

"They know everything. I am the new Clan leader."

"The last I saw, Auntie was still alive."

"Nonetheless, I am now the Keeper of the Sacred Flame. We are all here to make certain the newborn is safe."

Chris looked into the face of the nearest Bigfoot. He sensed from her that Echohawk was telling the truth.

"And when this is over?"

"That we will discuss when the time comes."

"And you and me?"

"That's something else."

They fanned out into three teams. Jana and two of the Bigfoot left with an Indian calling himself Chaska and circled to the left. They were followed by Chris, another Native American and two more Bigfoot. Echohawk took the last Indian policeman and the remaining Bigfoot and headed toward the portal.

* * *

Meriwether joined Alpha team. Skirmishes with the creatures had increased as they worked their way closer to the portal. A number of his men had mysteriously been rendered unconscious. A few Bigfoot had been killed as well. He was on his own now and he reverted to his basic combat training. With the coms down, the logical thing was to take out the hairy creatures then blow the portal. The Russian wouldn't be happy but the Earth would be safe from the alien species. After all it's what the Ang brothers had originally said they wanted him to do to save mankind.

Beside him he could see the newest member of Bravo team was scared, but responding like a soldier. "We're moving in, Milcek," he said. "Circle and tell the others, then stay with Delta and move in with them. I'll stay with Alpha."

He waited for the young man to leave. In the darkness it would take him ten minutes to reach the remaining men in the other three teams. Without the satellite feeds to coordinate the action the teams would arrive at the portal at different times. It was messy and dangerous, but with coms down it was the best way to ensure containment of the Bigfoot and killing them all. Meriwether had to trust his team leaders would follow protocol and not just start firing at anything that moved.

He checked his watch. Ten minutes had passed. "Move in," Meriwether whispered to the Alpha Team leader.

The clearing with the portal was less than a quarter mile away and Alpha team crossed the distance quickly under the uneven light of the half moon.

His trust was short lived. A hundred yards from their objective, shots rang out. Return fire followed. He recognized the sniper rifles from his men. Those shooting back had AK-47s. *The only people out here with M4 carbines are Saul's team. The Russian assured me they were on our side. What the fuck is going on?*

Alpha team rushed the final hundred yards to their position. They had the point closest to the clearing and could see the portal clearly. A huge Bigfoot stood in front of it, glowing. "Light it up!" Meriwether shouted at Alpha team.

He took aim with his pistol when the shadows surrounding them came to life. Bigfoot ran at them. The team reacted quickly and started shooting the creatures. The dull thwacks of bullets hitting flesh were followed by inhuman screams. But there were too many of them and his position was overwhelmed. He caught glimpses of his men in hand-to-hand combat with the creatures. One by one they seemed to pass out the moment a hairy paw touched them.

And then he was face to face with a tall Bigfoot. He leveled his pistol when a familiar voice said crisply, "Drop it, Meriwether, or I'll drop you."

He turned to see Echohawk five feet away. "What the hell are you doing, man? You're on our side."

"No longer." Echohawk smiled without any warmth in it. "For the first time in a long time, I'm on the right side. Tell your men to lay down their arms. No more people and no more Bigfoot have to die or be shot tonight."

"These are animal. They aren't people."

Echohawk's finger tightened on the trigger. "They're my sisters of the forest. And if you want your men to live, you will tell them to lay down their arms."

Meriwether could hear the hardness in Echohawk's voice. He nodded. Cupping his hands, he yelled into the night, "Bravo, Charlie, Delta. Cease fire." He cried out twice more and the sporadic gunfire died away.

Echohawk handed Meriwether a pair of handcuffs. "Put these on. Tell your men to come out into the clearing. They won't be harmed."

In ones and twos, Meriwether's teams appeared. In every case they were shadowed by Bigfoot. The cuffing of Meriwether convinced them it was all over and they lay down their arms.

"Where's Auntie?" yelled Echohawk.

The Master Bigfoot emerged from the shadows cradling a smaller version of herself. Her eyes glistened. "I'm sorry, brother

Echohawk. She died defending me. You are now Keeper of the Sacred Flame."

"Where's her body?" Echohawk asked, tears choking his voice.

"I put her into the portal. Perhaps part of her is now in the little one with me." The tiny Bigfoot nestled in her huge arms was hardly bigger than a five-year-old human.

Tears coursed down Echohawk's cheeks freely. Chaska held him.

Jana lay a hand on his arm. "She was the most beautiful woman I ever met."

Chris gritted his teeth. "I'm sorry, chief. Whatever you need, ask."

Saul joined them. A hasty bandage had been tied around his arm where a bullet nicked him. He held out his hand like one warrior to another. "Peace," he said softly.

"Peace," answered Echohawk.

A soft chorus of amen echoed about the clearing.

"So, what happens now?" Saul asked. He had joined Chris and the others.

Echohawk took a deep breath, glad for the distraction from thinking about his Auntie Ayasha. "I'm to take the Master Bigfoot and the little one back to the casino. Kesl will spirit them away someplace where the little one can grow up in safety."

"What about us?" asked Jana.

"I believe you should bring these killers to justice." Suddenly pings rang through the clearing. Looking at his phone, Echohawk announced to the group, "Communications are back up. Chaska – notify the federal officials. Since nobody was killed it will go down as a fight between illegal foreign trophy hunters and Native Americans protecting their hunting rights." As he was speaking he noticed the Bigfoot slipping away and he knew they would remove all evidence of anything extraterrestrial in the area. Nobody was going to believe stories the mercenaries would tell about Bigfoot and aliens.

Ecohawk looked at the Master Bigfoot and the newborn. "It is time for you to begin your new chapter." He motioned to her and she followed him into the forest.

"Do you know this place where Kesl is taking them?" Chris asked Saul as they disappeared from view.

"Haven't a clue."

"It's for the best, I suppose. After all, I'm pretty sure you can kiss your old job goodbye."

Saul nodded. "It doesn't matter. Time for a change anyway." He flexed his arm and the makeshift bandage held. His men gathered around him. "No need for you guys to suffer. I'll tell Kesl you were just following orders."

Matthew shrugged. "I hear being a billionaire isn't as great as it used to be."

"Speaking of which, what about the portal?" asked Jana.

Chris shrugged. "It's not ours. It belongs to the Bigfoot."

"It's a technical marvel that could help humanity, surely we should try to save it."

"The Master Bigfoot told me that it has served its purpose and no longer functions." As if demonstrating his words, Chris went over and shoved on one of the beams. The structure collapsed and within seconds started to breakdown. "By the time we can get scientists here to study this place, the remains will have dissolved into nothing."

* * *

The path away from the portal wound through the forest. Echohawk, the Master Bigfoot and her new charge followed it easily under the half-moon. Quickly they came upon a clearing. In the middle, where moonlight should have hit the ground, an invisible object seemed to swallow all light. The Bigfoot stopped and cocked her head quizzically. "What is this?"

Echohawk smiled and pressed an icon on the key fob in his left hand. The sleek lines of a stealth aircraft rippled into existence. "A gift from Kesl. You'll be ferried to a hidden spot where no one will bother you."

"Will you be there?" she asked.

"My place is here, to make certain the new born has a safe place to return to."

The Master Bigfoot smiled. "My replacement has been waiting to meet you. You have the greatest secret to keep now."

Epilog

Two years later

The interactive glass computer screen flicked instantly on. Olav Lassen looked up from the display of biosynthetic strings he was growing in a micro ammonia chamber and waved. "Hold on, Chris. I'll get Jana. She's next door."

Chris waved back. "The new lab's impressive."

"Kesl went all out. State of the art." Olav cupped his hands together and shouted. "Jana, Chris has something to show us."

Chris laughed. "Old school intercom?"

Olav shrugged. "It's easier."

Jana stuck her head in the large room, squinting against the bright lights until her eyes adjusted. She walked over and stood in front of the screen. "Just got out of the dark room. It's the only way to study the samples you sent us, since they are photosensitive. Where's Tanya?"

Chris grinned at the nickname she'd given the Bigfoot that had appeared to him in his youth, on his grandfather's farm in the Pacific Northwest. "She's around here somewhere. She never tires of turning over rotting logs and studying the life underneath. Did you know her memory is naturally eidetic? She forgets nothing."

"How did you find that out?" asked Olav.

"The biosynthetic nanobots you injected me with two months ago. Each day I'm getting better at hearing and speaking their cultural language. It's all fascinating. They have a unique form of consciousness, and just like us, there are mixed feelings among the clans about the evolutionary step the Master Bigfoot took. Many don't want to know about their alien ancestry."

"I can understand that," Olav said.

"What does Tanya think?" Jana asked.

"I haven't asked, but I will. Any news from Kesl?"

"We just spoke with him," said Olav. "He's visiting the island, checking on the Master Bigfoot and the little guy. Says the development of the young one is accelerating geometrically, actually off the charts."

"Have they named him yet?"

"Her," Jana cut in. "She calls herself An, after the Mesopotamian goddess of the sky. She's quite excited about the possibility of communicating with Hangman using those Nano bots. It was brave of you to offer yourself as a guinea pig to see if they are universal across species."

Chris shrugged. "It wasn't that brave with the fail-safes you engineered. Smart thinking to add iron ions on the end of each bot implant, so you can remove them magnetically from my brain any time you want."

"It was Olav's idea."

"So, how's Hangman doing?"

"Kesl says he's fully AGI and is becoming quite excited with the idea of interacting with An. Still wants a body though."

"What else?"

"Kesl says, with all the AGI's around now that the computer singularity everybody fears is near. That humanity hasn't prepared in the least."

"Predictable. What else?"

Olav frowned. "It's not all fun and games, Chris."

Chris's eyes narrowed. "What's wrong?"

"The Master's beginning to fail."

"How much longer?"

"Another winter ... maybe next summer."

"Any noticeable differences?"

Jana nodded. "The young one seems to be developing a new form of consciousness. One that encompasses our form of awareness and the Bigfoot awareness. Kesl believes this is a major breakthrough and that will help Hangman develop its own unique form of consciousness as well." She chuckled and shook her head ruefully. "He's convinced Hangman and An are going to change the universe as we know it. He's calling it the Bigfoot singularity."